dashing hero, and an undaunted heroine will find that Bowman fulfills their dreams of the perfect romance."

—*RT Book Reviews*

"Poignant, entertaining . . . this was a fun book to read."

—*Romance Reviews Today*

NEVER TRUST A PIRATE

"Thrilling, delicious, and suspenseful."   —*Kirkus Reviews*

"Wonderful, sprightly repartee, a fast pace, and delightful characters blend together in another enthralling Bowman romance. Always smart and sassy, Bowman's heroines delight in piquing the hero; taunting and tempting. Together they heat up the pages and turn readers' thoughts to what original story line she'll come up with next for their 'keeper' shelf."   —*RT Book Reviews* (Top Pick!)

THE LEGENDARY LORD

"A sweet and fulfilling romance."   —*Publishers Weekly*

"A deliciously witty, sexy historical romance that will keep readers turning the pages."   —*Romance Junkies*

THE UNTAMED EARL

"Bowman delights with a humorous tale that could come straight out of a Shakespearean play . . . enchanting romance."   —*RT Book Reviews*

"Valerie Bowman's stories sparkle with humor, and her

characters are absolutely adorable. *The Untamed Earl* is an engaging and romantic love story." —*Fresh Fiction*

THE IRRESISTIBLE ROGUE

"Bowman's novel is the complete package, filled with fascinating characters, sparkling romance, and a touch of espionage." —*Publishers Weekly*

"With its lively plot, heated sexual tension, surprising twists, engaging characters, and laugh-out-loud humor, Bowman's latest is another winner."
—*RT Book Reviews* (Top Pick!)

"You will find no greater romantic escapade."
—*Night Owl Reviews* (Top Pick)

"The story is filled with humor, a twisting plot, and vibrant characters that have become Bowman's hallmark."
—Sarah MacLean, *The Washington Post*

THE UNLIKELY LADY

"Bowman keeps her prose and characters fresh and interesting; her book is an entertaining renewal of a classic plotline and well worth reading." —*Kirkus Reviews*

"Quick, lively entertainment at its best"
—*RT Book Reviews*

"A joyous romp in Regency England, filled with bright characters, scintillating conversations, and just plain fun."
—*Romance Reviews Today*

No Other Duke but You

VALERIE BOWMAN

St. Martin's Paperbacks

This is a work of fiction. All of the characters, organizations, and events portrayed in this novel are either products of the author's imagination or are used fictitiously.

NO OTHER DUKE BUT YOU

Copyright © 2019 by June Third Enterprises, LLC.

For information address St. Martin's Press, 175 Fifth Avenue, New York, NY 10010.

ISBN: 978-1-250-12167-7

Our books may be purchased in bulk for promotional, educational, or business use. Please contact the Macmillan Corporate and Premium Sales Department at 1-800-221-7945, ext. 5442, or by email at MacmillanSpecialMarkets@macmillan.com.

Printed in the United States of America

St. Martin's Paperbacks edition / May 2019

St. Martin's Paperbacks are published by St. Martin's Press, 175 Fifth Avenue, New York, NY 10010.

10 9 8 7 6 5 4 3 2 1

For all the Playful Brides readers.

I began this series as a trio of books between three friends, Lucy, Cáss, and Jane, but the love you all showed for the series enabled me to continue it.

It's been a true joy to write these books.

Thank you for the hours you spend reading.

CHAPTER ONE
London, June 1827

Twenty-two-year-old Lady Delilah Montebank peered around the corner of the servants' staircase while her friends smuggled a small potted tree, an armload of paper moss, and a set of fake donkey ears down the back steps of her mother's town house.

"*J'adore* the donkey ears," she whispered, glancing over her shoulder to check for witnesses. Her chin brushed against the ruffles of her pink gown. "Shh. We cannot let Mother hear."

Her friends, Owen Monroe, the Earl of Moreland, Christian Forester, Viscount Berkeley, and Derek Hunt, the Duke of Claringdon, all dutifully slipped out the back door, their arms full, without making a sound.

"*Merci beaucoup,*" she whispered to Derek, as his boots crunched the gravel on the way to his coach. "Please tell Lucy I'll see her tomorrow." She waved at the duke.

Derek inclined his head by way of reply.

Delilah turned and let out a deep breath. She'd been skittish all morning, hoping her mother wouldn't find her friends smuggling the decorations for the play out of her bedchamber. But Mother hadn't discovered them. Job well done.

Delilah was about to close the door behind her when a small red squirrel dashed inside. The squirrel sprinted down the corridor toward the front of the house.

Delilah winced. She may have met this squirrel before. She *may* have fed it, which meant she may be responsible for its entrance into her home. And if Mother or Cook saw it first, the poor little animal would be doomed.

Delilah hiked up her skirts and took off after the squirrel. The rodent dashed back and forth down the corridor, leaping left and right, heading directly for the front of the house as if he knew the layout. Mother was in the front drawing room receiving visitors. The door to the gold salon was open. She might see the squirrel dash past. Of course, Delilah knew this because she'd thoroughly researched her mother's whereabouts before telling her friends to proceed with smuggling things out the back door.

The squirrel was already in the foyer by the time Delilah caught up to it. It paused and looked about. Delilah paused too, holding her breath. She stood panting and waiting, her skirts still hiked above her stockinged ankles. Mother's voice drifted from the salon. Delilah swallowed, her eyes darting to the side.

The squirrel dashed across the marble floor and ran under a rosewood table, the same rosewood table that housed the expensive crystal bowl in which visitors left their calling cards. The same crystal bowl Mother was excessively proud of.

Mother's voiced drifted from the salon again. She was

saying good-bye to someone, which meant she was about to emerge from the room. Delilah didn't have much time. She expelled a breath and eyed the squirrel warily. It sat under the table, sniffing the air and swishing its bushy tail. Delilah had no choice. Time was of the essence. She dove for the squirrel, catching her slipper in the hem of her skirt and ripping it, upending the table, and smashing the crystal bowl. She landed in an ignominious heap amid the jumble, her hands closed around the squirrel's tiny, furry body.

A shadow fell across her, and she hoisted herself up on one elbow to turn and look at the straight-backed figure looming behind her.

"Um, *bon jour*, *Mère*. I mean, Mother." Her mother disliked it when she called her *Mère*. Delilah's use of French—specifically, her *poor* use of French—drove her mother to distraction.

Her mother's dark, imperial eyebrow lifted. The frown on her face was both unmistakable and omnipresent. The Earl of Hilton stood to her right, an irritated smile on his smug face.

"She takes after her father, doesn't she?" He eyed Delilah down his haughty, straight nose. "Clumsy."

Lord Hilton had supposedly been Papa's closest friend. Ever since Papa died over ten years ago, the man had been hovering about Mother. Delilah had suspected for a while now that they were courting. He and his hideous son, Clarence, had begun coming around more and more of late. Delilah guessed they were interested in money, and unfortunately, her mother had a great deal of it. Her uncle was the earl now, but Papa had provided generously for both her and her mother's future.

Mother lifted her chin, her lips pursed. It was never good when her lips pursed. "This creature looks like my daughter, but I'm not certain I wish to claim her at the moment."

Delilah scrambled to her feet. Her hair had come out of the topknot and a large swath of it covered one eye and half of her mouth. Her grip still tight on the squirming squirrel, she tried to blow the hair away from her face, but the swath simply lifted momentarily and fell back into place.

Mary and Rose, the housemaids, had already begun cleaning up the mess she'd made. "I'm awfully sorry," Delilah said to them. They glanced at her, both offering sympathetic smiles. She'd been friends with them for an age, and they knew she was about to get a tongue lashing from her mother.

Mother's gaze fell to the squirrel, and she gave a long-suffering sigh. "What in heaven's name have you got there?" The countess's nostrils flared slightly as she glared at the squirrel as if it were a rabid rat.

Delilah clutched the little animal to her chest. "*L'écureuil*," she announced, hoping the word for squirrel sounded more acceptable in French. Most things sounded more acceptable in French.

Her mother turned sharply toward the front door. "I am going to see Lord Hilton out. I'll give you five minutes to dispose of that *thing* and meet me in the salon. I need to speak with you." She whisked her burgundy skirts in the direction of the front door.

Delilah glanced about. The front door was the closest exit. She rushed past Mother and Lord Hilton to reach the door before they did as Goodfellow, the butler, opened it. She hurried out into the spring air and glanced around. The park was across the street. It would be the best place for the squirrel. She watched for carriages and then dashed across the muddy roadway and into the park, where she found a spot in the grass to carefully release the animal. "Take care, *Monsieur Écureuil*," she said, as she leaned down and gently opened her palms against the soft, green grass.

She watched the squirrel scramble away to safety before she turned and rushed back across the road, further muddying her skirts in the process. *Mon Dieu*. Just another thing for Mother to disapprove of.

By the time Delilah reached the foyer again with a ripped, stained hem, she was breathing heavily and her coiffure had become even more unwieldy. At least the Earl of Hilton was gone. She quickly flipped the unruly swath of hair over her shoulder. Best to pretend as if she couldn't see it. She rushed into the salon and stopped short to stand at attention in front of her mother, who was seated, stiff-backed and imperious, like a queen upon a throne.

Mother eyed her up and down before shaking her head disapprovingly. "Take a seat."

Delilah lowered herself to the chair that faced her mother's. She'd learned long ago that if she kept her eyes downcast and nodded obediently, these sorts of talks were over much more quickly. Too bad she didn't have it in her to do either. "About the squirrel, I—"

"I do not wish to speak about the squirrel." Her mother's lips were tight.

"About the vase and the table, I—"

Mother's eyes were shards of blue ice. "I do not wish to speak about the vase or the table."

Poor *Mère*. She would have been beautiful if she weren't always so angry. Usually with Delilah. Her mother's blond hair held subtle streaks of white, her eyes so blue they would have been heavenly if they weren't so hard. She had a perfect, patrician nose and lines around her mouth no doubt caused by years of frowning at her only child.

Delilah looked nothing like her. Lord Hilton was correct. Delilah took after her father. She had Papa's dark brown hair and matching eyes. A butter stamp, they'd called her, meaning she looked exactly like him. Delilah was of medium height while her mother was petite. Delilah was exuberant and talked far too loudly and far too much, while her mother was always calm and reserved. Delilah was a failure on the marriage mart, while her mother (even at her advanced age of three and forty) had a score of suitors. Hilton was the most aggressive, and her mother's obvious favorite.

Delilah's mind raced. If Mother didn't want to chastise her about the vase, the table, or the squirrel, what could she possibly—

Delilah winced. "Is it about the donkey ears?"

Mother's eyes widened slightly with alarm. "Donkey ears?"

Oh, dear. Now was probably not the best time to tell Mother she'd been rehearsing a play for charity. The woman rarely approved of anything Delilah did, and joining the outrageous Duchess of Claringdon, Lucy Hunt, in a production of a play was certain to be another in a long list of things Mother disapproved of, even if they were performing Shakespeare's *A Midsummer Night's Dream*.

"Never mind," Delilah said in as nonchalant a voice as she could muster.

Mother delivered another long-suffering sigh. She touched one fingertip to each of her temples. "I don't even want to know what you meant by that. But no, it's not about any of those things." Her mother's hands returned to settle motionless in her lap.

Delilah watched with awe. She'd never been able to master the art of sitting perfectly still. She also hadn't mastered the arts of speaking fluent French, being patient, pouring tea without spilling it, keeping her clothing clean and rip-free, or any of a number of other things she'd tried. All of her shortcomings were a source of unending shame to her mother.

Delilah pressed her lips together, but she couldn't keep her slipper from tapping the floor. When would she learn it was always better to allow Mother to speak first? The conversation tended to be less incriminating that way. "What *would* you like to speak to me about, Mother?" she forced herself to ask in the primmest voice she could muster. Mother had always valued primness.

Mother straightened her shoulders and pursed her lips. "It's about your marriage."

A sinking feeling started in Delilah's chest and made its way to the bottom of her belly, where it sat, making her feel as if she'd swallowed a tiny anvil. She'd known this day would come, known it for years, but she had merely hoped it wouldn't arrive quite so . . . soon.

"You'll be three and twenty next month," Mother continued.

A fact. "Yes, Mother."

"That is *far* beyond the age a *respectable* young woman should take a husband."

That depended upon what one considered respectable, didn't it? It also depended on whether one's goal was respectability. "Yes, Mother."

"You've spent the last five Seasons running about with the Duchess of Claringdon, playing matchmaker for other young ladies."

True. "Yes, Mother." Delilah managed to stop her foot

from tapping, but her toes continued to wiggle in her slipper.

"You don't seem to have given so much as a thought to your own match."

Also true. "Yes, Mother." Was it her fault if it was much more diverting to find matches for other people than to worry about a courtship for herself? When she was a girl, she'd looked forward to being courted by handsome gentlemen. But that had been years ago, before she'd grown up to be entirely unmatchable. She'd always known she would have to try to make her own match eventually, however. Someday. Apparently Mother's patience was at an end.

"I daresay your friendship with Huntley hasn't been a good influence. He also refuses to make a match. And he's a duke, for heaven's sake. He'll need an heir someday."

Delilah winced. It was never good when Mother mentioned Thomas. The two could barely stand each other. "Thomas doesn't exactly believe in marriage."

"Yes, well, *you'd* better start believing in it." Mother's highly judgmental eyebrow arched again. "This is your *sixth* Season, and it's nearly over."

Yes, but who was counting? And why did Mother have to pronounce the word *sixth* as if it were blasphemy? She sounded like a snake hissing.

"I insist you secure an engagement this year," Mother continued. "If you do not, I shall be forced to ensure one is made for you."

Delilah shot from her chair. "No! Mother!" Her fists clenched at her sides.

Mother's brow lifted yet again, and she eyed her daughter scornfully until Delilah lowered herself back into her seat. She managed to unclench her fists, but her foot resumed the tapping.

Mother pursed her lips. "You fancy yourself the *ton*'s matchmaker, my dear. It's high time you made your *own* match."

Delilah took a deep breath and blew it out. Then she took another one for good measure. Aunt Willie had taught her that little trick when dealing with her mother. How Aunt Willie and Aunt Lenore, her cousin Daphne's mother, had grown up with Mother and been so different, so happy and nice and pleasant, Delilah would never know. The three sisters couldn't have been more dissimilar.

After the third steadying breath, Delilah forced herself to think. Marriage. Very well. This was actually happening. She would have to make a match by the end of the Season. She gulped. Next month.

"Of course, you'll have to find someone who is willing to put up with your . . ." Her mother eyed her up and down again. "Eccentricities. But there are plenty of young men of the Quality who are in need of a hefty dowry. I suggest you set your sights on one of them."

Delilah blinked back tears. She refused to let her mother see her cry. She hadn't allowed it since she'd been a girl. When Papa died. That was when Mother had informed her that crying was for people who had no control over their emotions, something Delilah had always struggled with. Her emotions tended to immediately register on her face. That was one of the many reasons she had always been a terrible disappointment to her mother.

But Delilah *had* always intended to make a good match. She had. She'd merely been . . . distracted. Why, together, she and Lucy had made splendid matches for all of Delilah's friends. Lady Eleanor Rothschild, Lady Clara Pennington, and Lady Anna Maxwell. Those young ladies had made their debuts with Delilah, and one by one they'd been married off to charming, handsome, titled gentlemen of the aristocracy . . . in love matches, no less.

"Don't misunderstand me," Mother continued, passing a hand over her perfectly pressed skirts. "I don't expect you to make the match of the Season."

Delilah blinked. "The match of the Season?" Surely, her mother didn't mean—

"I've heard the Duke of Branville is looking for a bride this year."

Drat. That's exactly who her mother meant. And it was true. The Duke of Branville had long been the most coveted bachelor on the marriage mart. Until this year, he hadn't shown an interest in finding a bride. She and Lucy had already spent the better part of the Season avidly discussing his prospects. It was one of their favorite pastimes actually. "Yes," she murmured in response to her mother. "The Duke of Branville is certainly eligible."

Her mother's lip curled. "As I said, I've no expectation that you could secure an offer from the likes of Branville, for heaven's sake. No. I think someone a bit more, ahem, reasonable would be best." She sat up even straighter if that were possible. "To that end, I already have chosen someone for you."

Delilah's stomach performed a somersault. "Who?" Cold dread clutched at her middle.

"Clarence, of course."

Delilah's jaw dropped and her brows snapped together. "Clarence . . . Hilton?"

Her mother directed her gaze skyward for a moment. "Of course, Clarence Hilton, who else?"

"Oh, Mother, no!" Delilah couldn't help the disdain in her voice. "I'm certain I can do better than Clarence Hilton."

"Oh, really?" Mother drawled, crossing her arms over her chest and regarding Delilah down the length of her nose.

"Yes, really." Delilah nodded vigorously. She'd rather marry a good-natured goat than Clarence Hilton. The man was portly, smelly, and rarely spoke, and when he did, he had nothing interesting to say.

"Very well." Mother stood from her seat and made her way toward the door. "I'll give you until your birthday to secure a better offer."

Delilah clenched her jaw. Her mother didn't think much of her. She certainly didn't think Delilah was capable of attracting a worthwhile suitor, and she obviously didn't think Delilah could attract anyone better than Clarence Hilton.

Anger bubbled in Delilah's chest. Normally, she did her best to keep it at bay. Anger was an emotion, after all. But sometimes, no matter how hard she tried, she couldn't stop such thoughts from throbbing in her brain. She was a butter stamp of her father in more ways than one, and the current way involved being madly stubborn and ridiculously determined once she set her sights upon something.

By God, Delilah would show her mother. She would prove to her that she wasn't the lost cause Mother thought. Besides, who better to make the match of the Season than she herself? She was a matchmaker, wasn't she?

"You'd do well to remember that Clarence Hilton is the heir to an earldom," Mother intoned.

"I'm well aware." Delilah tried and failed to keep the sarcasm from her voice.

"Don't be impertinent. You truly believe *you* can secure an offer from someone with better connections than that?"

Delilah raised her chin and met Mother's glare. She would die trying. Because her mother had just issued a challenge of sorts, and unfortunately, Delilah—emotional, too-loud, eccentric Delilah—had never been able to pass up a challenge.

Besides, her odds of success had to be better than average. Her best friend, Thomas, was always talking about odds. Numbers leaning this way or that. He put great stock in them. Delilah rarely gave odds much thought, but now she had to believe they were in her favor. After all, Delilah had the infamous Duchess of Claringdon, Lucy Hunt, in her corner, and that woman was undisputedly the best matchmaker in the land. "Yes," she declared. "I believe I can."

"Fine." Mother paused in the doorway and turned to regard her daughter, a hint of disdain in her forced smile. "Do you have anyone in mind? Any prospects?"

Delilah straightened her shoulders. Her mother's lack of faith in her hurt, but it also made her resolute. Her birthday was the twenty-first of July. She had just over a month to accomplish her goal. Her perhaps overly lofty goal.

"Yes, in fact." Delilah stood from her seat and met her mother's stare with her own highly determined smile. "I intend to secure an offer from the Duke of Branville."

CHAPTER TWO

Thomas Hobbs, the Duke of Huntley, eyed his older sister, who perched across from him in his study. He sat behind the large mahogany desk, while Lavinia remained seated primly on the edge of the chair in front of it. She looked innocent enough, and she was certainly well-dressed, but the greater the distance between them, the better. Lavinia was more like a wasp than a woman. But she was his sister, and he loved her as one must love family.

He was also responsible for her. Their father had died a decade ago. At the tender age of eighteen, Thomas had been forced to leave school and take up the daunting role of duke. He'd done his best to be worthy of the title. While his friends were off drinking, studying, and cavorting, Thomas had to learn how to run his vast estate and keep his tenants happy. He'd managed not only to keep his holdings running smoothly, but he'd increased his tenants' profits threefold.

In addition to his duty to his acreage, he'd had to watch over his mother and his unwed eldest sister. He'd taken care of his mother and provided Lavinia a generous allowance each month, with which to buy whatever clothing or fripperies she wanted. His family and the dukedom were the most important things in Thomas's life. He'd vowed never to let anyone important to him down. Lavinia included.

He eyed her carefully. "What did you want to speak with me about?"

Lavinia rarely spoke to him, and he had to admit he was somewhat intrigued as to what she wanted.

A scrawny, one-eyed cat jumped to the desktop and Lavinia gasped. "What in heaven's name is that thing?" She pushed herself back in her seat to put distance between herself and the animal.

Thomas stood and scooped the cat into his arms. He carefully let the cat down in the corridor outside the study and closed the door. Then he turned and made his way back to his desk. "That is Hercules."

"You own a cat?" Lavinia's voice dripped skepticism.

"No. I have agreed to house a cat for Delilah, who found it outside the mews near her town house badly injured by another cat. Hence its solitary eye."

"Why doesn't Delilah keep the cat at her house?" Lavinia asked, her nose still pinched.

"Her mother doesn't allow animals inside."

"I don't blame her. It could be flea-bitten."

"It most certainly was flea-bitten," Thomas confirmed. "But Delilah gave it a bath and assures me it's perfectly clean now."

"The things you allow that girl to talk you into," Lavinia sneered.

A grin spread across his face. "You don't know the

half of it. In addition to that cat, there is a three-legged dog living in the stables at Huntley Park, and a one-eared rabbit upstairs in the servants' quarters. All courtesy of Delilah's big heart."

"You cannot be serious," Lavinia intoned. "A one-eared rabbit?"

"Yes." Thomas sighed. "But something tells me my little menagerie of misfits is not what you've come to speak to me about today."

"You're right." Lavinia smoothed a finger over one dark eyebrow. "What I've come to discuss is quite simple, really." She lifted her chin. "I want to marry."

Thomas blinked. Surely, he'd heard her incorrectly. Lavinia had stopped searching for a husband long ago. They'd all assumed she was a confirmed spinster. He tilted his head to the side. "Marry?"

Her face remained blank. "That's correct."

Blast it. He *had* heard her correctly.

Lavinia barely shrugged one silk-encased shoulder. "It's your duty to find me a husband, Thomas. I'd like it to happen by the end of the Season."

"This Season?" Thomas tried to keep his face blank, but no doubt Lavinia could see the skepticism that was certain to be there. She was correct. He did have a duty to his sister, but he'd always assumed she would simply remain under his care indefinitely.

"That's right." Lavinia's lips tightened into a prune-like bunch. "I've waited long enough. It's high time I marry."

It was *beyond* high time. At thirty-two, Lavinia was five years older than Thomas, and firmly and solidly on the shelf. She'd had had a debut many years ago and had nearly been married to Thomas's good friend, Lord Owen Monroe. But his other sister, Alexandra, had been madly in love with Monroe for years, and had eventually convinced both Owen's parents and their parents to allow the match. Even though Lavinia hadn't given a toss about Owen, she had flown into a rage, as usual, and spent the next several years doing as she pleased. Thomas suspected the worry over Lavinia's behavior had led, at least in part, to the heart condition that had taken their father's life several years later.

In the years since he'd become duke, this was the first time Thomas had ever had a discussion with Lavinia about taking a husband. He'd merely assumed, as they all had, that she was completely . . . well, unmarriageable. His sister was beautiful, educated, and poised. But she had an adder's tongue and the disposition to match. The woman was a shrew, plain and simple.

He cleared his throat. "I'm not certain I—"

Lavinia held up a hand. "If you're about to refuse me, I suggest you rethink your words. We both know that I was Father's favorite. He would want this for me. I've been in mourning, perhaps longer than I should have been, but now I want a husband, and I intend to have one."

She was blaming her lack of a husband on her mourning? Convenient. Lavinia always got what Lavinia wanted. Or, more correctly, what she demanded. But she also knew exactly what to say to Thomas to affect him. Lavinia *had* been Father's favorite. And Thomas had been his least favorite. Or, more correctly, Thomas and his father had fought at nearly every opportunity. Including the last time Thomas ever saw him alive. Lavinia may have contributed to his father's heart problem, but Thomas had put the nail in the man's coffin, a fact he'd had to live with for the last decade, a fact he would carry with him the rest of his life.

Thomas tapped his fingers along the desktop in front of him. "Do you . . . have anyone in mind?"

Her face registered no emotion. She waved a hand in the air. "I assume you'll be able to come up with someone adequate."

Thomas racked his brain. None of the gentlemen of his acquaintance would be interested in Lavinia, and he frankly wouldn't wish his awful sister on any of them. The odds of Lavinia finding a husband calculated themselves inside his brain. Not favorable. Not at all. "I'm sorry, Lavinia, it's just that I . . . had assumed you were no longer interested in marriage."

Her eyes narrowed on him. "I may no longer be a lass of eighteen, but I'm still a member of one of the best families in London, and I expect you will provide me with a sizable dowry. One that will attract the sort of suitor I deserve."

Deserve? Thomas wasn't certain who she deserved. Or who deserved her. But she was correct about her dowry. If he raised it a bit, the odds of her finding a husband would increase. He might have to raise it substantially, he thought with a grimace.

"What else do I have?" Her voice took on a weepy quality, and she produced a handkerchief and dabbed at her eyes in an attempt to convince him she was crying. "Alexandra is already married. I expect you'll marry eventually, and when you do, I cannot imagine your new duchess will be pleased to have your elder sister lingering about the house."

Thomas settled back in his chair and watched her. He didn't believe for a moment she was truly upset, but she made a good point. Perhaps Lavinia was right. Perhaps it would help both of them to see her married.

The handkerchief quickly fell away from her face. "I expect to have an arrangement by the end of the Season." She stood and made her way to the door. "I'm depending

upon you, Thomas." She turned back slowly with a
snide smile on her face. Her false tears had quickly dried.
"If you fail, I can make your life quite unpleasant."

Thomas shook his head. Of course, she had to end
with a threat. Typical of Lavinia. "Have a lovely day,
sister dear."

She exited the room without sparing him another look.
Thomas leaned back in his chair, ran a hand through his
hair, and groaned. Damn. He hadn't seen *this* coming.
Lavinia wanted a husband? How the hell was he supposed to make *that* happen? He'd spent the last decade
of his life figuring out things he knew little about and
mastering them, but becoming a matchmaker just might
well be beyond his skills.

When he'd taken on the role of duke, his entire life had
changed. He'd gone from a carefree young marquess at-
tending Oxford, to a man with a slew of important and
varied responsibilities. He hadn't thought he could do it.
Not at first. But he'd studied and learned and made every
effort to become the man his father would have wanted
him to become. A man his mother and sisters could be
proud of. Not that Lavinia was proud. But Al was. And
so was Mother. His carefree days were cut short, and the
load of responsibility was placed heavily upon him, and
he'd managed it all, while being loyal to his friends, like
his good friend, Will.

He and Will had grown up together. Spent their child-
hoods together. Will had been the stable boy on Thomas's father's estate. After the former duke died, Thomas
had promoted his friend to the role of his valet. Will
was a questionable-at-best valet, but Thomas didn't
care. Will had been teased unmercifully in his youth for
his stuttering problem, and he and Thomas had got into
more than one fistfight with other boys over it. Thomas

had never let Will fight alone. The difference in their stations didn't matter to him and never had.

Thomas Hobbs was loyal and dutiful if he was anything, and if his sister wanted a husband, he would do his damnedest to find her one.

As luck would have it, his closest friend happened to be a matchmaker. Delilah would know what to do. He'd call upon her for assistance. He would ask Delilah to find a husband for Lavinia. It might be the most difficult match she'd ever make, but if anyone could do it, it was she.

Of course, it would open the door for Delilah and her friend Lucy to ask him for the thousandth time why *he* refused to take a wife. But he would simply continue to put them off. For Thomas had a very good reason for pretending not to be interested in marriage. A very good reason indeed.

CHAPTER THREE

Delilah flew into Lucy Hunt's library. The large room was lined with its requisite bookshelves, but it was also cluttered with the items they'd been collecting all summer for the set of their performance. The tree, moss, and donkey ears Delilah had contributed sat on a table near the center of the room, along with a host of similar things.

Cassandra Swift, the Countess of Swifdon—one of Lucy's closest friends—sat in the corner, painting a large tree on a swath of fabric. With her honey-blond hair and cornflower-blue eyes, Cass was a beautiful artist and had been commissioned to paint the sets for their production. Delilah's cousin by marriage, Danielle Cavendish, occupied another corner, where she and a team of maids had been tasked with sewing all of the costumes.

In addition to Derek Hunt, some of their other friends were there, including Lord Owen Monroe, Cass's husband, Julian, the Earl of Swifdon, and Lucy's cousin, Garrett, the

Earl of Upbridge. The men were busy carrying in additional items needed for the play.

"Delilah, there you are." Lucy floated over to greet her. The duchess was gorgeous and diminutive with black curly hair and two different colored eyes, one hazel, the other blue. She twirled in a circle, her green skirts flaring around her ankles. "It's coming together nicely, don't you think?"

Delilah nodded and glanced around at the chaos. "Yes, what else do we need?"

Lucy tapped a finger against her cheek. "A lantern, a bush, a scroll, and a toy dog, if we can get one."

Delilah raised one finger in the air. "I think I can get a stuffed dog."

"Perfect, dear," Lucy replied with a smile and a nod.

Delilah narrowed her eyes in thought. "A real one wouldn't be acceptable, would it?"

"I don't think so, dear. Seems like that might quickly turn into trouble."

"You have a point. I've been hiding everything in my bedchamber all summer," Delilah said with a smile. "Mother never comes to visit me in my bedchamber. *J'adore* the privacy, of course, but I do think if I were hiding an actual dog in there, she might find out."

At mention of Delilah's mother, Lucy rolled her unusually colored eyes. "Yes, well, I just came from the meeting of the Royal Society for the Humane Treatment of Animals, and Lady Rothwell was delighted when I told her the sets for the play were nearly complete. Step lively, boys," Lucy said to the men, "there are still many things in the carriages."

Owen and Julian shuffled out again. Derek stopped to give his wife a welcoming kiss on top of the head before following them.

Lucy wandered over to the moss that Garrett had left on the table. "We'll need more of this. I want the stage to look like a real forest in the middle of the night."

"Yes," Delilah agreed. "There's not much sense in doing it if we don't do it correctly."

Letting the paper moss float back to the table, Lucy crossed her arms over her chest and sighed. "I've had to keep the children away from the fairy wings for days. Mary and Ralph insist they want to be in the play."

Delilah clapped her hands together. "You should let them, Lucy. No doubt they'd be excellent and have so much fun."

"Yes, but, they're only five and six years old. I seriously doubt they'll be able to remain awake all evening. Otherwise, I would allow them to."

Delilah laughed. "I suppose a production of *A Midsummer Night's Dream* is a bit much for small children."

Lucy reached up to push away one dark curl from her forehead. "I'd love to cast Cass's daughter in it since she's older, but it seems the girl has no interest in performing. She's shy like her mother, the dear."

Lucy glanced over to Cass, who remained painting in the corner. Cass turned to them with a smile. "I'd much rather be painting than acting. And Bella would be a bundle of nerves on a stage."

"We know, dear," Lucy replied, smiling back. "We know. She's a gorgeous child, however, and quite as kind and lovely as her mother. Don't worry. We'll cast someone else as the last fairy."

"That reminds me." Delilah marched over to the desk in the corner by the window and picked up a board with a list tacked to it. "Let's go over the cast again. We only have a few small parts that still need to be filled and not much time to fill them."

"Very well." Lucy strolled over to the window and looked out at the men unloading more of the decorations from the carriage.

Meanwhile, Delilah held a quill against the paper. "You and Derek are Titania and Oberon, of course."

Lucy clasped her hands together. "Yes. I've always wanted to dress like a fairy princess. One has so little opportunity to dress like a fairy princess in life," she finished with a sigh.

Delilah tapped the end of the quill against her lips. "I quite agree. It's a situation of which full advantage must be taken."

Lucy came to stand next to Delilah and peered over her shoulder at the list. "Julian is Duke Theseus," she said. "Alex was supposed to be Hippolyta, but now that she's told us she's with child, we must find someone else for that part."

"Cousin Rafe is Nick Bottom," Delilah added. "And Jane is Hermia."

Lucy nodded. "Garrett is Lysander. You are Helena."

A smile spread across Delilah's face. "That leaves Thomas as Demetrius."

"I still say I should have been cast as Puck." Thomas strolled into the room carrying an armful of paper leaves. Delilah glanced over at him and laughed. Thomas was tall and slim with dark hair and blue eyes. He was dressed in the simple, unfrumpy way of his: dark gray trousers, a sapphire overcoat, a white waistcoat with a white shirt, and a cravat tied in a highly questionable manner. His polished black boots completed his ensemble.

They'd met at a ball when Delilah was thirteen and Thomas was seventeen and had been thick as thieves ever since. Delilah, who had been too young to be there in the first place, had snuck inside and said something cynical about Lady Hammock's turban. When Thomas made a similar comment, she asked him to sit next to her, and they'd spent the remainder of the ball talking and laughing uproariously together.

The smile remained on Delilah's face as she took him in from head to toe. He was the furthest thing from a Puck a man could possibly be. "There you are, Thomas. I thought I wouldn't see you today."

"I finished the meeting with my solicitor early," he replied, dropping his armful of paper leaves on the settee. "I wanted to see what else we need for the set. I also have a business proposition for the two of you. That is, if you'll allow me to play the role of Puck instead of Demetrius."

"It's far too late for that. You cannot be Puck," Lucy replied, waving a finger at him. "Cade has already memorized all the lines."

"Besides, you're a perfectly swoon-worthy Demetrius," Delilah assured him, gathering the leaves from the settee and depositing them next to the donkey ears on the table nearby.

Thomas cocked his head to the side. "Always thought Demetrius was more of an ass than Nick Bottom."

Delilah laughed and shook her head. "It's a play for charity, Thomas. And we're only doing the *one* performance."

Thomas shrugged. "Very well. Demetrius, it is."

"Thank you for being so agreeable." Delilah bit her lip. "I only hope my mother doesn't disown me when she finds out what I've been up to."

Lucy's face turned tender. She touched Delilah's shoulder. "Oh, dear. Your mother's always threatening to disown you for one thing or another. I daresay this will hardly register."

"Yes, but still, becoming an actress isn't something that will endear me to her. Not to mention Lord Hilton has been coming around more and more of late. I believe he's on the verge of making an offer, and she won't like anything that might cause him not to. For instance, having an actress for a daughter."

Lucy waved a hand in the air. "Who is an actress? We are putting on a one-time performance for charity at my country house, and the only way to see it is to offer a large sum to the Royal Society. It's not as if we're selling tickets at Covent Garden, for heaven's sake."

Delilah sighed, sinking onto the settee. "I know, but Mother remains the most difficult person in the world to please. If she's not rebuking me for my lack of patience and decorum, she's displeased that I've got through the last five Seasons with nary an offer."

Lucy rolled her eyes. "Who cares? You don't want *any* offer. You want a good one. Besides, I didn't have any offers my first several Seasons, and I ended up marrying a duke."

"I've tried to tell her that," Delilah replied. "She's not convinced."

Lucy plucked at her green cap sleeve. "Not to mention you've spent the last few Seasons helping your friends find good matches because you are loving and caring and excellent at matchmaking. You've been trained by the best."

"Wasn't she trained by you, Lucy?" Thomas asked, grinning. He toyed with the donkey ears as they spoke.

Lucy settled onto the settee next to Delilah. "Precisely my point."

Delilah poked at her coiffure with the tip of the quill. "Yes, but Mother insists I stop trying to matchmake others this Season and focus on myself."

"Really?" Thomas dropped the donkey ears he was fooling with.

A wide smile spread across Lucy's face, and she clasped her hands together. "Are you quite serious?"

Delilah nodded, uneasiness roiling through her middle. "Yes. And I agreed. I blame it on the crystal bowl."

"The crystal bowl?" Thomas echoed, frowning.

Delilah winced. "I was trying to collect a squirrel from the foyer and ended up breaking Mother's crystal bowl. Afterward, I was so flustered I believe I would have agreed to anything she asked of me."

Lucy hugged her friend with glee as she exclaimed, "Oh, Delilah, I've been waiting for years for you to tell me you're ready to find a husband. I could not be more thrilled. Now, who are the prospects?"

"Yes," Thomas said, his tone droll. He threw himself into the chair next to Delilah, stretched out his long legs, and batted his eyelashes at her in an overly dramatic fashion. "I'm on tenterhooks. Who *are* the prospects?"

Delilah shoved at Thomas's shoulder. "Do not make fun of me. *You* may not believe in marriage, but I have always been a proponent of it, and *I* must marry."

"I never said I didn't believe in it," Thomas replied, tugging at his cuff and still smiling. "I merely said I wasn't interested in rushing into it. And that's almost always after the two of you have begged me to allow you to matchmake for me."

Delilah rolled her eyes at him. "You're a duke, for heaven's sake, and you won't allow us to find you a duchess! It's positively maddening."

Lucy dismissed Thomas with another wave of her hand. "Don't let him dissuade you, dear. We'll find you an excellent match. In fact, I intend to make it my first priority for the remainder of the Season."

The look of pure joy on Lucy's face made Delilah laugh. "Had I known you'd be this delighted, I might have searched for a husband three Seasons ago."

"Nonsense." Lucy took the cast list and quill from Delilah's hands and set them back on the desk. "Three Seasons ago, we were hard at work bringing Lady Eleanor Rothschild together with the Marquess of Hinsdale."

"That was an excellent match," Delilah replied, nodding. "Those two are ever so happy together, and now they have baby Theodora and—"

"Ahem." Thomas cleared his throat. "I believe Her Grace asked you a question. Who are the prospects for *your* match, Delilah?"

"Yes, that's right." Delilah wandered over to the pile of costumes Danielle had created and picked up a glittery gold fairy wing. She turned to look at her two friends, a catlike smile on her face. "I've been such a disappointment to Mother. There's only one prospect."

Lucy furrowed her brow. "What do you mean?"

Thomas leaned heavily over the arm of his chair. "Yes, what exactly do you mean?"

Delilah twirled the wing in a circle. "I've decided to set my sights on the suitor who'll duly impress Mother. The most eligible bachelor in the *ton* this Season."

She didn't miss the skeptical glances Lucy and Thomas exchanged. Neither of them thought much of her mother. Or Mother's opinions.

"The most eligible bachelor of the Season?" Lucy echoed. "Who is that?"

Delilah stopped spinning the wing and allowed a small smile to pop to her lips. "The Duke of Branville, *bien sûr.*"

"Branville!" Lucy exclaimed with a little gasp.

"What? Don't you think he's eligible?" Worry skittered

through Delilah's middle. She needed Lucy's help to accomplish this feat.

Lucy blinked rapidly. "Yes. Of course he *is* eligible."

"He's also rich and handsome," Delilah added, carefully watching Lucy's face.

"I hear he's funny too," Lucy continued.

"I don't think he's particularly funny," Thomas interjected, a frown on his face. He stood and made his way to the window, looking out with great interest at something, as though the discussion did not hold his attention one bit.

"What's wrong with Branville?" Delilah asked Lucy, pointedly ignoring Thomas's remark.

Lucy glanced away, a hint of guilt in her eyes. "I . . . simply had no idea you would set your sights on him. And there . . . may be a problem."

"A problem? What problem?" Delilah's heart thumped faster. She leaned closer to Lucy and searched her face.

Lucy bit the end of her fingernail. "I recently learned that this Season's most eligible debutante, Lady Emmaline Rochester, has set her sights on Branville."

"Oh, no!" The sick feeling grew in Delilah's middle. Lady Emmaline Rochester was a diamond of the first water. She'd been cleverly entertaining a variety of suitors all Season and hadn't yet appeared to settle on any one of them.

"If I were you, I'd let her have him." Thomas's voice was grumbly.

Delilah sank to the nearby settee, still grasping the fairy wing. "I wish I had known that before I spoke with Mother this morning. I sort of . . . that is to say, I *did* promise her I'd secure an offer from Branville." She bit her lip. "By my birthday."

"Merely because he's purported to be the most eligible bachelor of the Season?" Thomas uttered a sound of derision in his throat and turned from the window to face her.

Delilah nodded miserably. "You know how I get when Mother issues a challenge. She said I'm to marry Clarence Hilton if I cannot secure a better match."

Thomas clenched his jaw. "You cannot be serious."

"Not to worry." Lucy folded her hands in her lap. "These things always have a way of working out. For all we know, Lady Emmaline is not Branville's sort." But a hint of concern sounded in her voice when she added, "When is your birthday again, dear?"

Delilah placed a hand on her roiling belly. She was certain she would cast up her accounts. "July twenty-first. The same night as our performance."

"Excellent." Lucy lifted her chin and presented a confident smile, the authenticity of which Delilah utterly doubted. "That will be plenty of time. You'll have me, Cass, Jane, and all of our other friends helping you. You cannot possibly fail. Besides, you know how much I love a challenge."

Delilah searched Lucy's face for the truth behind the bravado. "What about Lady Emmaline?"

Lucy shrugged. "What about her?"

"She's gorgeous and accomplished," Delilah replied.

"So what, dear?" Lucy blinked at her.

"So . . . I'm . . . not. That's quite a large problem, don't you think?" Delilah crossed her arms over her chest.

Lucy waved a hand in the air again. "Problems, large and small, have never stopped us before. We mustn't allow this one to. Be bold, I like to say."

"You two never fail to amaze me." Thomas threw himself into the chair again and blew out a breath of mild disgust.

"Thank you, dear." Lucy patted Thomas on the shoulder.

"I didn't mean that as a compliment," Thomas replied.

She winked at him. "Perhaps not, but I took it as one. I think all statements should be taken as compliments whenever possible."

"But I'm hardly competition against Lady *Emmaline*," Delilah said. "I'm inelegant, impatient, clumsy, and— let's see, what else does Mother say?—oh, yes, ungrace-ful." She counted off each fault on a finger.

"Rubbish," Thomas mumbled.

"That is not true, dear." Lucy pushed a dark curl away from her forehead. "Besides, I was hardly what anyone would call accomplished, and, again, I managed to marry a duke."

"With all due respect to His Grace," Delilah replied, "Derek is hardly your average duke."

Thomas laughed aloud at that. "What, pray tell, is an average duke?"

Delilah turned her head sharply to the side to eye Thomas. "You know perfectly well what I mean. The Duke of Branville comes from a long line of dukes who look for certain attributes in their future wives. If you were looking for a wife, I daresay you'd be looking for the same attributes."

"And being 'accomplished' is one of those attributes?" Thomas asked, skepticism on his face.

"Of course it is. You know it's true," Delilah replied with an impatient sigh.

"Wait a moment, dear." Lucy pointed a finger in the air. "If average dukes are looking for accomplished wives, what do you contend Derek was looking for?"

Delilah turned to Lucy. "I merely meant that Derek was given his title due to his valiance in battle, and while he is a highly respected war hero, he hardly had the same exacting standards when it came to choosing a wife, which is why he loves you while you're so . . . un-conventional." She patted Lucy's hand. "With absolutely no intention of offending you, Lucy, because you know how much *j'adore* you."

"No offense taken, dear. I suppose you and I are both unconventional. We're quite alike when you think on it." Lucy tapped a finger against her cheek again. "Which gives me an idea."

"What?" Delilah asked, straightening.

"I'm on tenterhooks again," Thomas added dryly, tug-ging at his cuff once more.

"Obviously, what we must do is find an unconven-tional duke." Lucy's eyes twinkled with laughter. "One such as Derek who will appreciate your, ahem, unique-ness."

Delilah rubbed the back of her hand across her fore-head. "That would be a wonderful idea if I hadn't already told my mother that I would secure an offer from the *Duke of Branville*."

Lucy patted Delilah's shoulder. "I completely un-derstand, dear. If I'd said something like that to my mother, I would die trying to accomplish it too."

"You've both gone mad," Thomas interjected.

"No, we're merely determined," Lucy replied. "Don't confuse the two." She turned back to Delilah. "Very well. If it's Branville you must have, then we shall employ every skill in our matchmaking arsenal to bring him up to scratch."

Delilah opened her mouth. "But what about—?"

"No!" Lucy held up a quelling finger. "We mustn't focus on the problems, dear. We must focus on the posi-tives." She cleared her throat. "To that end, what do you have going for yourself that Lady Emmaline does not?"

Delilah scrunched up her nose and contemplated the matter for a few moments.

"I honestly cannot believe I'm listening to this conversation." Thomas rubbed his temple. "If this is how ladies attempt to secure their matches, I'm frightened for my future."

Lucy shot him a conspiratorial glance. "Come now, Thomas. You mustn't run off and tell our secrets. That's the price you pay for having a close friend who is a matchmaker."

Thomas poked out his cheek with his tongue. "I suppose you have a point."

Delilah snapped her fingers. "I thought of something. While Lady Emmaline comes from a good family, mine is older, and my father was an earl while hers is a viscount. Not to mention I'm told I have an *indecently* large dowry and a healthy dose of spunk."

"You don't want to be loved for your dowry, Delilah. That's preposterous," Thomas said, disgust sounding in his voice again.

"Of course I don't," Delilah replied. "But I must use every advantage I have if I'm to win in a battle against Emmaline Rochester."

Lucy nodded and smiled. "Very well. That's perfect, dear. What else?"

Thomas crossed his arms over his chest and stared at them. "Truly?"

Delilah pushed her nose in the air. "If you're going to sit there and eavesdrop, Thomas, be helpful and think of ways in which I can compete with Lady Emmaline."

Thomas tossed a hand in the air. "I can think of a hundred reasons why you're better than Lady Emmaline."

"Now *I'm* on tenterhooks," Delilah replied, blinking at him. "Do tell."

Thomas scrubbed a hand through his hair. "You're funny, you're honest, and you're loyal to name three."

"That's true," Delilah agreed. "Lucy, perhaps we should be writing these down. Wait. I thought of another one," Delilah nearly shouted, pointing her finger at Lucy.

"Ooh, what is it, dear?" Lucy rubbed her hands together.

Delilah smoothed a hand over her unruly hair. "I am clever. I can only hope that cleverness counts for more than decorum in the game of love."

"Clever?" Thomas's frown included an eye roll.

"Yes," Delilah replied. "You know—cunning, wily, crafty?"

"I'm familiar with the word," Thomas replied. "But I don't see what that has to do with marriage."

Lucy shook her head at him. "So naïve."

"I'm naïve?" Thomas pointed at his chest.

"Yes, if you don't think cleverness and craft are involved in matchmaking, I'd say you're quite naïve," Lucy replied.

"Matchmaking and marriage are two different things," Thomas retorted.

Delilah exchanged an exasperated look with Lucy, then she nodded and patted Thomas on the shoulder. "I'm afraid Lucy's right, Thomas. You'd best leave the matchmaking to the experienced matchmakers." She turned back to Lucy. "You said to focus on the positives. In addition to my family, my dowry, and my cleverness, I intend to convince the Duke of Branville that I'm exactly the sort of unconventional lady he should like to marry."

Thomas groaned and rose to his feet. "That's it. I can no longer listen to this nonsense."

Lucy sighed. "No matter. We're done with the conversation for the moment." She turned to face the room and the rest of its occupants who had been quietly going about their business. She raised her voice so all could hear. "Everyone, now that the performance is getting closer, we intend to have rehearsal here three times a week instead of twice, before we go to my country house next month, where we'll practice for a day or two before the final performance."

There was a murmur of assent and approval from the group before they returned to their duties. Delilah allowed a wide smile to spread across her face. She glanced at Thomas first, then Lucy. "I have only a month to secure two goals. Ensure this production comes off without a hitch, and secure a proposal from the Duke of Branville."

Thomas cleared his throat. "Wait. There's something I forgot to add. Three."

Delilah and Lucy both blinked at him. "Three what?" they asked simultaneously.

Thomas scratched his cheek. "Three goals. Before you began this ridiculousness about Branville, I intended to ask you to secure a match for Lavinia as well."

"Lavinia!" Both ladies stared at him in shocked horror.

He stuck his hands into his pockets, a sheepish look on his face. "Yes. She's demanded it of me."

Delilah shook her head and blew out a deep breath. "I'm not certain we can—"

"Hold on, dear," Lucy replied. "As you recently pointed out, we *are* experienced matchmakers. And I just said how much I love a good challenge. If anyone can find a match for Lavinia Hobbs, it's us, don't you think?"

A slow smile dawned across Delilah's face. "Hmm. I

suppose you're right." She turned to Thomas. "Did your sister indicate whom she might like to marry?"

"She hoped I'd have some prospects, actually. Which is why I came in search of you two."

"So you're willing to admit that matchmakers do serve a purpose from time to time, eh, Huntley?" Lucy knocked her shoulder against his.

Thomas gave a long-suffering sigh. "I suppose I must admit it."

Delilah laughed. "As much as that no doubt pained you to say, Thomas, we would be happy to help Lavinia. It's just as well that she doesn't already have someone picked out. As I've recently learned, settling on someone too early makes the entire thing much more difficult."

"Agreed," Lucy added with a nod. "We always do better when there are more options. But don't let that worry you about Branville, Delilah. We'll make an exception in that case."

Thomas shook his head.

Lucy rocked back and forth on her heels. "It looks as if we're to have a busy month, Delilah. We must produce a play and make *three* matches."

"Three?" Thomas echoed.

Lucy nodded. "One for Delilah, one for Lavinia, and one for Lady Emmaline, if we're to get her out of our hair."

"Excellent." Delilah clapped her hands. "Let's get started immediately."

CHAPTER FOUR

Thomas slid into a chair at the Curious Goat Inn. He ordered a mug of ale for himself as well as one for his brother-in-law, Owen Monroe, the Earl of Moreland. Monroe hadn't arrived yet, but Thomas expected him at any minute.

When the barmaid returned with the drinks, Thomas took a large quaff of his and leaned back in his seat. It had been two days since he'd learned of Delilah's plans to wring an offer out of the Duke of Branville, and it still rankled him. Ladies could be downright . . . maddening. First, Lavinia had ordered him to find her a husband, a nearly impossible feat. Then Delilah had announced her intention to marry the Duke of Branville, of all bloody people. What had been a reasonably quiet Season, with only the production of a play to break up the monotony, had turned into a mess. One upon which he would have to get to work immediately to sort out. He took another large quaff from his mug.

Delilah. She was headstrong. She was willful. She was obstinate. Echoing her mother's words, she called herself loud, but the way he saw it, she was exuberant and full of life. She was playful and happy (when she wasn't around her mother). She was funny and fun, and he could always count on her to cheer him up and make him laugh. He'd known the day would come when the reality of their positions in life would catch up to them, and they'd both be expected to marry. But the years had passed in such a simple, easy rhythm. He'd been worried during her first Season that she'd immediately find a husband. But as soon as the Season began, it became clear that she enjoyed making matches for other people so much that she didn't spare a thought to her own. And so it had gone for the last *five* years.

He couldn't blame Delilah's mother for wanting her daughter to marry. Lord knew he had plenty of other things to blame the woman for. For instance, he certainly *could* blame her for frightening her daughter so much that she'd been forced into naming the Duke of Branville as the man from whom she intended to secure an offer. Very well. Perhaps *forced* wasn't the correct word, exactly, but Delilah had always wanted her mother's approval, and apparently she was willing to go to extreme lengths to finally get it. It made him sad for Delilah. It made him angry with her awful mother. And it made him apprehensive for himself.

"Afternoon, Huntley."

Thomas glanced up to see Moreland grinning at him. The earl slid into the seat across from him and pulled his mug of ale close.

"Good to see you, Moreland," Thomas replied.

"My apologies for being late. Alex asked me to deliver more decorations for the play to Claringdon's house.

She's so upset that she cannot be in the performance due to her condition that she's gone quite mad making as many of the decorations on Lucy's list as possible."

Thomas cracked a grin. "Tell her she should be glad she's with child and unable to participate. Jane Upton is quite the taskmaster when it comes to rehearsals."

Moreland's bark of laughter shot across the room. "Yes, well, I managed to get out of acting in the play, but thanks to my wife, I'm quite heavily involved in carting the decorations all over London. Let it be a lesson to you, Huntley." Moreland took a large draught of ale. "When you marry, you are obliged to do such things."

"Ah, but you're forgetting. I've been carrying decorations too, and I'm not married," Thomas pointed out. "Not to mention, Delilah cast me as Demetrius."

Moreland sighed and lifted his mug in a silent salute. "I suppose you're right. That's what you get for having a lady as a best friend."

Thomas laughed aloud at that.

Moreland shook his head. "You fell into step with Delilah Montebank and Lucy Hunt at an early age. There's no way to extract yourself now. Those two ladies are more domineering than all the others combined."

Thomas nodded and laughed again. "Yes, well. I don't know much different. I grew up with two older sisters. I suppose I'm used to domineering women."

Moreland laughed and took another draught. "I wouldn't say Alex is domineering. Lavinia certainly is, though, that's for certain. As for Delilah and Lucy, you may be friends, but watch yourself. They are known for fancying themselves the best matchmakers in the *ton*. How you've managed to escape their machinations with a dukedom, I'll never know."

Thomas thoughtfully stroked the handle of his mug.

"I've been clear with them for several years now that I'm not yet interested in taking a bride," Thomas said firmly. "I like to tell them I'd rather give up all the brandy in London than commit to one person for life."

Moreland arched a brow. "And that does the trick?"

"So far. At the moment, they're preoccupied with Delilah's prospects. Seems the matchmaker has finally decided to make her own match."

"God's sake," Moreland muttered. "I must warn my bachelor friends. With those two on the loose this Season, no eligible man is safe."

Thomas took another draught of ale. "Not to worry. They've already picked the man."

Moreland's eyebrows shot up. "Really? Who's the lucky chap?"

Thomas took another drink. "The Duke of Branville."

Moreland leaned back in his chair and contemplated the news for a moment. "Branville, eh? That's a lofty goal, even for those two. I hear he's got scores of mamas after him day and night."

"No doubt that's true. And it's part of the reason why I asked you to meet me here."

Moreland leaned forward again, his brow wrinkled. "Because of Branville?"

Thomas traced his finger along the cracked surface of the wooden table. "Partially. At some point, I may need your help. You and the other men. But you mustn't tell the ladies."

Moreland's brow furrowed deeper. "What? Why not?"

"Because the women are terrible gossips, and they'll tell Delilah."

"A secret, eh?" Moreland took another swig from his mug. "I can tell Alex, can't I? I don't keep secrets from my wife."

Thomas scratched his chin and contemplated the question for a moment. "I'll tell her when the time's right. Al can keep a secret. I know that."

"Very well. I'm game. What's the secret?" Moreland asked.

Thomas leaned back in his seat and crossed his booted feet at the ankles. "After spending all these years matchmaking her friends, Delilah is ready to take a husband."

"She's been Lucy's disciple for quite a while now. From what I understand, she's made some excellent matches too."

The barmaid returned, and Thomas ordered a second mug of ale. He was finally ready to tell this secret. The one he'd kept all these years. "Delilah hasn't seemed interested in making her own match. Until now."

Moreland shrugged. "Suppose it was bound to happen eventually."

Thomas nodded. "Yes, and her mother has demanded it. I've been waiting for this day. But also dreading it."

A half-smile touched Moreland's lips. "Worried that your friend will make the wrong match, Huntley?"

"Yes." Thomas met his brother-in-law's stare. "Because I want her to pick me."

CHAPTER FIVE

That same afternoon, Delilah sat on the settee in the middle of Lucy Hunt's drawing room. Lucy was there, of course, along with her closest friends, Cassandra and Jane. The three women sat around Delilah in a semicircle.

"Ladies," Lucy began, settling her clasped hands into her lap, "the issue at hand is most serious. I've gathered you here today for what is certain to be our most important matchmaking session in years."

"Delilah's getting married?" Cass exclaimed, a wide, dreamlike smile on her pretty face.

Jane poked her nose out of her ever-present book and took another teacake from the plate that rested on the table in front of them. The countess was slightly plump, with dark brown hair and eyes and silver-rimmed spectacles atop her nose. She had a biting wit and was rarely without a book in one hand and a teacake in the other. "I suppose we all must succumb at some point."

"That is not a particularly helpful comment, Janie," Lucy replied, her lips pursed.

Jane shrugged, stuck her nose back into her book, and continued munching on her teacake.

Lucy cleared her throat. "Now, our lovely, delightful Delilah here has finally decided to focus on her own match."

"Because Mother is at her wits' end with me," Delilah interjected with a nod.

"For whatever reason," Lucy continued, her nose in the air, "our lovely, delightful Delilah here has set her sights on the most eligible bachelor of the Season."

Cass gasped and placed hand to her breast. "The Duke of Branville!"

"One and the same," Lucy replied, smiling at Cass.

"I thought you were going to say Huntley," Jane interjected, not looking up from her book.

Delilah scrunched up her nose. "No. No. Branville is who I'm after. And it won't be an easy feat. I will need all of your help."

Jane pulled the book down low enough to eye Delilah over the top of it. "Do you love him?"

"Branville?" Delilah breathed.

"Yes, Branville," Jane replied. "Isn't that who we're speaking of?"

Delilah opened her mouth to answer and then blinked. Love? The Duke of Branville? She didn't even know him, and she only knew a bit about him. He was handsome and rich. He was eligible. Wasn't that enough? She might not be madly in love with the man, but that hadn't stopped anyone from marrying before. The fact was, she wasn't madly in love with anyone. Love simply hadn't seen fit to barrel her over as it had some of her friends. She could get to know the Duke of Branville. She would see if he

was someone she could spend her life with. But even if
they didn't suit, she would wring an offer from him. She
might be forced to turn him down, but she would get an
offer if it was the last thing she did.

"No, I cannot say I love him," she finally admitted,
clearing her throat.

"That's beside the point," Lucy announced, glaring at
Jane. "We merely want to provide her with the chance to
meet him and spend time with him."

"Oh, is that all? So you aren't hoping for a proposal?"
Jane clarified.

"I definitely want a proposal," Delilah replied. "I suppose I'm hoping we suit." There. That was good enough,
wasn't it?

"What about Lady Emmaline?" Cass asked, obviously
trying to change the subject from Jane's uncomfortably
direct line of questioning.

"We've already discussed it," Lucy said. "Lady Emmaline is—"

"Gorgeous," Delilah pointed out.

Lucy shook her head. "She's—"

"Accomplished," Delilah continued.

Lucy crossed her arms over her chest. "She's—"

"Demure," Delilah said.

"Stop it." Lucy touched her hand to Delilah's arm.
"Being gorgeous, accomplished, and demure are highly
overrated."

"No, they're not," Delilah replied, sliding lower in her
chair. "Oh, why is my mouth always so quick to say things
before my brain catches up? If only I hadn't promised
Mother I would secure a match with Branville, of all
people."

"You've as good a chance with Branville as Lady Emmaline does," Lucy continued. "You merely need the

opportunity for him to get to know you. Then, I've no doubt he will come to see your many qualities and love you as we all do."

Cass and Jane murmured their agreement.

"We also have another task," Lucy announced, straightening her shoulders. "One that may prove even more difficult."

Cass and Jane turned their attention to Lucy.

"*More* difficult?" Jane asked, raising her eyebrows.

"Yes." Lucy looked at Cass first, then Jane. "Thomas asked us to find a husband for . . . Lavinia."

"Lavinia?" Cass breathed, her mouth forming a wide *O*. She pressed a palm to her cheek.

"Lavinia Hobbs?" Jane's voice raised a good octave. She snapped her book shut and sat up straight. "Now that's a feat I'd pay to see. I daresay *that* will be more entertaining than the play."

"Stop it, Jane." Lucy leaned forward to reach for the teapot and pour herself another cup. "Thomas has asked for our help, and Delilah and I intend to help him."

"How in heaven's name do you think you can find a husband for *Lavinia*?" Jane asked, hugging her book to her chest.

"As our cook used to say, there is a lid for every pot," Lucy replied, studiously avoiding everyone's eyes. "Lavinia is lovely and rich. There's bound to be someone who'll want to marry her."

Delilah took a sip of tea. "I've been thinking about it, Lucy. We should invite Lavinia to join us in the play."

The room went silent. Cass's jaw fell open. Jane's eyebrows shot up. Lucy scrunched up her nose and narrowed her eyes, before saying, "I'm not certain Alex will approve, dear. They may be sisters, but you know those two only speak when they must."

"But Alex cannot be in the production, so she won't even have to see Lavinia," Delilah replied. "I'll discuss it with Alex. I'm certain she'll understand once I tell her how Lavinia threatened Thomas."

"Wait a moment," Cass interjected, blinking rapidly. "Lavinia threatened Thomas?"

"Yes," Delilah replied, shaking her head. "She told him she'd make his life difficult if she's not paired off this Season."

"That woman is frightening," Cass breathed, shuddering slightly.

"She certainly is," Delilah replied, raising her teacup to her lips again.

"Very well," Lucy said. "It's agreed. Delilah, you speak to Alex, and we'll invite Lavinia to the rehearsals to attempt to get to know her better. Perhaps she'll take a fancy to one of the bachelors in the play."

Jane grimaced. "God help the bachelors in the play."

"Wait a moment." Lucy tapped her cheek. "I may have the perfect gentleman for Lavinia."

"Who?" Cass asked, her cornflower-blue eyes round as saucers.

Lucy set her teacup on the table in front of her. "Do you remember Lord Stanley?"

"Stanley?" Jane narrowed her eyes in thought.

Lucy nodded, clearly warming to her subject. "Yes, a bit older. Nearly forty. He's good-looking, wealthy, from a decent family."

"Viscount, isn't he?" Cass asked.

"Yes, and a widower," Lucy added.

"I think I remember him," Delilah said.

Lucy dropped another lump of sugar into her teacup and picked it up again. "He's a good-natured chap, and one I don't think would allow Lavinia to run roughshod over him. He's the right age and comes from a good family."

"I suppose you know him," Jane said with resigned sigh.

"But of course. I know everyone," Lucy replied with a wink. "I intend to write him a note this afternoon, asking him to join us for the play as well."

"Do you think he'll say yes?" Delilah asked.

"Of course. Especially if I heavily imply that I may have a lady to introduce him to."

"Very well." Cass smoothed her hands over her skirts. "That may take care of Lavinia if we're fortunate, but what about Delilah and the Lady Emmaline problem?"

A catlike smile spread slowly across Lucy's face. "I've given that quite a bit of thought."

"And?" Jane leaned forward to grab another teacake.

"And . . . the Duke of Branville is not the only fox in the forest. We can present Lady Emmaline with a worthy alternative."

"Like who?" Delilah cocked her head to the side as she stared at Lucy.

The smile on Lucy's face widened. "Like our dear, beloved Thomas. He's a handsome, rich duke too, isn't he?"

CHAPTER SIX

"What exactly did your mother say when you told her you intended to secure an offer from the Duke of Branville?" Thomas asked Delilah later that week as they sat on a bench in front of a table in Berkeley Square, enjoying an ice from Gunter's.

Gunter's was one of the few places they could go to together without causing a scandal. An unmarried lady and an unmarried gentleman going about started gossip. It was ludicrous that they were only allowed out alone in certain places. Of course, Delilah's maid, Amandine, dutifully waited in the coach along with the coachman and the groomsmen, while Delilah and Thomas enjoyed their treats.

"At first she seemed amused by it. Later, she told me I was mad," Delilah said with a chuckle.

"Mad?" Thomas echoed. "She actually used the word *mad*?"

"Yes." Delilah shrugged. "I prefer *insensé*, of course. She didn't even use the French."

A muscle ticked in Thomas's jaw. "I'd say that's the least offensive thing she did."

Delilah studied her spoon, turning it over and over in the glass cup. "She's been through a great deal. My father's death was difficult on her."

Thomas shook his head. "It was difficult on you too. You were a child, but she only seems to care about herself." Thomas needed to change the subject. No good ever came of discussing Delilah's mother. Delilah was loyal and loving, and kept trying to get her awful mother to show her some affection, however slight. Delilah might make light of her mother's words, but he knew they affected her deeply.

Delilah flashed him a look of amusement. "Oh, Thomas, you've never liked her. Ever since she chastised you for throwing pebbles at my window when we were younger."

It was true. He used to toss pebbles at Delilah's window to get her attention. It was also true that Lady Vanessa had become incensed one night when she'd found him doing it, but that was *not* why he didn't like the woman. He didn't like the woman because she treated her wonderful daughter so poorly.

"Yes, well, I no longer toss pebbles at your window. Now, I simply pull my carriage to the door, but your mother remains not particularly motherly." It was the kindest thing he could say about the woman.

"Perhaps." Delilah took another bite of her ice. "But I've never been terribly daughterly either."

Thomas furrowed his brow. "What is that supposed to mean?"

Delilah shrugged. "I only mean that if I weren't such a disappointment to her, I'm certain she'd be more agreeable to me."

"I'm not certain about that at all." Thomas glanced away. Delilah was smart and funny and beautiful and unique and a hundred other wonderful things. If her idiotic mother couldn't see what a gem she had, she didn't deserve her. But, Delilah's intense loyalty was another thing he admired in her. Once she decided you were part of her inner circle, she would move heaven and earth for you if you needed her to. Her mother was no exception.

He stretched out his legs and laid an arm across the back of the bench. It was time to change the subject. "Do we have all the decorations for the play?"

"Nearly." Her spoon arrested halfway to her lips, Delilah stopped and blinked. A sly smile crept onto her face. "Did I tell you Miss Adeline shall be in the play?"

Thomas's smile faded. "No. You did not. May I resign my role in light of this news?"

Miss Adeline was Delilah's parrot. She'd insisted on procuring a parrot when she learned that Cade Cavendish, her cousin Daphne's brother-in-law, was a pirate. In truth, Cade was a privateer, but that version of events did not suit Delilah's penchant for the dramatic. She insisted she was related to a pirate, and further insisted that the family must own a parrot as a result. The cursed thing lived at Daphne's house, of course, because Lady Vanessa disliked animals. But Delilah had gamely offered to be the one to look after the bird. She'd had the thing for several months and had been calling it Miss Adeline before she discovered, to her chagrin, that it was in fact a *male* parrot. Delilah, never one to allow such mistakes to affect her greatly, decided it would be too confusing to the creature to change his name, and therefore insisted upon calling him Miss Adeline for the rest of his days. The parrot did not seem to mind.

Delilah rolled her eyes. "Must you fight with Miss Adeline?"

"I don't fight with him," Thomas replied. "He fights with me. Specifically by biting me every chance he gets. Plus, he has a ridiculous name."

She shook her head. "First, he's terribly jealous. And second, it's impolite of you to mention his unfortunate name given the fact that you yourself have a ridiculous string of names." She blinked at him innocently. "Thomas Marcus Devon Peabody Hobbs."

"At least all of my names indicate the correct gender," he said with a scowl.

Delilah stuck her nose in the air. "You're far too judgmental."

"Judgmental of a nuisance bird. What is he jealous of, at any rate?" Thomas leaned back and studied the leaves in the tree above them.

Delilah shrugged. "The time I spend with you, I suppose."

"Which is ridiculous because I am a person and he is a parrot."

"Don't tell him that." She took another bite of her ice.

Thomas rolled his head to the side and smiled at her. "You're right. It may scar him to discover he's a bird."

Delilah waved her spoon in the air. "He knows he's a bird, but he also knows he's a special bird."

"Yes, well, I for one cannot wait until that special bird bites the Duke of Branville."

Delilah gasped. "How positively unsporting of you. I don't want to do anything to jeopardize my chances with

Branville. Now, I must worry about Miss Adeline biting him, a possibility I had not before considered."

Thomas refused to be remorseful for his remark. "You know it's bound to happen."

Delilah plucked at her bottom lip. "I suppose you're right. I must make preparations."

Thomas narrowed his eyes as he studied her profile. "Do I even want to know what you're scheming?"

Delilah shook her head. "No, I don't suppose you do."

He regarded her down the length of his nose. "So tell me. What is your plan to lure Branville?" He waggled his eyebrows.

Delilah primly pressed her lips together. "Don't make it sound so suspect. It's not as if I intend to trap him in a large box."

Thomas propped an elbow on the table in front of them. "I wouldn't put it past Lucy. You'd better check with her before you make that claim."

Delilah laughed. "My plan is not complicated. I intend to attempt to be demure, ladylike, and charming. Isn't that what you men like?"

Thomas scratched his chin. "I suppose some men like it. I've always preferred a woman who speaks her mind, enjoys herself, and is friendly for the sake of being friendly."

Delilah offered him a fond smile. "I suppose that's why you and I have always been friends, Thomas. You're one of the few people who isn't put off by my being unconventional. And you're one of the few people who will make fun of the ridiculous strictures of the *ton* with me."

She went to take another bite, missed, and the chocolate concoction dribbled down the front of her gown. She rolled her eyes skyward. "See? This is the exact sort of thing I mustn't do in front of the Duke of Branville."

Thomas handed her a napkin from the tabletop. "Branville's never made a mistake before?"

She dabbed at the chocolate, which only served to smear it. "I highly doubt Lady Emmaline does things like drip chocolate ice on her gowns."

"Well, perhaps she should." Thomas rubbed the back of his hand over his eyes. He would have liked nothing better than to come out and tell Delilah how he felt about her, how he'd always felt about her. But he'd known her long enough to understand that she became easily anxious over ideas that were not ostensibly her own. Besides, he had no way of surmising whether she returned his affections in the least. The fact that she'd set her very determined sights on the Duke of Branville meant she would have to give up that plan before she'd so much as entertain another.

Thomas's plan at the moment consisted of hastening the end of her infatuation with Branville. It wouldn't be easy, of course, because of her desire to please her mother. The entire situation was one that needed to be handled with extreme patience and care. Which was fine with him, because while Delilah may not have patience, as she often liked to point out, Thomas had patience in spades.

He cleared his throat. "You don't actually plan to pretend you are conventional for the sake of attracting Branville, do you?"

She took the last bite of her ice and set the empty glass cup and spoon on the table in front of her. She tugged at the strings of her bonnet. "I must make some effort to act like a future duchess should. I'm not about to bring him up to scratch by being loud and lacking decorum."

Thomas eyed her carefully. "Do you *truly* want to marry him?"

She shrugged and glanced away. "I must marry *someone*, and marrying Branville will make Mother happy, at least."

Thomas expelled his pent-up breath, but when he turned to Delilah, he forced himself to roll his eyes. Delilah would be terribly suspicious if he was anything other than his normal sarcastic, devil-may-care self. "Sounds terribly romantic."

She plunked her hands on her hips. "You know these things aren't always romantic, Thomas."

"Really? Aren't you the one who bragged about the love matches you made for your friends?"

"Yes, well, those ladies were quite fortunate. It doesn't *always* happen that way."

"Name one couple you know who wasn't a love match," Thomas prompted.

Delilah furrowed her brow. "Let's see, there's Lucy and Derek. Cass and Julian. Jane and Garrett." She ticked off the couples on her fingers. "Cousin Daphne and Rafe. Alex and Owen. Christian and Sarah. Cade and Danielle. Meg and Hart."

"All love matches, correct?" He grinned at her.

She frowned at him. "There has to be *someone* who married first and fell in love later."

"I'm waiting." He propped his chin on his elbow.

"How do I know I'm *not* in love with the Duke of Branville?" she finally answered primly.

He eyed her from the side. "You can't be serious."

Delilah shrugged. "He's handsome, rich, and funny. I may well fall madly in love with him the moment I meet him."

Thomas's spine stiffened. "First, I do not believe he's

particularly funny. I don't know who told you that. Second, I suppose there's only one way to find out if you fall madly in love with him at first sight, isn't there?" The thought made Thomas feel as if he'd been punched in the gut, but he said the words with as much sarcasm as he could muster.

"I suppose you're right," Delilah replied with a resolute nod.

He pushed his own empty glass cup farther onto the table. It was time to change the subject again, to one he must handle with extreme care. Thomas scratched his cheek. "I suppose I must marry someday as well." He watched her from the corner of his eye.

Her eyes grew round as sovereigns. "You? Marry? I seem to recall that every time I've mentioned a potential match to you over the years, you've steadfastly declared yourself a bachelor and refused to even countenance the discussion. I believe you said something about giving up all the brandy in London. Or am I thinking of someone else?"

She had a point. Of course, he'd put off talk of his match over the years. He hadn't wanted to discuss it until Delilah was ready to marry. Only he'd envisioned the whole thing happening in an entirely different manner. He assumed that one Season, she would announce her readiness to find a husband. Lucy would immediately realize that Delilah should marry Thomas. The duchess would set up an elaborate plot to push them together, all the while having no idea that Thomas was quite ready and willing to oblige. In the course of Lucy's machinations, Delilah would come to realize how much she truly cared for Thomas, and how right they would be together as a married couple. He would choose a ring that sparkled nearly as much as she did, and he'd get down on one knee when the time was right, and that would be that.

It all made perfect sense. Only he hadn't counted on Delilah picking out a different husband before she'd barely decided to make a match.

"I suppose that sounds like something I may have said," he allowed, tipping his hat to the back of his head.

"All these years, whenever I've asked when you intend to take a bride and offered my services in matchmaking, you've refused."

Thomas folded his arms over his chest. "Just because I haven't been particularly eager to put the parson's noose around my neck doesn't mean I never plan to marry."

"Yes, well. That day may come sooner than you think," Delilah said, a sly grin on her pretty face.

Suspicion curled in his middle. "What do you mean?"

"Lucy has got the notion that *you* might be the best way to distract Lady Emmaline from the Duke of Branville."

Thomas straightened his spine. "Pardon?"

Delilah shrugged. "She pointed out that you're a rich, handsome duke too."

He expelled his breath slowly and painfully. "How did I become involved in this madness?"

"By proximity, of course." She giggled. "The same way anyone ever becomes involved in Lucy's plots."

Thomas wondered for the hundredth time if he should involve Lucy in his own plotting. It was tempting. The duchess would make a strong ally. On the other hand, Lucy was not known for her subtlety. Quite the opposite, actually. He could imagine her marching straight up to Delilah and pointedly asking her if she fancied Thomas. Then the entire plan would be ruined. Lucy Hunt had a long and storied history of making messes of people's lives. True, things tended to work out for the best at the end of her plots, but the last thing Thomas wanted was for his courtship of Delilah to become a mess, even temporarily. It was too important to him.

No, wooing Delilah had to be done with subtlety and patience. Neither of which were qualities the Duchess of Claringdon possessed. Even if he had been tempted to ask for Lucy's help, Delilah's claim that Lucy wanted to use him to distract Lady Emmaline from Branville had made the final decision for him. Once Lucy got an elaborate scheme in her head, there was no stopping her. He'd do much better to wait and allow their machinations to play out before he made his move. It was all right. He had time. Delilah hadn't even *met* Branville yet.

"Yes, well, I'm not convinced you should secure a match with the Duke of Branville," Thomas said, putting a snobbish, drawn-out emphasis on the man's title. He didn't necessarily mean to outwardly disapprove of the man, but he also had no intention of encouraging the match.

Delilah pushed a curl behind her ear. "Why don't you approve of him?"

Thomas crossed his arms over his chest again, a thunderous scowl on his face. "I never said I don't approve of him."

A seemingly helpless smile tugged at Delilah's pink lips before she pursed them solemnly. "Then why do you say his name in that painful way of yours?"

Thomas clenched his jaw and looked away. "Because dukes are snobs by nature. You'll be a snob if you marry Branville."

She laughed. "Need I point out that *you're* a duke?"

"Yes, but I'm not a snobby one. Quite rare, if you ask me."

"Derek is a duke and he's not a snob."

"As you've already said, Derek is a duke because he was a war hero. He wasn't raised in luxury."

A breeze blew a curl across Delilah's cheek, and she turned her head so it would fly away. "You're ridiculous. Dukes are not snobs, and Branville is a perfectly nice man. I've heard as much from several people. I'm not such a ninny that I would seek to engage myself to an awful person merely to please my mother."

"I'm glad to hear that, at least." And that was what frightened him. What if Delilah got to know the Duke of Branville and did fall in love with him? What would Thomas do then?

Delilah twirled her bonnet ribbon and nonchalantly added, "All I must do is find out if the Duke of Branville meets the criteria on my list."

Thomas's arms dropped away from his chest, and he stared at her aghast. "What list?"

Delilah left off plucking at her sleeve, met his eyes, and winced. "I got the idea from your sister, actually. Alex told me that Owen met every criterion on her list."

Thomas arched a brow. Oh, this was simply rich. His brows shot up, and he leaned forward over the table, his chin propped on one fist. "Dare I ask what's on your list?"

She trailed her pink reticule around the tabletop with one finger. She shot a glance at him. "Now that you mention it, it might help you to know. You may make yourself more pleasing to *your* future bride."

He almost laughed aloud. "Now I *must* hear it. Where is this list?"

Delilah eyed him carefully. Then she drew her reticule

into her lap, opened it, and pulled out a small sheet of paper that had been folded many times over. She carefully unfolded the paper and spread it on the table in front of her.

"Ahem." She cleared her throat. "Before I read it, you must promise not to make fun of it."

Thomas slowly shook his head with a smile on his face. "I can promise no such thing."

Delilah arched a brow at him. "Fine. But don't be mean."

He lifted his palms in a gesture of innocence. "I'm never mean. Sarcastic, perhaps, but not mean."

Shooting him a warning look, she lifted her chin and adjusted the paper just so for recitation. "Delilah Montebank's Future Husband Qualities List," she announced. "One must always title things properly."

He inclined his head. "Of course."

She lifted her chin higher. "Number one. Eligible."

"Obviously."

"Number two. Kind."

"Important," Thomas agreed.

"Number three. Intelligent."

"One would hope."

"Number four. Funny."

"I already told you he's not funny."

"Shut up." She paused. "Number five. Healthy."

Thomas frowned. "How on earth would you know for certain?"

Delilah lifted one shoulder. "I suppose I can request a doctor's report."

"This is ridiculous, you know? But go on." He nodded.

"Number six. Forgiving." She paused again and arched a brow over the top edge of the paper. "One must be forgiving if one is going to spend one's life with me. I often do things such as break expensive crystal bowls."

Thomas scowled. "No doubt Branville can afford a new bowl or two."

"Number seven." Her face turned an adorable shade of pink. "Ahem. Handsome and kissable."

Thomas cupped a hand behind his ear. "Pardon?"

She narrowed her eyes on him. "You heard me."

He gave himself a moment to swallow the urge to laugh, then schooled his expression into one of careful solemnity. "Handsome and kissable?"

She scrunched up her nose. "You promised not to be mean."

He cleared his throat. "It's an impressive list, but are you certain the fabled Duke of Branville can live up to all of those qualities?"

Delilah folded the paper and pushed it back into her reticule. "I've no idea, but I have every intention of finding out."

Thomas lifted a brow. "How do you intend to do that?"

"By spending time with him, of course. Lucy plans to introduce me to Branville at the Penningtons' ball tomorrow night."

CHAPTER SEVEN

Thomas unraveled his cravat for the second time. He wasn't particularly adept at tying the neckcloth, but he was better than Will. Thomas hated to embarrass his friend by making him attempt to tie his blasted neckcloth half a dozen times. They'd worked this way for years. Thomas did most of his own dressing with Will adding what he could to the process. It may have resulted in Thomas going out into the world wearing a few slightly wrinkled shirtfronts and some askew cravats, but Thomas would never hurt his friend's feelings by criticizing him.

He stood in front of the looking glass in his bedchamber and worked on the neckcloth while Delilah's Future Husband Qualities List repeated itself in his mind. He'd spent the better part of the day mentally checking off each of the requirements she'd cited. Specifically, ensuring *he* met all of them.

Eligible? Yes. Decidedly.

Kind? He'd like to think so.

Intelligent? He had gone to Eton and at least begun Oxford, hadn't he?

Funny? That was best left for someone else to determine, but he'd always been able to make Delilah laugh. That was promising. And Branville was *not* funny. He'd known Branville at school, and the man had never made him laugh.

Healthy? That was one criterion Thomas could resolutely say he met. He'd always been fit as a fiddle. Oh, he'd broken the odd bone a time or two doing things he probably shouldn't have in his youth, but he'd never had any lengthy illnesses or lingering health problems.

Forgiving? More forgiving than Delilah's awful mother, but that wasn't exactly saying much. Besides, he didn't agree with Delilah that she needed to be forgiven for anything. A crystal bowl could be replaced, but Delilah was a true treasure. All of her so-called detriments (according to her mother) would never add up to the joy she brought to her friends' lives.

Handsome? If others were to be believed. He certainly had never had any trouble attracting the opposite sex. But his heart had always belonged to Delilah, so he'd never much attempted to attract other ladies.

Kissable? That remained to be seen. It depended entirely upon who was on the other end of the kissing. He could only hope Delilah would want to kiss him when the opportunity presented itself.

He'd got himself in a bind. He'd always known he and Delilah were a perfect match for each other. Delilah, however, seemed to look at him as nothing more than a friend. That had been entirely appropriate given their age when they first met. However, now they were plenty old enough to marry, and he loved her madly. But he knew two things about Delilah. She was stubborn, and she didn't like anyone else to tell her what to do. She had enough of that from her mother.

He let the damnable cravat hang for a moment and rubbed his hands over his eyes. It would be awkward to be the first to divulge his feelings. Thomas was rather expecting she'd figure it out on her own. He always hoped that one day she'd look at him and realize he'd been there the whole time, her perfect match. The woman was a purported matchmaker, for God's sake, one who seemed to be frustratingly obtuse when it came to her own match.

The Duke of Branville was a decent man, but he would never appreciate Delilah's uniqueness. Branville would be the type of husband who would expect Delilah to become the perfect duchess, and Delilah wasn't conventionally perfect. Far from it. She ripped her gowns and stained her slippers and brought home all manner of strange creatures that needed to be healed or helped, and she did a hundred other outrageous things on nearly a daily basis. These were the things Thomas loved about her, the same things her ridiculous mother disapproved of so highly. Delilah needed a husband who would accept her exactly the way she was.

She needed Thomas.

He had to go about this carefully. No obvious proposals or declarations. He didn't want to ruin their friendship, after all, and an unwelcome proposal might do that. He'd rather live as her friend the rest of his life than lose her friendship because it had become uncomfortable between them. He couldn't lose her friendship. He wouldn't. She had been there on the worst day of his life and all the days since.

He'd been home from school on a break. His father had called him to the carpet in his study that evening. It hadn't been much different from the dozens of other arguments they'd had, but Thomas would never forget the words they'd exchanged that particular night.

Thomas had grown up doing mainly the opposite of anything his father asked of him. He'd been more interested learning how to gamble in the stables with Will, riding horses too fast, and imbibing too much brandy than taking his role as a marquess very seriously. His father, who expected his only son to be perfect, had never appreciated Thomas's fun-loving ways.

Thomas had stood in front of his father's desk that night, while the duke railed at him. He'd managed to crash his expensive new phaeton on the way home from school. "You're thoughtless," Father had thundered. "You're reckless. You're selfish."

Thomas had feigned disinterest, but each of the words had torn a hole in his heart. Standing at attention, he'd kept his jaw tightly clenched and his gaze trained on the wall behind his father's head. "You forgot useless," he ground out.

That reply had made spittle fly from his father's mouth. "You're supposed to be a bloody *duke* one day, but all you care about is gaming and drinking and riding hell for leather with your friends."

"And?" Thomas had drawled, crossing his arms over his chest and giving his father an insolent stare.

His father shook his head in disgust. "Is that all you have to say for yourself?"

Thomas had wanted to say he was young. He wanted to say he had time. He wanted to tell his father that he'd always intended to stop gambling and drinking and riding hell for leather after he graduated university, after he grew up a little, after he enjoyed himself a bit. But Father never listened. He preferred to criticize. He'd always chose to assume the worst about his son, so Thomas had done his best to live up to his father's low expectations. It had nearly turned into a sport for him.

"No," Thomas drawled. "I also wanted to say you can go straight to hell." He'd turned on his heel and stalked from the room.

He'd gone directly to a gaming hell with some chaps from school that night. He'd been half in his cups and had won nearly five hundred pounds with his penchant for odds-making when Owen Monroe found him. Monroe's face was pinched and pale.

"You must come home, Thomas. Immediately."

The tone of Monroe's voice had penetrated Thomas's drunkenness. It had to be serious, but he hadn't asked, and they'd ridden in silence the short drive from the gaming hell to Father's town house. They'd jumped from Monroe's coach, ran up the steps, and flown into the foyer. Soft voices sounded from the drawing room, and Thomas rushed inside.

Al was there with red-rimmed eyes. His mother sat stoically staring into the fireplace. Lavinia wasn't there. He later learned she had refused to come out of her bedchamber.

But Delilah had been there. Only a girl at the time. Al had sent a note to her house and she'd come right away, while Monroe was scouring the city's gaming hells for Thomas. Apparently, he'd gone to several before locating him.

"Father's dead, Thomas," Al had breathed. "He had an attack and . . . collapsed."

Thomas hadn't wanted to believe it. He'd doubled over as if he'd been punched in the gut. Bracing his hands on his knees, he'd fought the urge to vomit and forced himself to suck the pain into a reservoir deep inside. His father would not want him to show emotion.

From that moment on, he vowed to become the man his father had wanted him to be.

Two hours later, he'd been sitting on the back stoop staring blindly at the mews. The weight of his new responsibility had just begun to settle into his sobering brain, when the door opened behind him and Delilah came out.

Quietly, she settled on the stair beside him. She waited for several silent moments to pass before she said, "I hate wearing black." She plucked at her dark skirts. Her own father had died only months earlier.

"That's because pink is your favorite color," he'd replied absently.

"Yes, because pink is a happy color," she said. "Black is terribly unhappy."

Thomas groaned and rubbed the back of his neck. "I suppose I must begin to wear black now."

She pressed her small hand to his shoulder. "You must begin to do many things now. No doubt they will seem overwhelming at first, but I have every faith you'll do them splendidly."

Thomas nodded, not trusting himself to speak.

"Every day will be less awful," she continued.

"I . . . won't be going back to school." He'd already thought about it. Already decided. "Everyone will be counting on me now. Mother, Al, Lavinia."

Delilah leaned over and kissed his cheek, the sweet, soft press of her lips a cool balm to his soul. "I can think of no better person to count on."

Delilah had never known how much her simple words had meant to him that night. She believed in him. She always had. And because she believed in him, he'd had the confidence to believe in himself. He'd changed that night. Forever. He'd stopped drinking. Years passed before he'd been able to enjoy the odd mug of ale from time to time again. He'd stopped gambling altogether. He'd stopped being reckless when he rode, and he hadn't returned to school. He'd stayed in London and set about learning every detail of the estate, the lands, and the duties of becoming the Duke of Huntley.

With his father's solicitor's help, he'd become an expert with a single-minded determinedness no one had ever seen from him. Instead of using his proclivity for calculating odds to determine his chances at the gaming tables, he'd set about using them to improve the estate. Nine years later, the estate had never been so profitable. He used his skill at gaming, the numbers flying through his head and landing in all the right places, to improve the books for the estate.

And all the while, his friend Delilah had been at his side, quietly encouraging him and lending a friendly ear whenever he needed to talk. She made him laugh. She made him happy. And somewhere along the way, after she'd grown into a lovely young woman and made her debut, he realized that he was madly in love with her.

Delilah was special. Thomas had known it from the moment he'd met her. He had waited in the shadows all these years, knowing eventually she would have to take a husband and he would make his move. Only he didn't want to frighten her away. This was it, however. It was time. He would have to slowly convince her to see him in another light, while discouraging her courtship with Branville.

First thing was first. He was going to the Penningtons' ball tonight. To watch Delilah attempt to matchmake herself with the blasted Duke of Branville.

The first quality on Delilah's list was eligible. By God,

Thomas was going to have to prove himself a catch. It was certain to be excruciating.

He retied the cravat for the fourth time with slightly trembling fingers.

CHAPTER EIGHT

Lucy was Delilah's escort to the Penningtons' ball. The arrangement was nothing new. Delilah's mother had long ago allowed Lucy to take over as her daughter's chaperone. It served two purposes. It made Lady Vanessa less frustrated with her daughter's shortcomings, and it left the woman to her own amusements.

Delilah was only too happy with the arrangement as well. It allowed her to practice her matchmaking skills, and now it would allow her to attempt to secure an offer from Branville without having to worry about her mother's watchful eye.

Tonight, she wore a bright pink gown with a matching pink bow around the waist and one in her hair, with matching pink slippers and diamond ear bobs that her mother had reluctantly allowed her to borrow. Mother had told her many times that pink was not a good color for her complexion, but Delilah couldn't help but choose it when fabrics were displayed at the dressmaker's, despite her mother's condemning head shakes. The color had cheered Delilah since she was a small girl.

Lucy wore a gorgeous emerald gown, and her dark hair was piled atop her head. Her discerning eyes flitted around the ballroom, taking in everything. She snapped open her fan and spoke from behind it. "I have it on the best authority that Branville will be here tonight."

"Perfect," Delilah replied, trying and failing to use her fan to the same effect. She'd never quite mastered the art of proper fan use. "Will Lady Emmaline be here as well?"

"That is an excellent question," Lucy replied, her fan still fluttering in front of her lips. "And, of course, the first rule of matchmaking is to never underestimate your opponent. Lady Emmaline is quite set on catching Branville, so we must assume she will be here. I'd expect nothing less from a truly worthy adversary." Her eyes gleamed.

"I agree. I don't want my win to be *too* easy," Delilah said with as much confidence as she could muster, but inside her belly felt sick. It was simple to matchmake other people. It was fun, a lark. Doing it for herself was something else entirely. She wasn't convinced the Duke of Branville would want her or would even look twice at her. But she felt it necessary to at least feign confidence in front of Lucy. Her friend was her champion, after all. She didn't want Lucy to believe she was wasting her time.

Thomas came strolling up to them through the throngs of partygoers with his particular, easy stride. "Win at what?"

Delilah frowned at him. How had he managed to decipher their conversation from so far a distance?

Lucy eyed him up and down. "Don't you look handsome this evening."

Delilah glanced at Thomas. He was always well put together: tall, broad-shouldered, bright blue eyes, black hair, a perfect nose, high cheekbones, and a smile always resting on his lips. He was the precise image of a Society bachelor. Always talking, smiling, and laughing, with a drink in his hand—a drink he rarely finished—but never allowing any one lady to get too close. He would take the coat from his back to give to someone in need, whether pauper or prince. He was a good man, her friend. Quite a good one, indeed.

She waved the fan across her inexplicably warm cheeks. She'd been thinking of him more of late. Ever since Lucy had announced her intention to distract Lady Emmaline by offering Thomas as an alternative, Delilah couldn't seem to *stop* thinking of him. It was quite distracting, actually. *He's a rich, handsome duke too*, Lucy had said. Somehow in that moment, Delilah had realized that Lucy was right. Thomas, for all that he was her closest friend, was also a grown man—and a handsome, successful, rich one at that.

She'd tried to push away the thought. She'd tried to unthink it, but that had proved impossible. The most unsettling part, however, was the realization that the idea of Thomas with Lady Emmaline made Delilah . . . oh, she wasn't entirely certain exactly *what* it made her, but whatever the feeling was, she didn't like it. Not one bit.

She averted her gaze from his appraisal and fanned herself even more vigorously. She ought to be happy about Lucy's plan. She should be nothing but encouraging of the match. It stood to help her win Branville, after all. Instead, she'd been uncomfortable all week, and whenever she thought about Emmaline Rochester, the petty notion to . . . perhaps . . . trip her the next time she saw her, flashed through her mind. She'd finally decided she didn't *want* Thomas to distract Lady Emmaline. But how could she explain such ridiculousness to Lucy?

"You do look handsome, Thomas," she heard herself say, but was quickly forced to hide behind her fan as a wave of heat suffused her face anew. *Mon Dieu*. Was she actually *blushing* because she'd called Thomas handsome? She'd spoken the compliment to him a hundred times before. Why was tonight any different? She shook her head. This would not do. She needed to get control of herself. Immediately.

"I try." Thomas grinned from ear to ear as he smoothed his shirtfront with one hand.

"You tied your cravat yourself again, didn't you?" Delilah asked, shaking her head.

He shrugged. "Does it matter?"

Delilah bit back a smile. "Please allow me to have Cousin Rafe's valet come teach Will a few things. You'll both be better off."

Thomas frowned. "Will's fine just as he is."

Delilah shook her head again. That was something she'd always admired in Thomas. The man was exceptionally loyal. And thoughtful. He'd given his good friend Will the position as valet and didn't give a whit if his own appearance suffered as a result. "Very well, but don't cry to me when he picks the wrong coat for your appearance at court."

Thomas's brows shot up. "When am I making an appearance at court?"

"When you choose a wife, of course." Delilah turned to Lucy. "Lucy, didn't I tell you? Thomas has declared interest in finding a bride . . . finally."

"I did no such thing," Thomas stated baldly. "I merely admitted that I would need to find a bride *eventually*."

"That is excellent news," Lucy replied, "because we need you to distract Lady Emmaline. And speaking of Lady Emmaline, there she is." Lucy surreptitiously pointed her fan toward the entrance where Lady Emmaline and her mother had appeared.

Delilah's stomach dropped. This was it. It was time for Lucy to introduce her to the Duke of Branville, and for Thomas to try his hand at distracting Lady Emmaline. For some reason, Delilah wasn't looking forward to either thing. She glanced over at the gorgeous blonde and muttered to herself, "She's everything I'm not."

"Meaning?" Thomas prompted.

Delilah scowled. "Tall, blond, beautiful, accomplished."

"You may not be tall or blond," Lucy conceded, "but you are beautiful and accomplished."

Delilah eyed her friend. "No, I'm not. I'm cute, at best, and decidedly unaccomplished."

"It depends on what you consider an accomplishment," Thomas said with a snort of laughter.

"You know precisely what I mean," Delilah retorted. "I cannot play the pianoforte unless I wish to give offense, I cannot embroider, and I certainly cannot sing." She shuddered.

"How do you know Lady Emmaline can do any of those things?" Thomas asked.

"Look at her." Delilah nodded in Lady Emmaline's direction. "She just looks as if she can."

Thomas laughed. At least she could still make her friend laugh.

"It doesn't matter how accomplished she is," Lucy interjected. "Remember what I said about focusing on the positive, dear. We merely need Branville to see *your* desirable characteristics."

"Which are?" Skepticism nearly dripped from the look Delilah gave her friend.

"Intelligence, humor, good-natured robustness," Lucy responded.

Delilah fanned herself again and managed to hit herself in the nose, making her blink. "Robustness is a nice way of saying I'm loud. And I just hit myself with my own fan. I'm the opposite of graceful."

"No, robustness is not a nice way of saying you're loud," Lucy replied. "And if you hit yourself with your fan again, you must not mention it. Pretend as if nothing happened."

Good advice.

"Besides," Lucy continued, "Lady Emmaline may be beautiful, but she doesn't have your pluck. And pluck counts for a great deal in this world, dear."

"I agree," Thomas declared loyally.

Delilah snapped her fan shut and shoved it into her reticule. Better not to have the thing at all than worry about slapping herself with it while addressing Branville. "I hope you're right because pluck is about all I have in my favor at the moment."

"Pluck and a large dowry, dear," Lucy replied with a wink. "And that never hurts."

A footman walked past carrying a tray of champagne flutes. Lucy took one and Thomas took two. He handed one to Delilah.

"What's this for?" she asked, blinking at him.

"To drink, of course," he replied. "And calm your nerves."

She squinted at him. "How can you tell that I'm nervous?"

"I've seen you do many things before, but hitting yourself in the nose with your fan isn't one of them."

Delilah whimpered and took a long, fortifying sip from the flute. "I'm going to make a complete fool of myself, aren't I?"

"Not at all," Lucy replied. "Though it may be a good idea to finish the glass of champagne, dear, before I introduce you."

Thomas turned to look about the room. "Where is Branville?"

"He's over there." Lucy pointed with her fan once again. "He's been surrounded by young ladies and their mamas all evening. I've been waiting for a break in the crowd."

"Yes, well, don't wait too long. One of those young ladies and their mamas might cart him off right under your nose," Thomas said, grinning.

Delilah didn't look at him. Instead, she concentrated on draining her glass. "Shut up," she told him belatedly, pressing her empty glass against his shirtfront. "I am attempting to become engaged."

Lucy snapped her fan shut and lifted her skirts. "I'm afraid Thomas is right, dear. We might as well go make our introductions. The crowd around Branville is not likely to thin."

"Wait," Delilah said, stopping, nearly in a panic. "My mind has gone blank. What should I speak to him about?"

"How about the play?" Thomas gamely offered.

"Oh, yes," Lucy interjected, a twinkle in her eye, "better yet, let's invite him to join us. He can play Hermia's father. We still haven't filled that role. What better way to keep you in his company for the remainder of the Season? What an excellent idea, Thomas. Thank you. Let's go, dear."

Feeling a slight surge of courage due to the lovely glass

of champagne, Delilah also lifted her skirts. She glanced at Thomas. "Wish me luck."

Thomas shook his head as he watched Delilah follow Lucy into the crowd. The Duke of Branville did indeed have a large group of women hovering around him. Half were lovely young ladies who'd recently made their debuts, and the other half were their obviously hopeful mamas.

Branville had made his intentions clear that he was looking for a bride this Season. If Thomas had made a similar declaration, no doubt he'd be surrounded by ladies and their mamas as well. Was that what it would take to get Delilah to notice him as more than a friend? He shuddered. Encouraging a crowd of marriage-minded misses was hardly something he relished. Hopefully it wouldn't come to that. He'd briefly entertained the idea of spending time with Lady Emmaline. After all, doing so also might serve to make Delilah look twice at him. But he discarded that notion for three reasons. First, it didn't sit well with him to flirt with a woman he had no intention of courting. Second, if he occupied Lady Emmaline's time, she wouldn't be there to compete with Delilah for Branville. Third, and perhaps the most unsettling, Delilah had seemed nothing but pleased by the notion of Thomas distracting her rival while she moved in on Branville, so it hardly stood to make her jealous.

Thomas glanced across the crowded ballroom. He could kick himself for bringing up the play. Now Lucy intended to invite Branville to join them. Thomas's gaze fell on Lady Emmaline. He had to admit, she did look as if she was probably accomplished in all of the things Delilah had mentioned earlier. She was indeed tall, blond, and beautiful, but she didn't have a hint of a smile on her face, he noted with disappointment. Delilah, on the other hand, possessed an infectious love of life. Being in a room with Delilah was like sucking down a mouthful of champagne. She was bubbly and delightful, and she always had a kind word for everyone and a laugh on her lips. Lady Emmaline looked . . . disapproving. Humorless. No doubt she would be perfect for Branville.

Thomas handed his half-finished champagne glass to the next footman who passed by, and took a deep breath. He needed to prove his eligibility tonight. He might as well get started. In the meantime, he intended to do whatever he could to push Emmaline and Branville together.

CHAPTER NINE

"Your Grace," Lucy exclaimed as she and Delilah made their way into the center of the Duke of Branville's social set. Delilah practically had to elbow the young ladies out of the way to get anywhere near the man. She could kick herself for the hundredth time for promising her Mother she would secure an offer from *the most popular bachelor of the Season*. But there was no use for further recriminations at the moment. She'd made up her mind, and she was nothing if not determined.

The duke looked up and smiled the moment he saw Lucy. Ooh, he was handsome, with close-cropped blond hair and bright blue eyes. Not to mention the absolutely adorable dimple that appeared in his cheek when he smiled. His teeth were good too. That was promising.

"Your Grace," he replied in kind to Lucy, executing a perfect bow. Very well. In addition to being handsome, the man was also charming. It was obvious why he'd gathered such a crowd. Of course, the fact that he was a *duke* purportedly looking for a wife didn't diminish his appeal. Now that she'd seen him up close, Delilah honestly couldn't understand why his crowd wasn't *twice* as large.

Lucy wasted no time. She pulled Delilah out from behind her with a solid jerk. "There's someone I would like you to meet."

Delilah gulped and did what she could to still the pounding of her heart as Lucy pushed her toward the duke. "This is Lady Delilah Montebank, the late Earl of Montford's daughter."

"Lady Delilah," the duke said smoothly, bowing over her hand. She sniffed at his head when he did so. He smelled good and his cravat was not askew in the least. No doubt he had a perfectly trained valet. She shook her head. She needed to concentrate on impressing the man, not worrying about the state of his valet's training.

"*Enchanté*," she said, curtsying, before immediately regretting two things. First, she realized that *enchanté* was something *he* should have said to *her*. Second, her curtsy had been far too enthusiastic. She'd lowered herself farther than she'd intended to, which resulted in her getting stuck in the curtsying position. She could *not* pull her left foot from behind her and right herself. Adding to her misery, she was in imminent danger of tipping over.

She remained crouched in that awkward position, her face heating, until Lucy glanced over. The duchess must have recognized her distress because she casually moved to Delilah's side, grasped her around the waist, and hoisted her up as elegantly as she possibly could, which wasn't elegant at all. It worked, however, and Delilah sprang back into place, hoping Branville hadn't noticed the awkwardness . . . much.

Never one to allow much silence, she said far too loudly, "*J'adore* a ball, Your Grace. *Ne pas vous?*"

The hint of a smile passed over the duke's fine features. "Yes, I, um, too, enjoy such parties."

Delilah twirled her hand in the air. "*J'adore les fêtes, les boissons, et les écureuils.*" She tended to rattle off poor French when she was nervous.

The other ladies surrounding the duke tittered with laughter.

Lucy grabbed Delilah's elbow, which thankfully served to stop her stream of French. The duchess leaned over and quickly whispered, "You just said you love parties, drinks, and squirrels, dear."

Delilah's heart thundered. "I know," she whispered back, through tightly clenched teeth, doing her best to keep the smile on her face for the duke's sake. "I was trying to impress him, but I'm so nervous I could vomit. Please say something more nonsensical to make what I just said less so."

Lucy waded into the silence. She began by clearing her throat. "Lady Delilah and I, along with a set of our friends, are performing a play for charity. We hoped you might like to join us, Your Grace."

Branville's bright eyes widened slightly. "For charity, you say?"

Lucy nodded. "Yes, it's *A Midsummer Night's Dream*, and all the profits will go to the Royal Society for the Humane Treatment of Animals."

"Ah, a charity near my own heart," Branville replied, inclining his head to both of them. "I do love animals."

"*J'adore aussi les animaux,*" Delilah continued before Lucy pinched her on the back of the arm. She squelched her *ouch*.

"Yes," the duke replied. "You mentioned that. Squirrels in particular, correct?"

The other ladies laughed again. Delilah's face heated. Why had she mentioned squirrels? Why squirrels? She could have easily mentioned dogs or cats or even parrots without sounding too mad. Squirrels, however, introduced an undeniable element of madness.

Soon the other ladies in the flock began murmuring about how much they also adored animals, and Delilah nearly swooned with relief. No one mentioned squirrels, of course, but the talk served to distract the duke until Lucy cleared her throat again.

"Our next rehearsal is tomorrow night at my husband's town house," she said to the duke. "I hope you'll join us. Eight o'clock?"

"I'd love to," Branville said, inclining his head and smiling. There was that diverting dimple again.

The next thing Delilah knew, she was nearly bowled over as the flock swarmed Lucy in their attempts to gain entrée to the rehearsal as well. Clearly they were all willing to do anything to spend more time with the duke. Lucy spent the better part of the next quarter hour patiently turning down offers to play any remaining female role in *A Midsummer Night's Dream*. One young lady even went so far as to offer her services as a reserve fairy, which apparently was a fairy who learns all of the lines in case one of the other fairies couldn't perform for some reason.

"You're all more than welcome to purchase tickets to the event to see the duke perform in the play," Lucy, ever the diligent saleswoman, informed them all with a huge smile. "Go see Lady Rothwell at the Royal Society. She has all the details. I understand nearly all the tickets have been sold, however, so don't linger."

Delilah feared the crowd of women would turn en masse and rush out of the ballroom and down to the offices of the Royal Society to break in the doors.

"You'd do well to warn Lady Rothwell of the flood that is certain to come her way," she whispered with a laugh, just after Lucy had made their excuses and pulled Delilah away from Branville's crowd.

"I will," Lucy said with a smile and a wink. "I'll also suggest that she ask them all to make a donation even if they cannot purchase a ticket. Inviting Branville to join the cast has got to be the best idea we've had all Season. Thomas is brilliant. Not only will it serve to allow Branville to have more time with you, we're certain to sell the remainder of the tickets in a matter of hours."

Delilah shook her head. Lucy was nothing if not one to take advantage of an opportunity. "I suppose that's one way to look at it. All I could do was worry about how much competition I obviously have."

"Pish posh," Lucy said, as the two of them made their way back to the middle of the ballroom. "Competition never hurt anyone. I'm convinced it makes me perform at my best. Now, how did you find the duke?"

Delilah bit her lip. "He's ever so handsome, and entirely charming." And if his comment about adoring animals was true, he was probably kind, as well. That boded well. He already met at least two of the criteria on her list.

"He is, isn't he?" Lucy said with a sigh. "And it was quite nice of him to agree to be a part of the play."

"It was," Delilah agreed. "I only hope he doesn't think I'm a complete ninny for my less-than-elegant curtsy and my comment about squirrels."

"Nonsense," Lucy replied. "You made yourself memorable, which is important in a crowd that size. Besides, you mentioned the squirrel in French, and as you always say, everything sounds better in French."

"I suppose you're right," Delilah replied, "but the squirrel comment may be *too* memorable. I barely got a chance to say anything else to him."

Lucy clucked her tongue. "Ah, ah, ah. You're forgetting the second rule of matchmaking: Never overstay your visit. It leaves him wanting more."

Delilah nodded. That sounded good, but she wasn't certain Branville would want more of inelegant curtsies and inane comments about squirrels, whether spoken in French or English. Lucy was eternally confident, however, and Delilah did her best to mimic that emotion.

"Now," Lucy continued, grabbing a flute of champagne off the tray of a passing footman and spinning in a circle. "I shall keep my eye on Branville to see if he glances at you, while you pretend as if you've forgotten all about him and go have fun. Dance with as many eligible gentlemen as you can."

Delilah glanced around. Normally at such events, when forced to find a dancing partner, she looked for one man. "Where's Thomas?" she asked, turning in a wide circle in search of her friend.

"He's over there, dear." Lucy motioned with her chin while lifting the champagne glass to her lips. "I'm off to find my husband. I expect to see you dancing within minutes."

Delilah barely heard Lucy's last words as the duchess floated off in search of Derek. Instead, Delilah's gaze was trained on the crowd that she'd just realized Thomas was standing in the center of. Admittedly, his crowd was not the size of the Duke of Branville's, but a crowd of any size was something new for Thomas.

Delilah stood there, dumbfounded, watching him smile

and laugh in the middle of a group of ladies. She cocked her head to the side as if she were a puppy trying intently to understand something her master was saying. A flash of something that felt suspiciously, unexpectedly, and unhappily like . . . *jealousy* shot through her chest. She tried to shake it away. She would find another gentleman with whom to dance. It wouldn't be such a chore, would it? At any rate, she refused to fight a crowd for Thomas's time. Besides, the debutantes surrounding him were silly. They were wasting their time trying to flirt with Thomas. He'd already told her he wasn't interested in a finding a match this Season. Hadn't he?

She shook her head, forcing herself to look away and find another group of people to talk to. Relief flooded her when she spied Cousin Daphne and her husband, Rafe, standing near the refreshment table. Delilah lifted her skirts and was about to take off toward them when her friend Lady Rebecca Abernathy sauntered up to her.

"There you are, Delilah," Rebecca said, a wide smile on her face. "I saw you speaking to the Duke of Branville a few minutes ago."

Lady Rebecca was pretty, with brown hair and light green eyes and a figure most of the town's debutantes would die for, Delilah notwithstanding. She'd always liked Rebecca.

"Yes, the duke seems quite nice," Delilah said, eyeing Rebecca with suspicion. Why was Rebecca asking about Branville? *Mon Dieu.* She didn't need any *additional* competition for him.

"Handsome too," Rebecca added, swinging her hips back and forth.

Delilah narrowed her eyes on the woman. "He's the most eligible bachelor of the Season for a reason."

Rebecca blinked. Then she shook her head. "The

Duke of Branville isn't the most eligible bachelor this Season."

Delilah frowned at her. She liked Rebecca, but the woman was obviously a few pence shy of a pound. "What do you mean? Of course he is."

A sly smile popped to Rebecca's full lips. "No, he's the *second* most eligible bachelor. The *real* catch of the Season is the Duke of Huntley."

Delilah's frown intensified. "The Duke of Hunt— Thomas? Are you mad? Thomas isn't eligible. Well, to be precise, he is, but . . . he's not looking for a wife this Season. I have it on the *best* authority." But even as she said the words, she had the sinking feeling she might be wrong. Or worse, that while Thomas might not be looking for a wife, by the size of his ever-growing crowd, a wife might well be looking for *him* this Season.

Lady Rebecca smoothed a hand over her elegant dark chignon. "Nevertheless, he's more handsome than the Duke of Branville, he's richer than the Duke of Branville, and his family is older than the Duke of Branville's. That makes him more eligible."

Delilah blinked at her. Everything Lady Rebecca had said was true, but still . . . they were talking about *Thomas*. Why was this happening? How had her perfectly ordered world become upended this Season?

"I was hoping you'd introduce me to him," Lady Rebecca continued with a sly smile.

Delilah glanced over to where Thomas continued to hold court with a bevy of gorgeous young ladies. Something small and unhappy unfurled in her chest. What, precisely, did she like about Lady Rebecca again? "I . . . well . . . I suppose I could do that. Someday."

Lady Rebecca's mouth fell open as Delilah marched away from her without another word. She made her way directly to Thomas's court, pushed through the small crowd, and settled herself by his side. She even found herself giving the ladies a tight smile. What was happening to her?

Thomas glanced down at her and smiled. "Delilah? There you are. How was your dance with Branville?"

Delilah scrunched up her nose. "I didn't exactly . . . dance with him." That admission hurt.

"No?" Thomas grinned. "Too popular, was he?"

Delilah waved her hand in the air and glared at a young woman who seemed to be trying to push her out of the way to regain her position by Thomas's side. Too bad for the young lady, Delilah was skilled in the judicious use of her elbows. "Something like that." She lifted herself up on her tiptoes to get closer to Thomas's ear so he could hear her over the din of the annoying ladies twittering. "I'd love to dance *now*, however."

Thomas did not mistake her meaning. He inclined his head toward her, offered his arm, and excused himself from the ladies. A series of long sighs and unhappy murmurs followed them as he escorted Delilah to the floor.

A waltz began to play, and he bowed to her before they began their dance. He'd always been a lovely dancer. As a result, he'd always made her look like a much better dancer than she was. When she forgot a step and landed on his foot, he had a way of making it look as if it were planned. He always maneuvered her back into the proper steps without missing more than one beat.

"I thought perhaps you'd stay at Branville's side longer," Thomas said, as they stepped together in the familiar pattern they'd practiced for years.

Delilah swallowed. She'd got a whiff of Thomas's cologne, and if she didn't know any better, she'd swear it smelled better than whatever the Duke of Branville had been wearing. She forced herself to push that unwelcome thought from her mind and concentrate on what Thomas had said. "Lucy said I shouldn't overstay my introduction. Meet and elude, or something like that."

Thomas grinned. "Ah, so you're being elusive?"

There was no doubt about it. Thomas smelled good. *Mon Dieu.* "Trying to, at least," she forced herself to say. Delilah glanced over to where Branville remained talking to his entourage. This time, she noted with some pique, the crowd around him included the lovely Lady Emmaline. "Lady Emmaline obviously doesn't know about being elusive. She's been at his side all evening."

"All evening? I only saw her go over there a few minutes ago."

Delilah arched a brow. "You've been watching Lady Emmaline?"

Thomas laughed and shook his head. "Lucy did ask me to distract her."

"Oh, yes." Delilah bit her lip and glanced away. "I suppose you should be doing that instead of dancing with me."

His grin widened. "Should I abandon you here, then, directly on the dance floor?"

Delilah fought the urge to stick out her tongue at him. Instead, she glanced over his shoulder to Branville's crowd. "I wonder if he will ask Lady Emmaline to dance."

"Well, if you're the one being more elusive, you should have the upper hand, according to Lucy."

Delilah scrunched up her nose. "Do I have the upper hand, or am I being shortsighted?"

Thomas inclined his head. "What would you tell a lady you were trying to matchmake?"

Delilah pursed her lips. "I'd tell her to be elusive."

"Then surely you should take your own advice."

"I am." She shook her head. "But I don't have to like it." She forced herself to smile, then contemplated her next words before deciding to go ahead and say them. She wanted to see his reaction. "My friend Rebecca asked about you."

He was gazing across the ballroom and hardly seemed to give a toss. "Rebecca who?"

"Lady Rebecca Abernathy."

He frowned. "She asked about *me*?"

"Yes. And she said you were"—Delilah cleared her throat. She wasn't entirely certain she should say this next word—"eligible."

Thomas pressed his lips together and arched a brow. "What do you think? In your expert opinion, *am* I eligible?"

She lifted her chin. "Don't be ridiculous. Of course you're eligible. You're an unmarried duke, aren't you?" She'd meant it to sound nonchalant, but she suspected that it sounded petulant. *Mon Dieu* again.

"But not as eligible as Branville?" he asked, waggling his eyebrows at her.

Delilah stepped on his foot. Perhaps on purpose. He grinned at her and swung her easily back into the steps before she said, "On the contrary, according to Rebecca, you're *more* eligible."

"Ah, is that so?" He blinked his ridiculously long, dark eyelashes at her.

"Don't be smug. After all, there is a large difference between you and Branville."

Thomas's eyebrows shot up. "Really? What's that? Hair color?"

She wanted to step on his foot again. "No," she answered primly. "Branville is looking for a wife, and you are not." She wanted to add, *Are you?* but that seemed the slightest bit too interested.

"But do you agree? *Am* I more eligible than Branville?" he prompted.

Delilah did not like this conversation. She didn't like it one bit. It made her uncomfortable discussing Thomas's potential eligibility with him. How had they even got into this—Oh, right. *She'd* been the fool who'd brought up what Lady Rebecca said. "Who am I to say which duke is more eligible than the other?" she replied, still doing her best to sound nonchalant.

The waltz ended, and Thomas bowed to her again before escorting her off the floor.

They'd barely made it to the sidelines when Lucy came floating over to them.

"Let's ask the duchess," Thomas continued. "What do you think, Lucy? Am *I* more eligible than the Duke of Branville?"

Lucy blinked as if momentarily surprised by the question. Then she narrowed her eyes and tapped her finger against her cheek for a moment. "Yes, without a doubt."

"Lucy!" Delilah exclaimed, plunking her hands onto her hips.

"What?" Lucy shrugged. "I'm merely being honest. Thomas's family is older, his estate is greater, and his looks are certainly comparable."

"Only comparable?" Thomas asked with a mock-offended gasp.

"Depends upon whether one prefers the dark sort or the blond sort," Lucy replied with another shrug.

"Ah, so you prefer the blond sort," Thomas said to Delilah.

Delilah scowled at him. "Think what you're saying.

It's *you*. I've known you since you were a boy. The Duke of Branville is . . ."

Thomas batted his eyelashes at her. "What? A blond god?"

"No." She crossed her arms over her chest. She continued to detest this conversation. "I was going to say . . . he's not my friend."

Lucy fluttered her hand in the air. "Yes, well. I've come with news. I've had a chance to watch Lady Emmaline at work." Lucy leaned in and lowered her voice. "She's good. Quite good."

Delilah bit her lip.

"I'm afraid we're going to have to employ all the tricks of the matchmaking trade to accomplish this feat," Lucy continued.

"Dare I ask what the tricks of the matchmaking trade are?" Thomas said.

Lucy used her fingers to count them off. "Being elusive, pretending you aren't interested, and most important of all, employing a bit of competition."

"I'm not certain I've got much competition, Lucy," Delilah replied.

"Not at the moment, dear, but you will before I'm finished with you. By the by, these same methods will work for Lavinia's match too."

Thomas inclined his head toward Lucy. "I'm pleased to hear it. The sooner Lavinia is matched, the better." He turned toward Delilah. "Now, I'd like you to introduce me to your friend, Lady Rebecca. Perhaps it is time I find my own match this Season."

Once again, the tiny anvil sunk to bottom of Delilah's belly.

CHAPTER TEN

"All right, everyone, gather round. We'll begin with the scene where Nick Bottom turns into the ass," Jane Upton called to the group at rehearsal the next night in Lucy's library.

The center of the large library had been transformed into a woodland arbor at night, dominated by a foot-high wooden stage that Derek and Christian had erected. The furniture that had previously been in the center of the room had been moved out. The large desk had been pushed into a corner where it served as the location for the costumes. The other corner was filled with Cass and her canvases. There were small groups of players practicing their lines in groups of two or three throughout the room, while Jane stood in the center directly in front of the stage, raising her voice to be heard above the din.

It turned out Jane was a formidable stage manager and director. No one dared cross her, and she knew the text as if she'd memorized every word. Delilah secretly suspected she had. Jane kept everyone in line and on time for their rehearsals, and thanks to her excellent organizational skills and directorial talents, the production was coming together quite nicely.

The play was perhaps the only thing going well of late, as far as Delilah was concerned. She'd been out of sorts all day after spending the night tossing and turning, unable to erase the feeling of uneasiness caused by last night from her mind. First, the crowd of ladies surrounding Thomas had irked her. Thomas had never had a crowd before. Why did one suddenly appear last night? Then, Rebecca's comments had made Delilah want to stamp her foot. It was ridiculous of Rebecca to say Thomas was the most eligible bachelor of the Season. Everyone knew *Branville* was the most eligible. Finally, after announcing that he might indeed be looking for a wife, Thomas had trotted off in Lady Rebecca's direction, leaving Delilah no choice but to follow him and make the introductions.

The resulting scene had been nothing but awkward, with Rebecca nearly swooning over Thomas, and Thomas enjoying it like an ice at Gunter's. Rebecca giggled and Thomas preened, and then the two of them went off to dance, leaving Delilah standing alone with her half-empty champagne glass and a frown on her face. Worse, she'd been forced to contemplate, for the remainder of the evening and the entire day today, why, precisely, she was so offended by the notion that Thomas was not only eligible, but seemed to be enjoying the company of other ladies for the first time in . . . well, forever. Not to mention the fact that he should have been trying to distract Lady Emmaline from Branville, instead of dancing with Lady Rebecca.

After a great deal of introspection, Delilah came to the conclusion that she wasn't jealous. No. She was not. She'd examined the feeling a hundred different ways and decided resolutely that jealousy *was not* the emotion she was experiencing. She still didn't know what the emotion was, exactly. But it couldn't be jealousy. That would be preposterous. It was more like . . . offense. Yes. That was it. *She'd* known Thomas was a wonderful person and an excellent man for years, why were other ladies only noticing now? Besides, she'd been spoiled all these years by having his company to herself, essentially. As for Lady Rebecca, Delilah simply didn't appreciate being told that her closest friend was more eligible than the man she'd set her sights on. That was all. Nothing more.

Delilah stared out the window into the gardens behind Lucy's house, plucking at her lip while such thoughts churned over and over in her mind. As if she'd conjured him, Thomas came strolling up next to her, his script in his hand. He glanced over both shoulders before grinning at her. "I don't see Branville here."

Delilah's hand dropped to her side, and she turned to face him. "He, er, he said he'd be here. It's not yet eight o'clock."

Thomas leaned a shoulder against the wall and stared down at her. "Ah, is that the hour of his stately arrival?"

"That's when Lucy invited him." *Mon Dieu*. Why couldn't she stop sniffing Thomas's cologne? It was madness.

Thomas nodded. "He's playing Hermia's father, eh? I suppose he'll be especially handsome with a long, white beard."

Delilah pursed her lips. "Don't be smug. It doesn't become you. Besides, how did you manage to extricate yourself from all those ladies last night? I feared I'd never see you again."

He sighed. "It *was* difficult, but I managed."

"Meet anyone you fancy?" She couldn't stop herself from asking. "Lady Rebecca, perhaps?" She hated herself for asking that last part.

His smile softened a little. "Not to worry, my lady, you'll be the first to know if I meet anyone I fancy. By the by, I brought Lavinia with me tonight as Lucy instructed."

Delilah glanced around. "Where is she, then?"

Thomas shoved a hand in his pocket. "Last I saw her, she was in the foyer, rebuking one of the servants for stepping on the hem of her new gown."

Delilah nodded. "That sounds like Lavinia."

One moment later, the woman in question came sweeping through the doors of the library. She wore a gorgeous yellow silk gown that was obviously expensive, and her dark hair was piled high atop her head. She glanced around the room until her blue eyes lit on Thomas, then she marched over to him.

"Good evening, Lady Lavinia," Delilah said as she loomed closer. She'd done her best throughout the years to keep her distance from Lavinia, but they'd met upon occasion. Lavinia had never been particularly nice to Delilah, but then, she wasn't particularly nice to anyone.

"Lady Delilah," Lavinia intoned. "My brother tells me you and the Duchess of Claringdon are sponsoring a play." She sneered the word *play* as if it were a curse word.

"We aren't only sponsoring it. We're acting in it. It's entirely for charity, of course. Lucy and I were hoping you would join us, actually," Delilah added, hoping she had made the offer sound enticing enough.

One haughty eyebrow lifted. "Join you? Are you mad? The daughter of an earl, in a play?" Lavinia stared at her aghast.

Delilah did her best to squelch her smile. "I'm the daughter of an earl, and I'm doing it," she pointed out.

"I suppose there's no accounting for taste." Lavinia tilted her nose in the air. "Time was when birthright *meant* something."

Delilah pressed her lips together and glanced at Thomas who merely winced and shook his head behind his sister's back. They'd had many conversations about Lavinia's waspishness. The woman was beyond preposterous and insulting, but from living with her mother, Delilah had plenty of experience dealing with angry women who said mean things. Besides, Delilah had forgotten the most important aspect of dealing with Lavinia. One must always let Lavinia know what *she* stood to gain.

Delilah shared another quick commiserating look with Thomas and turned her attention back to Lavinia. "We also have three dukes and a duchess in our performance. I'd say you'd be in excellent company if you'd join us. There are several eligible *gentlemen* in the performance as well."

Lavinia glanced around as if sizing up the company. "Well, I do try to do what I can for charity, of course." She turned in a circle and crossed her arms over her chest. "And there *are* several members of the Quality here, I see. What part would you have me play?"

"We thought you'd be an excellent Hippolyta," Delilah replied.

The barest hint of an actual smile tugged at Lavinia's thin lips. "Hmm. The duchess? That sounds like me."

Delilah was about to open her mouth and agree with

Lavinia when Lucy swept into their circle. "Lady Lavinia, there you are. It's lovely to see you."

"Your Grace," Lavinia intoned, nodding regally toward Lucy.

Lucy glanced over both shoulders and lowered her voice. "Thomas tells us you're in the market for a husband this Season."

Lavinia raised one dark brow. "Did he?"

Thomas cleared his throat and glanced away.

"Yes," Lucy continued, "and I have to say I'm delighted. You know I fancy myself a matchmaker, and so does Lady Delilah."

Lavinia's narrowed gaze darted to Delilah. "Do you?"

Lucy nodded. "Yes, in fact, I'd love to introduce you to my friend Lord Stanley. He's just over there."

Lavinia's face lit with obvious interest, and Lucy twined her arm through Lavinia's and led her off toward Lord Stanley.

Thomas turned to Delilah. "I do hope she hits it off with the chap."

"So do I," Delilah replied. "Lord Stanley is a nice man."

Thomas winced. "I'm not certain *nice* is the best fit for Lavinia."

Delilah smoothed her hands down her sleeves. "We'll see. These things take time."

"Ah, but your courtship of Branville is on quite a short time schedule, is it not?"

She pretended to read her script. "Yes, but that is because I have no choice. Now, would you care to practice our lines?"

He opened his mouth to reply when Jane Upton shouted, "Delilah! Please come fetch your bird. He's repeating everything and impacting the performance."

Delilah hurried over to the stage to get Miss Adeline

from his perch nearby. She brought him back to where Thomas stood. Thomas and the parrot exchanged scornful looks before Miss Adeline leaned over and unceremoniously bit Thomas on the wrist.

"Ouch!" Thomas rubbed his wrist. "You'll be looking for some new feathers if you bite me again, bird."

"Bite me again, bird," Miss Adeline squawked, flapping his bright blue wings.

Delilah sighed. "Must you fight with Miss Adeline?"

Thomas narrowed his eyes on the bird. "I fight with anything that bites me as many times as he has. And for the thousandth time, his name is not Miss Adeline."

Delilah rolled her eyes. "As he is *my* bird and I have named him Miss Adeline, I must tell you for the thousandth time that it *is*, in fact, his name. Now come over here. We'll practice our lines before Branville gets here. I daresay I'll be distracted afterward."

Thomas followed her to the corner, keeping a watchful eye on the bird, who was balanced on Delilah's forearm and had the temerity to look smug. "Very well, but tell that lump of feathers to pipe down."

Delilah turned to face Thomas and glanced at her script. "This is the scene where Helena follows Demetrius into the forest." She cleared her throat. "Stay, though thou kill me, sweet Demetrius."

Thomas cleared his throat too. "I charge thee, hence, and do not haunt me thus."

"Oh, wilt thou darkling leave me? Do not so," Delilah replied.

"Do not so!" shouted Miss Adeline.

Thomas gave the bird a dark look, but continued with his next line. "Stay, on thy peril. I alone will go."

Delilah rolled her eyes and momentarily abandoned

character. "I must say, I would find this difficult to play if I didn't know that Demetrius ultimately sees the error of his ways and falls in love with Helena. He's positively awful to her otherwise."

"Awful to her!" Miss Adeline squawked.

"Miss Adeline, shush," Delilah commanded.

"I'll come and get him, Delilah," Danielle Cavendish said from her seat in the opposite corner of the room.

"Demetrius doesn't see the error of his ways," Thomas pointed out. "He's charmed by the juice from the flower."

"Yes, it's all quite ridiculous, isn't it? *J'adore* such silliness," Delilah said with a laugh.

"*J'adore*!" Miss Adeline squawked.

"He speaks French now?" Thomas said, glaring at Miss Adeline.

"Regrettably, he speaks better French than I do," Delilah pointed out dryly.

Thomas laughed.

Danielle crossed to them and generously took the parrot from Delilah. "It's not so ridiculous, you know?"

"What do you mean?" Delilah asked.

"Being charmed by the juice of a flower. There are many inexplicable things in this world." Danielle winked at Delilah and walked away, taking Miss Adeline with her.

Delilah watched her go. What the devil did that mean? She shook her head. Danielle was slightly mysterious. Perhaps it was her Frenchness. Or the fact that she was a spy. Delilah had always admired the woman, but every once in a while she'd say something that Delilah didn't understand. Usually, it was in French, however.

Regardless, Delilah wanted to finish the scene before Branville arrived. She glanced at her script again. "I do wish Demetrius didn't compare Helena to food."

Thomas suppressed his smile. "I don't believe that is your next line. We cannot rewrite Shakespeare's words. I highly doubt Jane would take kindly to that."

Delilah exhaled. "Very well, first Theseus agrees to their marriages, and then Helena says, 'So methinks. And I have found Demetrius like a jewel, mine own, and not mine own.'"

Thomas barked a laugh. "You don't sound convinced I am your own jewel."

Delilah arched a brow. "I suppose I must work on sounding more convincing. What's next?"

Lucy, having left Lavinia in Lord Stanley's company, strolled over to join them. "Helena and Demetrius should kiss."

Delilah blinked. "Pardon?"

Thomas's brows shot up.

"A kiss," Lucy replied, as though it were the most reasonable thing in the world. "I was speaking with Jane about it earlier. She agreed that Demetrius and Helena and Lysander and Hermia should each kiss after declaring themselves."

Heat instantly suffused Delilah's cheeks. She steadfastly refused to glance at Thomas. "That wasn't in the original play."

Lucy pushed a curl behind her ear. "Perhaps not, but they've all been granted their wish to marry and declared their love. A kiss is in order, is it not? Besides, Jane says it may help increase the value of the tickets, and I quite agree."

Delilah scratched her chin. She was nothing if not practical. "I suppose you and Jane have a point, though Mother will not be pleased if she finds out." She finally stole a glance at Thomas. He was watching her with an unreadable expression. "What do you think?"

He shrugged. "I suppose we must do what we must for charity."

Lucy serenely glided off, while Delilah resisted the urge to squirm. She continued to stare at her script for wont of something to look at while she wrapped her mind around the thought of kissing Thomas. Her friend. Her best friend. Wait—no, not Thomas. He was Demetrius! How silly she was to forget this was all merely a play. Her spine straightened, and she regained her perspective. "Very well, but get it over with quickly."

The corner of Thomas's mouth curled up. "I don't kiss quickly."

"Oh, really," Delilah shot back, one hand on her hip. "How do you kiss then?"

"You're going to have to wait and find out, aren't you?"

The heat that had suffused her cheeks began to spread to other more intimate parts of her body. "Very well. Do what you must, then." She squeezed her eyes closed, puckered her lips, and waited.

CHAPTER ELEVEN

Thomas took a deep breath. His gaze slid over Delilah's familiar face, her creamy skin, her dark brows, her slightly crooked nose. He wanted their first kiss to be special, even if it was a pretend kiss.

He quelled the pounding of his pulse, carefully wrapped his fingers over her slender shoulders, and breathed in her familiar, delicious scent. Then he pulled her toward him and leaned down, closer, closer, his eyelids sliding shut.

His lips skimmed hers, the brush light, ephemeral. She was about to pull away—he could sense it—and everything in him railed at the realization. Before he knew it, he had drawn her closer, heart to heart, and claimed her lips completely. This time, she didn't try to pull away. With a jolt of delight, he felt her little intake of air, a partial gasp, and when her lips parted, he boldly coaxed them farther apart with his tongue.

Her hands fluttered and came to grip his forearms as

though to hold her upright. Her head tipped back, an offering for him to take more. And so he did. Mindless of their fellow cast members, he deepened the kiss, and shuddered at the sound of the tiny moan that came from the back of her throat. It was so soft, but there it was. For his ears only. And for a moment, he knew with utter certainty that he had claimed her as completely as she had claimed him all these years.

Then came the realization that the room had fallen quiet, too quiet, and Thomas forced himself to release her and step back. He folded his hands behind his back—they were shaking—and searched her face for its reaction. Only, Delilah's eyes were still closed, and the dreamlike expression on her features made him want to laugh with joy and grab her in his embrace once again, onlookers be damned.

Lucy had returned. She cleared her throat, and the spell was shattered. Delilah's eyes flew open. "Delilah, dear," the duchess murmured, averting her gaze.

"What is it, Lucy?" Delilah's voice was dreamlike too. Good.

"Ahem, the Duke of Branville has just arrived," Lucy continued.

To Thomas's dismay, Delilah jolted to life, turned, and hurried toward the door, sparing him not a single backward glance. Then she must have thought better of it and paused. She walked carefully back to the spot she'd recently left. "I'm going to count ten," she announced.

"Probably best, dear," Lucy replied.

"Why?" Thomas asked, chagrined by the speed at which she'd run away from him at the mention of Branville's name.

"Because I just remembered that galloping about like a pony is hardly the way to endear oneself to a duke."

Delilah pressed her palm against her belly and took three deep breaths. She always took three deep breaths when she wanted to calm herself.

Thomas scowled. Obviously, the need for oxygen had nothing to do with his kiss, as he would have liked. This was all about Branville.

"I'll escort you over to him," Lucy said.

"Don't wait too long," Thomas added. "Mustn't keep the *duke* waiting."

Delilah nodded to Lucy. "I'm ready."

Thomas casually followed the two women as they made their way out into the corridor in front of the library, where the Duke of Branville was holding court. Thomas's heart was still pounding in his chest, his throat, and other traitorous parts as well. When Lucy had first suggested it, Thomas had been concerned that kissing Delilah so soon (even under such pretenses) might be a mistake. Surely she would recognize the pent-up longing in his kiss. But in the end, he'd been hard pressed to resist the temptation. The kiss he'd given her was far more than what Jane Upton's script had called for, but once he'd started, he could barely control himself.

He was playing a dangerous game, and he knew it. Last night when Delilah had mentioned Lady Rebecca had asked about him, he'd intended to do nothing more than gloat a little. He'd obviously made his point that he was eligible, and he'd been pleased with his quick success.

Then Lucy had gone and given him the *best* idea when she'd told him the tricks of the matchmaking trade. The most important one: employing a bit of competition. He'd used Delilah's own trick against her. He'd taken off in search of Lady Rebecca, and Delilah had followed him and introduced the two of them. Lady Rebecca was a

gorgeous young woman who had obviously been interested in him. He had no intention of falsely encouraging
her, but flirting never hurt anyone. Hell, before Monroe
had married his sister, the earl had practically been a professional flirt. Besides, wasn't that what young, healthy
eligible people were supposed to do at *ton* balls? Thomas
had proceeded to do just that.

The corridor outside Lucy's library was filled with the
majority of the company. After watching Thomas and
Delilah's kiss, they had exited the room en masse to
greet Branville. They were all good-naturedly welcoming him to the group.

"Ah, Your Grace," Branville said as soon as he caught
sight of Lucy. "You didn't tell me, when is the performance
to be?"

"The twenty-first of July, Your Grace," Lucy replied.
"Lady Delilah's birthday." Lucy pushed Delilah slightly
ahead of her.

"*Mon anniversaire*," Delilah repeated in a high, anxious tone.

Thomas hid an involuntary smile behind his hand.
Delilah always blurted things in French when she was
nervous. Not to mention her skin was turning an unfortunate shade of red, with blotches, another unlucky side
effect of her nerves. Thomas shook his head. Despite his
growing resentment of her interest in Branville, he wished
he could somehow take the embarrassment away from
her. She had nothing to be embarrassed about, of course,
but he'd gladly feel the emotion in her stead if he could.

Branville smiled at Delilah, and a damned dimple—
of all bloody things—appeared in the man's cheek.
Thomas cursed under his breath. In addition to blond
hair, he also had to compete with a dimple.

"Ah, Lady Delilah," Branville said, bowing to her,

"good to see you again. You're performing a play for charity on your birthday?"

"My birthday is on a midsummer's night," Delilah replied. "What better way to celebrate?"

Branville inclined his head toward her. "A lovely sentiment, my lady."

Delilah blushed on top of her red splotches, and Thomas couldn't help but roll his eyes. Who went around bowing and saying things like, *A lovely sentiment, my lady*? Though from Delilah's reaction, apparently ladies liked that sort of talk.

Lucy sidled up to Branville and wrapped her arm through his. "Come into the library with us, Your Grace. You can see for yourself all the trouble we've gone to in order to create the lifelike scenes."

"Lead the way," Branville replied, nodding.

Delilah fell into step on the other side of Branville, and they all marched back into the library. The large room had nearly emptied, save for Jane, who was directing a scene with Derek and Cade; Lavinia, who was staring at herself in a looking glass; Danielle Cavendish, who continued to sew; and Cass, who remained quietly painting in the corner.

"Come this way, Your Grace. We'll show you the fairy wings." Lucy led Branville to the desk on the far left side of the room where the costumes were piled.

Thomas stuck his hands in his pockets and reluctantly followed their little entourage. Had Branville actually agreed to be in the play yet? Or was Lucy still trying to convince him? Nauseating.

"Ah, yes, fairy wings," Branville said with a laugh, picking up one of the wings and examining it. "I suppose a performance of *A Midsummer Night's Dream* must include fairy wings."

"And a lion," Delilah blurted. "A fake one, of course."
Thomas watched as she pinched herself on the inside of
her arm and turned bright red again. "I mean, of course
the lion would be fake. What else would it be?" she added,
turning redder. "Er, um, *que pensez-vous des perroquets*,
Your Grace?"

Thomas winced. She'd just asked Branville how he felt
about parrots. Bringing up the parrot was probably not
her best choice. Thomas situated himself with his back
leaning against the nearest wall and continued to watch
the awkward interaction.

"Parrots?" Branville's brow furrowed. He obviously
wanted to ensure he'd heard her correctly.

"Yes, you know, brightly colored birds. Tend to speak.
Friendly with pirates," Delilah continued.

Thomas pressed his lips together to keep from chuck-
ling, while Branville narrowed his eyes. "Pirates?"

"Yes. My cousin Cade is a pirate," Delilah declared.

"I am no such thing, Delilah," Cade chimed in from
atop the stage. "Besides, at the moment, I am attempting
to be a woodland sprite." He grinned at Branville. "I'm
playing Puck."

Cade turned his attention back to his scene while Delilah pressed her hand to the side of her mouth and whispered to Branville, "He *used* to be a pirate. And that
inspired me to procure a parrot. He's just over there. Miss
Adeline."

Branville turned to look in the direction Delilah
pointed. Miss Adeline sat on his perch only a few paces
away. Thomas was convinced the bird wore a self-
satisfied look on his face.

"You do actually have a *parrot*." Surprise registered
in Branville's voice when his gaze landed on the fowl in
question.

"This particular version of the play includes a parrot," Lucy hastened to add.

"I don't seem to recall a parrot from my study of the play at Cambridge," Branville said narrowing his eyes again.

Of course, he would mention his time at Cambridge. Bloody braggart. Branville moved toward Miss Adeline's perch. He stopped in front of it and contemplated the bird.

"Watch out, Branville," Thomas drawled from his spot against the wall. "The parrot bites."

"Not always," Delilah shot back, her eyes glaring daggers at Thomas.

Branville offered his arm, and Miss Adeline immediately hopped over to it.

"I quite like birds," Branville said.

"Quite like birds," Miss Adeline echoed. There was no question about it. The bird was smug.

"He looks like a fine bird to me," Branville continued. "What did you say his name is?"

Delilah shot a guilty look toward Thomas before lifting her chin. "Ah, Miss . . . Adeline."

"She's lovely," Branville replied. "I think we shall be fast friends, Miss Adeline and I."

Thomas opened his mouth to correct His Grace on the matter of the bird's sex, but Delilah stopped him with a hasty "Thank you, Your Grace."

Still holding Miss Adeline on his forearm, Branville turned back to Lucy. "What part did you mean for me to play?"

Lucy clapped her hands. A smile lit her features. "We were hoping you would be Hermia's father."

Branville raised his brows. "Hermia's father? The awful man who stands in the way of true love?"

"One and the same," Lucy replied, smiling.

Thomas fought the urge to roll his eyes again. Who said things like, *stands in the way of true love*? Who really stood in the way of true love? Blond dukes with dimples who didn't appreciate the most wonderful young lady in the room. That's who.

"Would you like to see what you'll be wearing?" Delilah asked. Her cheeks were less red than they'd been a few moments ago, perhaps because that bag of feathers she called Miss Adeline had yet to bite Branville. Thomas remained hopeful, however, that an assault was imminent.

"Yes, please," Branville replied.

"I'll take Miss Adeline and go fetch the costume." Delilah held out her arm for the parrot. Apparently, she didn't want to take her chances leaving the bird alone with Branville. Probably clever on her part. "I'll be right back."

Miss Adeline on her arm, Delilah hurried away to consult with Danielle, and was back moments later with a robe hanging over one arm. She was about to open her mouth to speak when Miss Adeline squawked, "*J'adore le duc.*"

Thomas choked down a bark of sheer, shocked laughter. Silence fell over the rest of the party, and Delilah's face went up in flames. It was obviously something she'd said just before, and Miss Adeline had repeated.

"I, er, . . ." Delilah rushed the bird back to his perch so fast, feathers went flying in every direction. She all but dumped the bird, then hurried back to Branville with the robe. She'd extended her arm to give him the robe when she tripped over one of the boxes of decorations and flew straight into Branville's arms. The duke caught her, but apparently her hand had become entangled in his waistcoat. As she pulled away, she ripped his shirtfront straight down the middle.

The shirtfront flapped open, and Branville's chest was partially bared to all present. Poor Delilah's face was nearly purple. She pulled away from Branville and stood gaping at him as if she'd shot him.

"I beg your pardon," she said, pushing the robe toward him so he could cover himself.

"I daresay this is a first," he said with a laugh, but his cheeks were decidedly red.

Lucy lunged forward. "My apologies, Your Grace. If you'd like to repair to the salon, one of the servants can bring you one of Derek's shirts to change into." She stepped in front of her guest to shield him from prying eyes while he pressed the robe to his chest.

"Yes, um, perhaps that would be best," the duke said. "Excuse me, won't you?" he added to the rest of the party before hurrying out of the room on Lucy's heels.

Delilah slunk over to the corner, pressed her back to the wall, and slid down to sit on the floor. What had she done? Her mother was always telling her what a clumsy oaf she was, but usually she injured herself or inanimate objects. She'd never tripped and ripped a duke's shirt half off before. And not just any duke, but the duke she was trying desperately to impress.

She briefly considered going to the salon to find him and apologize again, but quickly thought better of it. No doubt she'd only embarrass the man further by walking in on him while he was changing his clothing.

Instead, she concentrated on planning what she should say to him when next she saw him. *You look better with a full shirt.* No, that would only call attention to it.

I should have ripped off the entire thing. No. Too bold. Although from the slight glimpse she'd got, the man did have a fine physique. And wasn't Lucy always telling her to be bold?

I'd wager you've never had your shirt ripped off before. Too obvious.

Perhaps it would be best if she simply acted as if it had never happened. She'd begged his pardon, what more could she say?

A shadow fell across her, and she looked up to see Thomas standing over her, his face inscrutable. Normally Thomas would give her a ribbing for such a performance, but he squatted down and chucked her under the chin. "You're being hard on yourself, aren't you?"

Thomas always seemed to know exactly what she was thinking. "Yes," she admitted in a small voice that she hated.

"You shouldn't, you know," he replied.

"Why shouldn't I?" she mumbled.

"Because it won't change what happened."

She leaned her head back against the wall and blinked at him. "I suppose you have a point."

Thomas turned and lowered himself to sit next to her with his back against the wall too. "If it makes you feel any better, I can rip my shirt half off too and pretend it's the new rage."

Delilah had to smile at that. Then she let her head drop. "I made a complete fool of myself in front of Branville."

Thomas pushed his shoulder against hers. "No, you didn't."

"Yes, I did."

He shrugged. "So what if you did?"

"So what? I'm trying to impress him."

Thomas pulled up his knees and propped his wrists atop them. "He should be trying to impress you."

A half-smile popped to Delilah's lips. "You're only saying that because you're my friend."

"I'm saying it because it's true, but look on the bright side. At least Miss Adeline didn't bite him. That was a success."

Delilah reached over and slowly patted his hand. "Thomas, you are kind."

A surge of satisfaction rolled through Thomas's chest. Another check off the list. Of course, he hadn't said those things to gain her favor. He meant every one of them, especially the part about how Branville should be trying to impress Delilah, not the other way around. But he would take his successes, however slight.

The door to the library cracked opened, and Lucy came hurrying over to them. The Duke of Branville was not with her. "Thomas," Lucy said, "Lady Rebecca is in the foyer, and she's asking for you."

CHAPTER TWELVE

When Branville returned from the salon with a fresh, unripped shirt, Delilah was too busy glaring at Lady Rebecca to hardly spare him a glance.

Rebecca had come marching into the library after Branville had left and spied Delilah sitting on the floor next to Thomas. She'd wasted no time. "Lady Delilah, it's so good to see you," she gushed, hurrying toward them. "Thank you for inviting me to the rehearsal."

Delilah *hadn't* invited her to the rehearsal, Rebecca had insisted upon coming. But Rebecca was her friend, and Delilah reminded herself that she *did* like her, despite the woman's recent brash interest in Thomas.

Thomas helped Delilah to her feet and then turned to Rebecca. "Good to see you again, my lady." He bowed.

"I'd hoped you would be here this evening, Your Grace." Rebecca's grin was ridiculously wide, and she performed a perfect curtsy. One from which she did not need to be rescued, Delilah noted with mild pique.

"I bet you did," Delilah mumbled under her breath.

"What's that?" Rebecca asked, frowning.

"Nothing." Delilah forced a smile to her lips.

Delilah watched them together. She tried to picture how Thomas must see her friend. Rebecca was a beautiful young woman. Well-mannered. Good family. No doubt she was precisely the type of young woman Thomas should marry.

And Rebecca definitely seemed enamored of Thomas. Delilah had simply never thought about it before—Thomas, her friend, her closest friend, falling in love and marrying someone . . . a woman. Perhaps she'd been terribly naïve not to have envisioned this moment, but she'd somehow thought she and Thomas would go on forever as they always had, talking and laughing and ribbing each other. She'd matchmake, and he'd avoid marriage, and they'd both grow old together. It wasn't that she'd planned for it to happen that way. It was only that she hadn't specifically considered it happening any other way.

Delilah watched with narrowed eyes as Rebecca laughed at Thomas's jests and reached out to touch his sleeve. Twice. She also noted that Rebecca did not rattle off poorly pronounced, nonsensical French, nor did she rip any of Thomas's clothing. How a courtship should be, Delilah thought with intense chagrin.

Moments later, Lucy swept toward them with a welcoming smile. "Lady Rebecca, it's good to meet you."

"Yes," Delilah said, happy to have someone else to introduce Rebecca to in order to divert her attention from Thomas. "Lady Rebecca Abernathy, the Duchess of Claringdon."

Rebecca and Lucy began talking as if they'd been friends for an age, and soon the Duke of Branville came strolling toward them in his new shirt. As he made his way over to their little group, Delilah tried to scrunch herself into a ball in the corner as if she might hide from him.

"Your shirt looks better," Lucy said. "I do hope the incident didn't put you off from playacting."

"Not at all," the duke replied graciously.

Delilah still wanted to hide.

Branville smiled and turned to Rebecca. "Won't you introduce me to your friend, Your Grace?" he said to Lucy.

She nodded. "Ah, yes, my apologies. Your Grace, this is Lady Rebecca Abernathy. Lady Rebecca, the Duke of Branville."

Rebecca smiled and curtsied and was perfectly polite, but she didn't show Branville half the attention she'd lavished upon Thomas. Which, of course, was good because with Lady Emmaline as her competition already, the last thing Delilah needed was more rivalry for Branville from Rebecca. But when Rebecca turned her attention back to Thomas, Delilah couldn't help but find herself even more irritated.

"Will you join our company, Your Grace?" Lucy asked Branville. "Will you play Hermia's father?"

The duke inclined his head. "Thank you for the invitation. I do believe I will accept."

Lucy clapped her hands this time. Thomas rolled his eyes. And Rebecca's focus remained on Thomas.

"Excellent," Lucy replied. "We meet three nights a week. See you tomorrow."

"I do hope there's room in the company for one more," Rebecca blurted. "I would so like to be a part of this wonderful performance for charity."

Delilah opened her mouth to decline even the mere thought, but Lucy was faster. "Of course, Lady Rebecca. We'll find you something. Peaseblossom, perhaps."

Delilah snapped her mouth shut. What was Lucy thinking? No good could come of having Rebecca in the play.

"I would be honored to join," Lady Rebecca said. "Thank you, Your Grace." She stepped closer to Thomas and gave him an inviting smile.

"Ah, I hadn't realized you were not already a part of the play, Lady Rebecca," Branville said, the dimple appearing in his cheek. "We'll both be new to the production, then."

Delilah frowned. At least Branville had agreed to join them, despite the embarrassment with the shirt. Perhaps he'd said yes because two other dukes were already in the performance. Perhaps he'd agreed because he truly did value the Royal Society for the Humane Treatment of Animals. Perhaps it was because Lucy could be uncannily convincing when she wanted to be.

Regardless of his reasons, Delilah breathed a sigh of relief. Branville would be coming back three times a week. She would have an opportunity to make up for her ridiculousness to date. No more mindless French. And no more shirt-ripping. She'd also do well not to bring Miss Adeline around. She glanced at the parrot from across the room and found him watching her with a particular glare in his eyes, as though he could read her thoughts.

"In addition to Peaseblossom," Branville said, "I wonder if there are any more roles for females as yet unfulfilled."

Lucy's smile faltered slightly. "Why do you ask, Your Grace?"

"I told Lady Emmaline Rochester about the play last night, and she also expressed her interest in joining."

CHAPTER THIRTEEN

"What do you think of pairing Lord Berwick with my friend Rebecca?" Delilah asked Lucy the next afternoon over tea in the duchess's drawing room. Delilah had *nearly* got over her acute embarrassment from the day before. Her outrage over Lady Emmaline joining the production had served to burn off a great deal of it.

The nerve of Lady Emmaline to ask Branville if she could be a part of the company! Clever and cunning of her, yes, but still, Delilah was smarting from being outwitted at her own game.

Lucy dropped a fourth lump of sugar into her teacup. "Berwick. The man playing Snout?"

"Yes," Delilah replied. "He's eligible. He's an earl."

Lucy cast her a wary glance. "Why are you interested in pairing off Rebecca? Did she ask you to?"

"No, but . . ."

"But what?" Lucy prodded. "I daresay we already have our hands full this Season."

Delilah eyed her friend surreptitiously. "I thought you enjoyed a challenge."

"I do, dear, but something tells me you have another reason for wanting to pair off Lady Rebecca."

Delilah cleared her throat and sat up straighter. "Fine. I think she has her sights set on Thomas, and I . . . don't want her to be disappointed."

Lucy shook her head. "No. Not Thomas. Not with Lady Rebecca."

Delilah expelled her breath. She was relieved she didn't have to explain or think too closely about why she didn't like the match. "I'm glad you agree."

"Yes, if Lady Rebecca is setting her sights on Thomas, let's be certain to pair her with Berwick."

Delilah smiled and nodded. "Agreed. Now. What about Lavinia? How did she get on with Lord Stanley last night?"

Lucy winced. "She wasn't awful to him. For Lavinia, that's something. However, it remains to be seen if Stanley will overlook her shrewishness for the purse Thomas's settled on her."

"Did Lord Stanley seem interested?" Delilah asked, studying the steam curling off the top of her tea.

"He asked if he might pay her a call, and she agreed." Lucy snorted. "I'd say they're halfway to the altar."

"That is promising," Delilah replied with a laugh.

"Now . . ." Lucy peered hard at her friend. "What about you and Branville?"

Delilah shook her head. "What about us? It hardly seems encouraging that he invited Lady Emmaline to join the company."

A catlike smile appeared on Lucy's face. "But that is why we cannot possibly pair Lady Rebecca with Thomas.

We still need Thomas to distract Lady Emmaline from Branville to give you more time with him."

Delilah didn't particularly like that idea either, but that was hardly the point at the moment, and she couldn't explain her feelings to Lucy, who was working so diligently at putting her in Branville's path. "After my disastrous turn with him yesterday, I'm not certain he wants more time with me."

Lucy pointed a spoon in Delilah's direction. "Don't tell me you're giving up."

"No, of course not. I merely thought perhaps we could give it time so he forgets some of the more poignant points of what happened. Such as the part where his shirt was ripped half off."

The smile returned to Lucy's face. "You want to be memorable to a man."

Delilah winced. "Not that memorable."

"Memorable is always better than forgettable," Lucy replied, picking up her teacup again.

Delilah took a sip from her own cup. "I'm not certain how you intend to use Thomas to distract Lady Emmaline when he has shown absolutely no interest in doing so."

"Yes, I know," Lucy said thoughtfully. "It's quite frustrating. He told me he doesn't want to lead her on."

"How does he know he wouldn't like her if he hasn't given her a chance?" Delilah asked, even as the very thought made her feel sick in the middle.

"Precisely what I told him. And you know, I do think it worked, dear."

"What?" Delilah coughed when she realized how panicked she sounded. She tried again, forcing herself to remain calm. "What do you mean?"

"I mean, it seems we have yet another goal this Season."

"What goal?"

"Last night after rehearsal, Thomas officially asked me to find him a match."

CHAPTER FOURTEEN

The Hillards' ball two nights later *should* have been the perfect place for Delilah and Lucy to put some of their plans in motion. All the players were there. Thomas, Emmaline, Lavinia, Lord Stanley, Rebecca, Berwick, and Branville. But the moment Thomas escorted his sister to where they stood near the refreshment table, Delilah knew something was amiss. Thomas looked as handsome as usual, with buff-colored breeches, a black coat, and white waistcoat and cravat. Delilah had chosen to wear a gown of light green for a change. Her mother had insisted on the fabric, but she thought she looked like a leaf.

"Lavinia, has something to say to you both," Thomas announced.

Lucy, who was wearing a gorgeous red silk gown, raised her brows. "Yes?"

Lavinia, dressed in a lovely lavender gown with diamonds at her ears and throat, pursed her lips. "I've settled upon a certain gentleman."

Lucy's eyes lighted. "Wonderful. We were hoping you'd fancy Lord Stanley. He's an excellent choice, and—"

"Not Lord Stanley," Lavinia declared, narrowing her eyes. She snapped open her fan and fluttered it in front of her face.

Delilah sucked in her breath. Oh, no. This did not bode well. "Who then?" she asked, a sinking feeling in the pit of her stomach.

"I fancy Lord Berwick." Lavinia snapped her fan shut and smoothed her long sleeves one after the other.

Delilah and Lucy exchanged worried glances.

"But don't you think Lord Stanley is more your . . . sort, dear?" Lucy attempted. Delilah knew she'd wanted to say *age*, but had obviously thought better of it.

"Lord Stanley is dull," Lavinia replied. "He spent the better part of an hour talking to me about drainage. Drainage! Can you imagine? Besides, he's merely a viscount. I daresay an earl is more my sort."

"It's true. Lord Berwick is an earl," Delilah said inanely, but she was already thinking about how difficult it would be to interest Lord Berwick in Lavinia, not to mention the fact that Delilah had already decided Lord Berwick would be the perfect man to distract Rebecca from Thomas.

"I know that," Lavinia replied with a tight smile. "I'd like to dance with him this evening. See to it, please."

She floated off into the crowd then, leaving Delilah, Lucy, and Thomas alone.

"I tried to tell her she cannot order you both about as if you are her servants," Thomas said sheepishly, pressing his palm to his forehead.

"We're matchmakers. It's what we do," Lucy replied with a sigh. "It does make it difficult, however. I've no idea how Berwick feels about Lavinia. Have they even met?"

"Yes," Thomas replied. "They met at rehearsal the other night, apparently, and Lavinia took a liking to him."

"But we've picked Berwick for Rebecca," Delilah said to Lucy with a note of desperation in her voice that she couldn't quite seem to quell.

"Rebecca?" Thomas echoed. "I thought she fancied me," he added with a grin.

Delilah lifted her chin. "I'm trying to do you a favor by distracting her."

"Who said I wanted such a favor?" he countered, raising his brows.

She opened her mouth to retort, but then snapped it shut, averting her attention from his handsome face. She'd found herself inexplicably perturbed with Thomas ever since her teatime conversation with Lucy. After all these years, he had finally decided to look for a match, and he'd chosen the exact same Season *she* was looking? That seemed entirely selfish to Delilah. Thomas knew she was quite busy this Season. The least he could do was wait till next Season to find his bride. Not to mention it had hurt her feelings to know that he'd asked Lucy to aid him and not her. Didn't he know Delilah and Lucy were a pair? Didn't he want *her* help?

And not only had he not asked her, he hadn't even mentioned it to her. He'd left Lucy to tell her. Over the last two days, Delilah had struggled with her feelings, and hadn't yet decided exactly what to say to Thomas about it or even if she should say anything. Too bad it wasn't in her nature to keep silent.

Lucy crossed her arms over her chest and eyed Delilah and Thomas. "We may have picked Berwick for

Rebecca, but we're forgetting one of the essential truths of matchmaking."

"What's that?" Delilah asked, her gaze scanning the ballroom for Branville.

Lucy tossed her head. "Sometimes the matchees are not agreeable to the matches. If that's the case, it can make things nearly impossible."

"We must convince them," Delilah retorted, frowning. She and Lucy had participated in some complicated matchmaking in the past, but this Season's antics were becoming troublesome indeed. None of their plans were materializing the way they'd hoped.

"Convincing rarely works, dear," Lucy pointed out.

"Yes, best of luck with that," Thomas replied, scrunching up his nose.

"But isn't part of being a good matchmaker making the matches realize that sometimes you know better than they do?" Delilah was not ready to give up on the matches she'd already settled in her mind.

"That's also true," Lucy replied with a sigh.

"Then I refuse to give up," Delilah declared.

Lucy waved a hand in the air. "All we can do at present is continue with the plans we have made and hope for the best."

"What plans?" Thomas asked, scratching his cheek.

Lucy eyed him up and down. "Are you quite certain you don't want to help us distract Lady Emmaline Rochester from Branville?"

"Quite," Thomas replied with a nod.

"Very well, Huntley," Lucy said. "Who would you like me to match you with?"

CHAPTER FIFTEEN

One hour later, Thomas escorted Lucy across the ball-room in order for her to introduce him to Lady Emma-line Rochester. After Lucy had put him on the spot in front of Delilah, he'd been forced to lie and say he had no idea who he should be matched with, and that had only served to make Lucy steadfastly talk him into meeting Lady Emmaline. How could he possibly know she wasn't the love of his life, Lucy argued, when he'd never so much as met the woman? In the end, he'd been forced to concede the point or explain why he was so ad-amant in his refusal, and it had seemed the easier of the two choices to agree to meet Lady Emmaline and get it over with.

Of course, the last thing he wanted was to help put Delilah in Branville's way, but Thomas supposed he owed it to Lucy to assist in her scheme at least temporar-ily, since she was doing her best to help pair off Lavinia.

"Lady Emmaline," Lucy said, a wide smile on her face

as soon as they approached the stunning blond. "Have you met my dear friend, the Duke of Huntley?"

Lady Emmaline nodded and smiled and said all the correct things, but Thomas knew immediately she was barely paying attention to him. Nevertheless, he dutifully asked Lady Emmaline to dance, he laughed at her unfunny jests, and he willingly trotted off to get her a glass of lemonade, while the blonde shot longing gazes across the room toward the Duke of Branville.

Lucy was right. You could put two people in each other's paths, but you certainly couldn't force their feelings. If that were possible, he would force himself to forget about a match with Delilah. Everything would be much simpler that way. Instead, he kept glancing across the room at her, where she hovered at Branville's side. It rankled him. What happened to her plan to be elusive? Had she discarded that notion entirely? Here he was playing attendant to a young woman who clearly didn't give a toss about him, while the woman he was desperately in love with threw herself at another man. How had he got himself into this situation?

At least spending time with Lady Rebecca was enjoyable. That young lady was interesting to talk to, and her interest in him was certainly preferable to Lady Emmaline humoring him.

Thomas had the sinking feeling that he'd gone about handling the entire situation incorrectly. Perhaps it had been a mistake to declare to Lucy that he was ready for a match. He'd partially hoped she would take the hint and pair him with Delilah. Instead, the duchess had immediately pushed him toward Lady Emmaline, which made him wonder how seriously she was taking his request. He'd really only told Lucy he wanted a match in order to attempt to make Delilah jealous. He'd assumed Lucy would try to match him with Lady Rebecca, and he'd hoped the more time he spent with Lady Rebecca, the more Delilah would look at him as a potential suitor.

None of it had gone the way he'd planned, however. At least he'd managed to demonstrate to Delilah that he was both eligible and kind. Well, hopefully, she already knew he was kind, but it didn't hurt to reiterate it, especially when she was in the market for a husband and had a specific list of qualities she wanted. He hoped she'd piece it together and figure out that *he* was all the things she'd been looking for. What was next on her list? Oh, intelligence. He *had* to have Branville there.

Thomas was contemplating whether he should ask Lady Emmaline to dance once more before giving up his halfhearted courtship of her for the night when someone tapped him on the shoulder.

"There you are, Your Grace," Lady Rebecca said when he turned. "I've been looking for you."

Thomas gave her his widest smile. "You have?"

"Indeed. I was hoping you'd ask me to dance."

Thomas arched a brow. She was bold. He liked that about her. She was friendly and bright and pleasant as well. Too bad he didn't feel much for her other than friendship. He hated to turn her down, but he also didn't want to give the lady false hope. His decision was made, however, when he glanced over to see Delilah watching them. Suddenly, he decided he would indeed like to dance with Lady Rebecca.

Thomas led Rebecca to the floor, and as they danced a quadrille, he surreptitiously darted glances at Delilah to find her staring at them, arms crossed over her chest. She looked none too pleased with being left on the sidelines. A smile threatened. Dare he hope she was . . . jealous? There was one way to find out. As soon as the dance ended, he maneuvered Lady Rebecca toward where Delilah stood.

"Good to see you, Rebecca," Delilah said, her voice prim.

"How did we look dancing together?" Rebecca asked Delilah, fanning her flushed, happy face and smiling up at Thomas.

Delilah's face turned slightly purple, and it seemed for a moment as if she might choke, but she quickly regained her wits. "Lovely. Quite lovely," she managed in a strained voice, studiously avoiding Thomas's gaze.

"I saw you dancing with the Duke of Branville," Rebecca continued.

"Yes, he asked about you, actually," Delilah said. "I believe he intends to ask you to dance."

Surprise registered on Rebecca's pretty face as the Duke of Branville himself materialized at her side.

"Lady Rebecca," Branville said. "May I have this dance?"

Rebecca agreed, and the two took off toward the dance floor as a cotillion began to play. Left alone together, Delilah and Thomas stood silently watching the couple dancing. Thomas resisted the urge to fidget like a child, painfully aware of her presence so close to him as never before, the soft fragrance of her perfume.

Finally, Thomas cleared his throat. "The waltz dates back to the sixteenth century, you know. It was recorded in 1580 in Augsburg."

When he glanced at her, Delilah frowned. "I thought it came from Vienna."

"No. I believe Vienna was where the name was changed, but the actual dance is really much older."

"I never knew you to have such an interest in the history of dancing, Thomas," she said with a hint of a smile.

He folded his hands behind his back. "I may not have finished my schooling, but I greatly enjoy reading."

"Of course you do," she replied. "I daresay you're more educated than those who took a first with all the reading you've done."

Thomas nodded and willed his cheeks not to warm. Delilah had always known he had a sore spot over not officially finishing his work at Oxford.

"They do make a lovely couple, don't they?" Delilah said after another awkward silence, watching Lady Rebecca and Branville dancing.

"Careful," Thomas replied. "You may have more competition there."

"No, I don't. Rebecca is merely trying to make you jealous." Delilah sighed. "She already told me she intended to do it. She knows I've got my sights set on him."

"She'd best watch herself. Lady Emmaline may well scratch out her eyes. She couldn't keep her attention off Branville while she was dancing with me. I'm afraid Lucy's little plan to keep her away from him isn't working well."

"How did you find Lady Emmaline?" Delilah asked, her eyes still trained on Branville and Rebecca.

"She's quite lovely for a woman who is obviously in love with another man," Thomas replied aridly.

As he'd known she would, Delilah glanced around the ballroom and immediately zeroed in on Lady Emmaline, who was staring longingly at Branville as he danced with Lady Rebecca.

Delilah shook her head. "Why must everything be so very complicated?"

Thomas frowned. "What do you mean?"

She tugged absently at the strings to her reticule

that hung from her wrist. "Nothing is going right. Absolutely nothing."

"Like what?"

Delilah tossed her free hand in the air. "Lavinia wants Berwick. Rebecca wants you. Emmaline wants Branville, and I've frankly no idea who Branville wants."

"Not to worry," Thomas said with a grin, "I haven't entirely given up on my attempts at Lady Emmaline."

Delilah blinked. "You haven't?"

He shrugged. "You're not the only one who enjoys a challenge. As to the others, why do you care if Berwick courts Lavinia?"

She fluttered a hand in the air. "It simply ruins the whole plan. That's all."

"What plan?" Thomas frowned again.

"The plan for Berwick to court Lady Rebecca."

He shook his head in confusion. "Berwick is courting Lady Rebecca?"

"No, but we'd hoped for him to."

"Why?"

"Because . . . because . . ." Her cheeks reddened. "Oh, it's too complicated to explain."

"Far be it from me to interrupt your and Lucy's grand schemes, but it seems to me that as long as Lady Rebecca doesn't have her sights set on Branville, what does it matter who she chooses?"

Two tiny lines appeared between Delilah's brows. "It matters because she obviously fancies you, and you're supposed to be distracting Lady Emmaline."

Thomas chuckled. "I have many talents, perhaps I can manage to distract both of them."

Delilah put a fist on her hip. "Don't tease."

"Who's teasing? I may fancy one of them," he replied with a sly grin.

"Yes, and that's another thing," Delilah declared.

Thomas pivoted to look at her. "What?"

"You asked Lucy to find you a match, and not me." Her voice was small, and he could hear the hurt in it. It threw him so off guard he was momentarily wordless.

"Lucy told me you asked her to find a match for you this Season," Delilah reiterated. "Why didn't you ask me?"

Thomas blew air into his cheeks. He had to handle this carefully. He'd never considered the fact that it might hurt Delilah's feelings if he didn't ask her. "I thought perhaps you were too busy this Season chasing Branville around."

"I'm not chasing Branville around, I'm . . ." Her face fell. "Oh, *mon Dieu*. I am chasing Branville around, aren't I? He's supposed to be courting me. Instead, I'm chasing him around like a lovesick fool."

Thomas cocked his head to the side. He tried to keep the emotion from his voice. "Are you lovesick?"

"No," Delilah replied miserably, "but for all the advice I've given others on the subject, I'm woefully unprepared for my own courtship. I obviously don't even know what I'm about."

Thomas cracked a grin. "What do you want to know? Perhaps I can help."

The sound that came out of Delilah's throat was a most unladylike snort-laugh.

"What's that for?" His smile grew as he studied her expressive features.

"*You* can't help me learn how to be courted."

"Why can't I? I'm a man, aren't I?"

"For one thing, you've never courted anyone," she pointed out.

"Not yet. But the time is fast approaching." He leaned closer so that his lips were nearly against her ear and, in a conspiratorial tone, said, "Perhaps we both need practice. Tell me what you want to learn, and we can try it."

Delilah rubbed her forehead. "This is preposterous, you know."

He nudged her shoulder. "No, it's not. Why shouldn't we help each other? Tell me."

She took a deep breath and contemplated the matter for a moment. "Very well. I suppose a proper courtship would involve walking in the gardens together at some point."

"The gardens?" Thomas scratched his chin, wrinkling his nose. "Why?"

She rolled her eyes. "Don't be naïve. Couples often sneak into the gardens at balls to talk. It happens quite often, according to my friends. It's called a rendezvous."

Thomas choked back a laugh. "You think couples sneak into the gardens to *talk*, and you're calling me naïve?"

Her brows lowered. "They don't talk?"

"There might be some talking, but I suspect they, ahem, do other things as well."

"Like what?" She blinked at him with those big, brown, naïve eyes.

Thomas shook his head. "Your lady friends haven't told you?"

Delilah put her hands on her hips and eyed him warily. "Do you mean . . ." She lowered her voice. "Kiss?"

He gave a solemn nod. "That's exactly what I mean."

Her eyes widened. "Are you telling me you've sneaked into the gardens at a ball and kissed someone?"

"Can't say I have," Thomas replied, scratching the back of his neck directly above his cravat. "Suppose I need the practice too."

She narrowed her eyes on him. "Why haven't you done it yet?"

"Why haven't you?" he countered.

She pointed her nose in the air. "I've been busy arranging assignations for my friends all these years. I haven't given a thought to my own until now."

"And now you want to try it?" he prodded.

"I suppose I must. I refuse to make a ninny of myself in front of Branville again."

Thomas arched a brow. "Have you asked Branville to take you to the gardens?"

"See? That merely demonstrates how naïve you are. You don't ask a gentleman to take you to the gardens. You secretly *meet* him there."

"Is that how it works?" His voice dripped sarcasm.

Delilah nodded primly. "Yes, he implies that he would like to meet you in the gardens, and you pretend to consider it for a moment and then agree."

"And then you meet and kiss?" Thomas batted his eyelashes at her. He teased her even as his heart thrummed in his chest, and perhaps other areas too.

"Well, I'm certain you don't kiss immediately." She waved a hand in the air. "There's bound to be a bit of small talk or some flirtatious exchange."

"Ah, yes, the flirtatious exchange," Thomas replied with an irrepressible grin.

"I only wish I could practice with someone who doesn't set off my nerves as the Duke of Branville seems to." She wrung her gloved hands, casting an unsettled glance in the other duke's direction.

"Very well." Thomas sighed as though the idea cost him dearly. "Meet me in the gardens. I'll kiss you. There may even be a flirtatious exchange."

Delilah thought he was jesting. Thomas had to be jesting, didn't he? Only she didn't have a chance to find out because he added, "See you there in a quarter of an hour," before he essentially bolted from the ballroom.

She was left to stare after him, blinking and wondering what she'd got herself into. She hadn't meant to imply that *Thomas* should be the one to kiss her. The notion was ludicrous, but now she had to go out into the gardens to tell him so. She didn't want to leave him out there waiting. That would be unkind.

So, she did what any good debutante with a planned rendezvous would and waited twenty minutes, to be safe, before she sneaked out the French doors on the far end of the room and scurried around the side of the house.

The Hillards' gardens were particularly well-designed for a rendezvous. They happened to include a maze of hedgerows, and everyone knew hedgerow mazes were the perfect place for an assignation.

Delilah bit her lip and glanced back toward the house with its glowing windows. No one was outside on the wide stone patio at the moment. She turned to contemplate the large hedgerow. The maze was lit with tiny white candles, glancing off the shiny dark green leaves of the hedges. She presumed Thomas had already made his way into the maze. Where else could he be?

She took the first tentative step onto the gravel path and forced herself to inhale a deep breath. Why was she nervous? This was nothing to be nervous about. Only Thomas would be at the end of this path, not Branville. She lifted her skirts and hurried forward.

He was standing in a patch of moonlight next to a stone bench in the center of the maze. The soft light highlighted his dark hair, one cheekbone, one bright eye as he casually rested a hip against the side of the bench. *He's gorgeous.* The realization nearly made her take a step back. What was she doing? She had no business thinking Thomas, of all people, was gorgeous. He was her friend. Her closest friend. They'd enjoyed making sarcastic comments about members of the *ton* together for years. He finished her sentences. He knew her thoughts. He indulged her love of chocolate ices at Gunter's, and helped her when she brought him yet another hurt puppy or kitten she found on the streets.

Thomas wasn't supposed to be handsome. He was Thomas. Only he *was* handsome. She had to admit it. Very well. He was a man, full grown, and she was a woman, full grown. But they were still friends, and that was what they would remain. However, if he wanted to help her feel less nervous by giving her a kiss, she would take him up on the offer. It didn't hurt that he happened to be handsome, did it?

The memory of their kiss during the scene at the rehearsal briefly flitted through her mind. She'd managed to force it from her thoughts for the most part, due to sheer stubborn will. But the truth was, that kiss had made her feel funny inside. It had sent butterflies winging through her belly. She'd told herself a hundred times that the act of kissing itself must be responsible for such a reaction. She'd find out tonight if he kissed her again, wouldn't she? If she had that same reaction, she'd know. Kissing was simply a highly enjoyable pastime.

"What took you so long?" he asked, jolting her from her shameful thoughts.

She smoothed her hand down her middle and cleared her throat. Why was she shaky? She was never shaky around Thomas. "Ladies must wait an extra five minutes before arriving at their assignations."

"I see. I believe you failed to tell me that part."

"You hardly gave me a chance to explain."

"Very well." He folded his hands behind his back and

paced a few steps. "Would you like to begin with the flirtatious exchange?"

"With you?" She laughed.

He stopped to look at her. "Yes, I'm told that's part of this. And we want to do it correctly, don't we?"

"You're being ridiculous, you know." She said it accusingly, but she could have sworn at least one butterfly was flitting around her middle.

"I'm not going to count that as part of the flirtatious exchange," he replied.

"Thomas, I—"

He took two long strides and pulled her into his arms. Her heart beat so loudly where her breast pressed to his coat she was certain he could hear it.

"I believe I should begin by telling you that you look beautiful tonight," he said in a husky-soft voice. His face had changed, and his expression looked downright . . . serious. He was a good actor. He was going to be a wonderful Demetrius.

"Thank you, Your Grace." She'd never called him *Your Grace* unless she was making a jest.

Those kind, solemn eyes—the eyes of a handsome stranger, suddenly—searched her features. "You smell like . . . lilies."

Her perfume was made from lilies. Thomas wasn't acting. He had actually sniffed her perfume. Disconcerting, to be certain. She swallowed hard.

He leaned down, and his lips brushed the side of her face, her ear, her temple. Goose bumps rushed along her skin. What was happening to her? *This is Thomas. This is Thomas. This is Thomas.* She couldn't remind herself enough because the feelings in her chest and . . . lower, were anything but friendly. Or perhaps they were too friendly.

His lips touched hers, lightly, lightly, and the breath caught in her throat. That wasn't so bad. It wasn't nearly as embarrassing as—

Then his mouth slanted across hers, and his tongue slid between her lips. White-hot sparks of something that felt nothing at all like friendship shot through her body.

She clung to him, fingers clutching his finely made coat and then inching up slowly to wrap around his neck.

His mouth on hers was like fire, lapping at her. It licked her everywhere and made her feel both hot and cold all over. Deliciously melting in places she barely knew existed.

She held as still as a fawn, soaking in every new jolt of sensation as his tongue explored the recesses of her mouth. His lips owned her, shaped hers, and when she tentatively touched her tongue to his, a strange sound rumbled in his chest, and he kissed her harder, deeper. He pulled her against his rock-hard body, and she moaned in the back of her throat, leaning into him, wanting more of him somehow, more, more, more.

And then, just like that, it was over. When Thomas drew away from her, she was breathing heavily—panting, in fact. And completely dumbfounded. *Mon Dieu.* What had happened? Kissing, it turned out, was magnificent. It was her favorite. Better than riding a horse too fast. Better than ices at Gunter's.

Thomas's hands lingered, warm and gentle, at her waist, and he pressed his forehead to hers as though he couldn't help himself, drawing breaths more ragged than her own. His eyes were closed, his lashes resting dark against his cheeks, and she was glad. For in that moment, she could freely stare at him as if he were some sort of magical beast. Like a Centaur who had emerged from the hedgerows to passionately kiss her.

At last she took a step back, studying him with wide eyes. "Oh my goodness. Have you done that before?" Wonder slid into suspicion.

He shook his head slowly. "No."

"Wh . . . why not?" She could barely speak. The man had stolen her breath.

"Because I'm saving myself," he replied, his expression grave, more sincere than she'd ever seen it. And maybe a bit vulnerable.

She finally caught air enough in her lungs to ask, "F . . . for who?"

"For the lady I'm madly in love with."

CHAPTER SIXTEEN

An entire week had passed since her rendezvous in the gardens with Thomas, but Delilah still could not focus on her lines. She kept forgetting every one of them. Her head was a mass of confusion. And she had quite a lot to be confused about. First, Thomas had kissed her, and second, Thomas was madly in love with someone? Who? He'd refused to say. He'd acted as if he hadn't meant any-one in particular, but the very notion had gnawed at Delilah's mind ever since he'd said the words, and the possibilities had plagued her for days.

He'd laughed it off as if it were a jest. She'd wanted to believe he was jesting or still acting, but something told her he hadn't been doing either. This served to further complicate her well-laid plans. Not to mention it made her insides feel sick. Who in the world could Thomas be madly in love with? It wasn't Lady Emmaline, was it? Oh, what if it was? Or even worse, what if it was Lady Rebecca who clearly returned his affections?

Her confusion over Thomas wasn't the only thing plaguing Delilah either. She'd begun tonight's rehearsal with an excessively unpleasant conversation with Lavinia, in which the lady had demanded that Delilah force Lord Berwick to pay attention to her. The Duke of Branville had barely said two words to Delilah all evening. She'd attempted to flirt with him, hoping he'd ask her to meet him in the gardens, but he'd done no such thing, and she couldn't exactly be the one to ask. That would be outlandishly forward. To add to her misery, she was becoming half-nauseated watching Lady Rebecca flirt with Thomas. Delilah was contemplating fleeing the rehearsal to go hide in her bed. She regretted leaving it this morning.

Thomas scanned the library where the actors were practicing their lines in small groups scattered here and there. Lavinia had poor Lord Berwick cornered. Branville was nearly shouting his lines onstage, and Jane was trying to get everyone to settle down and focus. They only had a bit over a fortnight before their performance in the country.

Thomas had watched earlier as Delilah made her way over to Branville and tried to talk to him. He had to admit, it didn't bode well for her. Branville seemed barely aware of her presence.

Thomas rubbed his chin. Last week when he had kissed Delilah in the Hillards' gardens, he'd half expected her to know how much he loved her merely from the kiss itself. It had certainly seemed to surprise her. The look on her pretty face when he'd pulled away from her had been a combination of surprise and . . . dare he hope . . . lust?

He'd kept his distance from her for the last week. They'd seen each other at rehearsals, but other than the lines they'd recited together, he'd hardly spoken to her. He didn't trust himself. His entire future with the woman he loved could be ruined if he made a muddle of this.

He still wanted to kick himself for telling her he had been saving himself for the woman he was madly in love with. That was far too risky a thing to say. He hoped she'd interpreted it more as a *one day* sort of thing instead of a current state of affairs. But she'd narrowed her eyes in suspicion when he'd implied he'd been jesting, and he could tell she was skeptical. That was another reason he'd kept his distance from her. What if she asked again? Knowing how determined she could be, he fully expected her to interrogate him if given the chance.

What had he hoped to accomplish by telling her? If he was being honest with himself, he'd admit that he'd wanted her to see the love shining in his eyes and fall equally in love with him, which, of course, was ludicrous. He should simply come out and tell her. Why the hell was it proving so difficult? He was handling this entire thing poorly. He needed to regroup and make a better plan.

He'd gone off with a half-cocked notion that if he paid attention to Lady Rebecca, Delilah might see him as a man and a possible suitor. Hadn't Lucy told him that was an effective way to gain a lady's attention? The kiss had been more of the same, an attempt to get Delilah to see him differently. More than a friend. Instead, he suspected he'd only confused her. Not to mention he had no intention of leading Lady Rebecca on for the sake of making Delilah jealous. That would be ungentlemanly.

To add to his troubles, Lavinia was on the warpath of late. Lord Berwick had not asked her to dance with him at the Hillards' ball, and she'd been in a rage over it ever since. Tonight, she was following the poor man around, doing her best to get his attention. At the moment, they were steps behind Thomas, close enough for him to over-hear their conversation.

"Lord Berwick," Lavinia said, "I thought we'd practice our lines."

"I don't believe we have any lines together, my lady. Snout and Hippolyta don't speak to each other." Berwick sounded puzzled.

"Perhaps not." Lavinia's voice held an edge of annoyance. "But that doesn't mean we cannot practice our lines *at the same time*."

"I suppose we could." Berwick had to realize she was being ridiculous, but the man was obviously too much of a gentleman to continue to point it out to her.

Thomas watched them drift off into the corner together. He and his sister weren't as different as he'd like to think, were they? Apparently they both wanted someone who wasn't interested in them. He'd already shown Delilah he was eligible, kind, and intelligent. That ridiculous speech about the origins of the waltz had to count for something, didn't it? He hoped she had found him kissable and handsome. Now, he needed to show her that he was funny. Or remind her, at least. They'd always laughed together. She seemed particularly unhappy today. He wanted to see her smile again.

Thomas turned to find Delilah approaching him. She nodded in the direction in which Lavinia had just left. "She threatened me, you know?"

Thomas's brows shot up. "Who?"

"Your sister."

He closed his eyes and shook his head. "Of course she did. I'm sorry."

Delilah crossed her arms over her chest and gave him a rueful smile. "She's a woman who knows what she wants and intends to get it."

"I suppose that's one way of looking at it. I say she's a spoiled termagant."

Delilah laughed. "Or that. I'm nearly certain she threatened Miss Adeline too, but unlike me, Miss Adeline threatened her back."

Thomas's bark of laughter followed. "I'm not certain who I'd bet upon to win that particular fight."

Delilah pursed her lips. "I had to tell Miss Adeline he was not allowed to pull out her hair."

"That seems reasonable." Thomas let his gaze wander over her softened features. "By the by, how did Lavinia threaten you?"

"She told me if I didn't get Lord Berwick to come up to scratch, she'd spread rumors about me to Branville."

Thomas rolled his eyes. "God. She's awful. What was your response?"

Delilah shrugged. "I told her I was doing my best and that she must be patient, which of course is completely hypocritical coming from me because I have no patience whatsoever."

"Did you put in a good word for her with Berwick?"

"No. Instead, I had a discussion with Lord Stanley and told him he cannot talk about drainage anymore if he hopes to capture her attention."

Thomas laughed again. "Did you give him any suggestions for suitable conversation?"

"I told him to talk about Lavinia's favorite subject."

"Herself?"

"Precisely," Delilah said with an impish grin.

They both laughed. And Thomas found some tension draining from him.

"How's it going with Branville?" Thomas asked next, thinking the slightly unkempt curls brushing her forehead were especially fetching tonight.

"How's it going with the woman you're madly in love with?" Delilah countered.

The tension returned. Thomas took a deep breath. He could either keep pretending he'd been jesting or attempt to use what he'd already said to his advantage. "It's not going particularly well."

"Nor mine," she murmured, her attention drifting across the room to the object of her affection. "Nor mine."

CHAPTER SEVENTEEN

"Call you me fair? That fair again unsay. Demetrius loves your fair. O happy fair! Your eyes are lode-stars, and your tongue's sweet air. More tunable than lark to shepherd's ear. When wheat is green, when hawthorn buds appear. Sickness is catching. O, were favor so. Yours would I catch, fair Hermia, ere I go. My ear . . . My ear . . ."

It was no use. Delilah could barely remember her first lines. All she could think about as she uttered them was how she might be playing Helena speaking to Hermia, but she might as well be herself speaking to Lady Emmaline Rochester.

Precisely three days ago, Delilah had been told by her maid, Amandine—who was friendly with the other French ladies' maids about town—that the Duke of Branville had been paying regular calls to Lady Emmaline. That unwelcome news had thrown both Delilah and Lucy into a whirlwind of action. They'd scrambled to come up with a plan to attempt to gain Branville's attention and favor.

As a result, over the last three days, Delilah had been shamelessly throwing herself at Branville. During rehearsal, she'd hinted that she would very much like him to pay her a call the next day. She'd waited impatiently at home all afternoon with only the regular call from her cousin Daphne. At the Mortons' soirée, Delilah had been forced to ask *him* to dance, a situation that still caused her cheeks to heat every time she thought of it, especially when she recalled that during their dance, she stepped on his feet no less than three times. And last night at the Cranberrys' ball, she'd managed to convince him to walk in the gardens with her, only to have been paying scant attention, resulting in her being whacked in the face by the branch of a particularly low-hanging tree. She'd barely had five minutes alone with him, not to mention the ridiculous incident had left her with a large scab on her forehead. The opposite of attractive. It could easily be said that not only was her courtship with Branville not progressing, it was, in fact, deteriorating daily, and Delilah was at her wits' end. Adding to her sense of failure, she also hadn't managed to drag a name out of Thomas as to whom he might fancy.

She tried her line again. "Yours would I catch, fair Hermia, ere I go. My ear . . ."

"My ear should catch your voice, my eye your eye. My tongue should catch your tongue's sweet melody," Danielle Cavendish said softly as she came to stand next to Delilah in the corner of Lucy's library.

Delilah gave her a tentative smile. "Yes, thank you, Cousin Danielle."

Danielle inclined her head toward her and returned the smile. "How are you, Helena?"

Delilah opened her mouth to say she was quite well, but shut it quickly. "Quite miserable, actually," she admitted, blowing out a deep breath.

Sympathy shone in Danielle's bright blue eyes. "Why's that?"

Delilah leaned her back against the wall and hugged her script to her chest. "You know I've been trying to make an impression on the Duke of Branville."

Danielle nodded. "I'd guessed as much."

Delilah dabbed at the scab on her forehead with one finger. "Well, I fear I've made an impression, but the exact wrong one."

Her cousin winced. "If you mean the incident with the shirt, he cannot possibly hold that against you."

"The shirt, the abysmal French, the parrot, then this." She pointed toward her scab. "I don't see how he cannot hold some of it against me." Delilah sighed and hugged the script closer.

Danielle folded her arms over her chest. "If he does, he's a bigger ass than Nick Bottom." She finished with a nod.

Delilah tried to smile, but couldn't quite manage it. She peered over the script at her slippers. They were already scuffed, of course. Poor Amandine had spent hours cleaning them. "I don't know what to do. I'm failing miserably at the one thing I'm supposed to be good at."

"What's that?" Danielle asked, her kind eyes filled with sympathy.

Delilah dragged one slipper along the floor. "Matchmaking."

"It must be difficult to matchmake for yourself."

"It should be simple. I've had a great deal of practice." Delilah lifted her head and pressed it back against the wall, searching the ceiling as if that large area of plaster might give her the answers she sought.

"You're being far too hard on yourself." Danielle laid a comforting hand on her shoulder.

"I suppose so." Delilah shrugged. "If only there was some way to make it easy."

Glancing over both shoulders, Danielle lowered her voice. "What if I told you there is?"

"Is what?" Delilah asked, blinking.

"A way to make it easy. Or easier, at least." Danielle's eyes sparkled with mischief. Delilah knew mischief when she saw it. Her pulse quickened.

She searched the Frenchwoman's face. "What do you mean?"

Danielle took a step closer and whispered, "You know I'm a connoisseur of perfume."

Delilah nodded. Danielle was half-French and had the best-smelling lavender perfume. She'd even helped a few friends buy perfume that would suit them. But Delilah failed to see what that had to do with matchmaking.

"I met a woman in Sweetings Alley who sells . . . special perfume," Danielle continued.

Delilah frowned. "I'm not certain I understand. You mean perfume that will draw Branville's attention?"

Danielle glanced around again. They were quite alone, but it was obvious the Frenchwoman did not want to be overheard. "If I tell you, you must promise to keep it a secret. It may sound quite mad."

A strange emotion uncoiled in Delilah's chest. It felt like hope. "I'm excellent at keeping secrets, and I'm also half-mad myself, or so my mother tells me, which means I am in no position to judge the madness of others."

Danielle smiled. "Very well. The woman who makes the perfume is a Roma woman named Madame Rosa.

The perfume is purported to make the person it's sprinkled upon fall in love with the person who administers it."

Delilah narrowed her eyes. "Cousin Danielle, you *do* know that sounds ever so much like what Oberon's up to in our play?"

Danielle smiled and nodded. "I told you it would sound mad."

It did sound mad. Entirely mad. But that didn't keep excitement from racing through Delilah's veins. Because in addition to sounding completely mad, it also sounded . . . perfect. "How do you know it works?"

Danielle shook her head. "I don't know that it works. I haven't purchased any. Madame Rosa told me about it when I visited her shop last year. But it cannot hurt to try, can it?"

Delilah's jaw fell open. The greater implications of this news were beginning to filter through her mind. "You've known about a love potion all this time, and you've failed to tell me or Lucy, the best matchmakers in town?"

Danielle laughed. "Honestly, I thought you'd scoff at it."

Delilah shook her head. "Lucy might scoff, but I won't. I'm completely desperate. Madness begins to sound like sense when one is desperate."

Danielle gave her a warning look. "You cannot tell Lucy. You can't tell anyone. You promised."

Delilah nodded and crossed her fingers over her heart. "It shall be difficult, to be certain, but I promised and I will keep that promise. The secret is safe with me, but you *must* take me to see Madame Rosa."

CHAPTER EIGHTEEN

Delilah sincerely hoped she was dressed appropriately to go to a magical perfume shop and buy love potion. She wore a light pink gown with matching slippers and no jewelry, save for her prized possession, a small golden heart pendant her father had given her the Christmas before he died.

Guilt tugged at her when she considered how she was keeping this scheme from Lucy (Lucy so adored a scheme), but Delilah had promised Danielle that she wouldn't tell, and she intended to keep her promise. The entire premise was completely mad, of course, but Cousin Danielle was an intelligent woman who had traveled the world and seen many things that Delilah had little idea about. How did she know there *wasn't* some sort of magical love potion in existence? Besides, as Danielle had pointed out, it couldn't possibly hurt to try it. Could it?

Danielle's coach arrived at Delilah's town house at precisely one o'clock in the afternoon the next day.

Delilah had already decided it best to keep the details to a minimum when describing her outing to her mother. She could picture the look of horror on her mother's face if she were to call out, "I'm going out to buy love potion," as she headed for the door. It was tempting, but she wasn't quite that brave. Besides, even if her outing seemed perfectly reasonable, she didn't want her mother to know she needed any help capturing Branville's attention.

On her way to the front door, Delilah stuck her head into the gold salon. "I'm going out shopping with Cousin Danielle," she announced. "I'll be back later."

"I don't approve of Danielle," Mother replied from her perch on the settee, where she sat looking at pictures of gowns in periodicals and sipping ginger tea.

Delilah had to fight her eye roll. Of course Mother didn't approve of Danielle. She didn't approve of any of the Cavendishes.

"Your Cousin Daphne could have made a much better match," Mother continued. "I don't know *what* my sister was thinking when she allowed that marriage to take place."

"Yes, well, I'll see you when I return." Delilah had long ago learned it was best not to argue with her mother about things like whom she did or did not approve of. Mother never changed her stance, and she enjoyed telling Delilah how wrong she was.

Mother's opinion had never stopped Delilah from being great friends with the Cavendishes. She'd always adored her Cousin Daphne and her husband, Rafe, his twin brother Cade, and Cade's wife, Danielle. Rumor had it, they were all spies. They were certainly all interesting and well-traveled, and had a great many fascinating stories to tell. Stories like knowing where to purchase magic perfume, Delilah thought with a smile.

She hurried out to the coach and allowed Danielle's groomsmen, who'd been riding on the back of the conveyance, to help her up into the interior.

"Good afternoon," Danielle said, as Delilah settled herself into the seat across from her cousin and her cousin's maid.

"Good afternoon," Delilah replied, patting her reticule. "I've got all my pin money saved and ready."

Danielle laughed. "I've already given the coachman the address." She called out to the groomsman, who let the coachman know they were ready to leave. The coach took off at a clip toward London's main shopping district.

"You haven't told anyone about this, have you?" Danielle asked, eyeing Delilah carefully.

"No. Mother only knows I'm going shopping," Delilah replied.

"And Lucy?" Danielle asked, drawing out the duchess's name.

"Not a word." Delilah crossed her fingers over her heart. It was true. It had nearly killed her not to tell Lucy, but she'd bit the inside of her cheek and kept her secret to herself when she'd spoken to Lucy last night.

"Did you tell your mother you were going out with me?" Danielle asked, a sly smile on her face.

"Yes."

"No doubt she disapproves."

"She disapproves of most of what I do."

"You haven't told her about the play yet?"

"Not yet. She's heard there's a play, but I've managed to remain silent every time she rails about how tasteless and vulgar such a thing is."

Danielle swallowed a laugh. "You didn't?"

Delilah shrugged. "It's quite amazing how people

assume you agree with them when you merely remain quiet."

"You're quite right," Danielle said, patting Delilah on the knee. "I assume you still want an offer from Branville, or we wouldn't be on this little trip today."

Delilah nodded, turned her head, and stared out the window, watching the sights of the busy town pass by. She'd barely had time to contemplate what she was about this afternoon. It was ridiculous to buy magic perfume. But she was desperate. Not the mild sort of desperate that called for trying to make the Duke of Branville jealous. No. The mad kind of desperate that resulted in a head injury from a tree limb and a trip to buy magic potion. She thought about her cousin's question. Delilah *wanted* an offer from Branville, but she didn't expect one. She hadn't expected one for days now. Oh, why couldn't she be brave enough to tell her mother to go to hell? Thomas had done that once with his father. But she knew it was a statement he'd regretted the rest of his days.

She closed her eyes and leaned her head back against the seat. She'd come home from play rehearsal quite late last night, and Mother had been waiting up in the gold salon. She'd reminded Delilah that she only had a matter of days to secure an offer from Branville, thus ensuring Delilah's involvement in this insane outing today.

Before Delilah had turned toward the door to go to bed, she'd asked her mother, "How's your courtship with Lord Hilton coming?"

A sly grin had quickly spread across her mother's lips. "I daresay I shall secure *my* engagement before you secure yours."

Delilah had nodded again and quietly left the room.

Why did Mother always have to be so competitive? Why did she have to be so unloving? As a child, Delilah had dreamed of having a mother who tucked her into bed at night and sang to her. One who worried over her when she was sick. Instead, her mother had always told her to stay away from her if she was ill, so she wouldn't come down with the same malady.

Father had been there instead. Kind. Loving. He'd called her his little butter stamp and kissed her forehead when it was hot with fever. If only Father hadn't got sick. If only Father hadn't died. How would her life be different now if he were still here? Mother would be nicer. Less angry. Less judgmental. Or at least she'd keep her angry, judgmental thoughts to herself.

Father had never allowed Mother to say anything unkind to Delilah. She hadn't begun doing so until after he'd died. Mother had always been quietly disapproving. She'd always sighed or rolled her eyes whenever Delilah tripped or spilled something on her clothing. But she'd never said anything truly awful to her until after Papa had died.

Delilah would never forget the night her mother had said the most awful thing of all. It had been the night of her debut. She'd been dressed in a gown of white, her mother's choice, not hers. She'd managed to keep the gown white too. Not a mark on it. Not a scuff on her pristine white kid slippers or her gloves either. It had taken every bit of her concentration to keep her clothing pristine, but she'd managed to make her way down to the foyer in a perfectly pressed, unwrinkled gown. She'd been waiting impatiently for her mother to meet her in the foyer on their way to her very first debutante ball. Delilah had been filled with hopes and dreams of meeting a man and falling in love and having the perfect courtship.

Mother had come down the stairs, looking as regal as

the queen descending to her court. She wore a gown of plum silk and stood silently while Goodfellow helped her on with her gray fur pelisse.

Delilah, ever impatient, couldn't wait a moment longer to discover how her mother thought she looked. She twirled in a circle and asked, "What do you think, Mother?"

"You haven't stained anything yet, have you?" was Mother's clipped reply.

"No," Delilah answered with a wide smile, thrilled to be able to honestly report such a thing for once.

"Good," Mother replied. "For heaven's sake, *try* to keep it that way."

Delilah nodded obediently, while Goodfellow opened the front door for them. On the way toward the coach, she glanced down at her finery and an unexpected thought made tears well in her eyes. "Mother," she asked quietly. "Do you think Papa would be proud of me tonight?"

Her mother had turned to her without a hint of emotion in her eyes. "It's probably best he's not here to see it, don't you think? That way he wouldn't be disappointed."

Mother had turned and made her way to the coach. The groomsmen had helped her up and Delilah had quickly followed, but she could barely breathe. Her mother's words had crushed her. She sat in stone silence all the way to the ball.

Once they arrived, Delilah had forced a false smile to her face. She danced and talked and ate refreshments. She went through all of the motions of being a normal, carefree young lady at her first ball. But she'd already tucked away the desire to find a match deep, deep inside. She wasn't good enough and she never would be.

Instead, she set about doing her best to make matches

for all of her friends. She'd already learned some of it from Lucy Hunt as a child and enjoyed it. Being a matchmaker was the next best thing to making one's own match, wasn't it? The last thing she wanted was to be an embarrassment to her mother. She'd already caused her enough shame. And Delilah truly couldn't bear the thought of being a disappointment to the memory of her dead father. It was safer not to try.

Delilah's penchant for matchmaking had made her happy all of these years. Only it hadn't. Not entirely. She'd always felt there was something missing, but she'd also always been scared senseless at the notion of making her own match. Now that her mother had forced the issue, Delilah was nearly as miserable as she'd been that first night. She was on her way to buy magic perfume, for heaven's sake.

The traffic in London was surprisingly light that afternoon, and it felt as if only minutes had passed before the coach rolled to a stop on Lombard Street. The coachman pulled down the steps, and the groomsman helped both ladies to alight. Danielle's maid remained in the coach.

As soon as Delilah's slippers touched the ground, she glanced around in search of the magical perfume shop. Unless she was missing it, however, there didn't appear to be a perfume shop nearby.

Danielle nodded toward the end of the street. "We have to walk the rest of the way."

Of course. A shop that sold magical perfume wouldn't be sitting about in the open, would it? Stood entirely to reason. Delilah, Danielle, and an accompanying footman made their way down the street and through a narrow alleyway, past a small white picket fence, to the back of a set of mews. They turned once more to locate a small green door nearly hidden behind a mass of dark ivy.

"Please remain here, Henry," Danielle said to the footman, who nodded and stood facing away from the door, his hands folded behind his ramrod-straight back. "We shan't be long."

Nerves clawed at Delilah's middle as Danielle lifted her gloved hand and slowly knocked on the door.

After a distressing length of complete silence, an old woman's voice finally called, "Enter."

Danielle grasped the handle and pushed open the rickety green door. She held it open for Delilah to precede her into the shop.

Delilah stepped inside and sucked in her breath. The interior was dark and cool with a heady mixture of scents she couldn't quite identify. She didn't realize she was holding her breath until they'd been in the shop for what felt like five minutes. She stared at all the strange and wonderful things inside, lining narrow shelves along every wall. The space was small and cramped and completely filled with all manner of items, including tin lanterns hanging from the low ceiling, beads, candles, and wooden tables filled with rows and rows of perfume bottles and vials.

The dimness was illuminated by the flickering light of candles. Delilah turned in a wide circle to take in everything and accidentally knocked into a table full of perfume bottles. The bottles teetered. Danielle caught two of them before they fell on their sides.

"Sorry," Delilah whispered, wincing. She scrambled to right the rest of the bottles.

"This way," came the old woman's voice again, and Delilah turned to see a tiny old lady sitting behind a table piled high with candles and vials of perfume. She was dressed in colorful robes and wore at least a dozen golden chains of varying lengths around her neck. Golden bracelets jangled on her wrists. Her curly gray-and-black hair was piled high atop her head and secured by a colorful scarf.

Danielle took Delilah's hand and led her over to where the woman sat. "Good afternoon, Madame Rosa. This is my cousin, Delilah."

"Come closer, girl," the woman said, squinting at her.

Delilah swallowed and took a step closer.

"Sit," Madame Rosa ordered, and Delilah dropped into one of the two rickety wooden chairs that faced the woman's table.

"Let me see your bare hand," Madame Rosa said.

Tentatively, Delilah pulled her white kid glove from her slightly shaking fingers and held out her hand, palm up.

Madame Rosa slid open a drawer to her right and pulled out a looking glass. She grasped Delilah's wrist and pulled her hand closer. When she bent over it, the heat of her breath warmed Delilah's palm. "Hmm," she murmured. "Quite interesting. But ye didn't come here for a palm reading, did ye, lass?"

"Palm reading?" Delilah glanced uncertainly at her cousin. Danielle shook her head almost imperceptibly.

"I read palms," Madame Rosa explained. "I can see the future in the lines of yer skin."

Delilah simultaneously wanted to snatch her hand away and push it closer to the woman's craggy nose. "What do you see in mine?" she asked, curiosity clawing at her insides.

"Want a palm reading, eh, lass?" The old woman laughed.

Delilah pulled her hand back into her lap. She swallowed. "I only wondered . . ."

"I'll tell ye one thing for free, lass," Madame Rosa said.

Delilah leaned forward so far she nearly toppled off the edge of her chair. She searched the old woman's face. "What?" she breathed.

"True love is in your future," Madame Rosa said, nodding sagely.

Delilah sighed and closed her eyes. She clenched her palm and rubbed her knuckles with the thumb of her other hand, nearly overcome with relief. "I cannot tell you how happy I am to hear that, Madame. In fact, it's why I've come. Well, not for the palm reading, but for . . ." She glanced tentatively at Danielle again. "The special perfume."

A frown descended over the old woman's face. "Special perfume?"

Danielle cleared her throat. "The elixir you told me about, Madame. Last time I was here."

Delilah nodded eagerly. *Elixir* sounded so much more official—and admittedly more insane—than perfume. "Yes. Yes. That."

Madame Rosa's eyes widened. They were extraordinary eyes, jade green with black rings around them. Eyes that had seen a great many things. "Ah, yes, the Elixir of Cupid."

Delilah caught her breath. Of course it was called the Elixir of Cupid. What else could it possibly be called? She bit her lip to keep from smiling. She did not want this fascinating woman to think she didn't take her work seriously. But she couldn't stop herself from asking, "Does it . . . really work?" As soon as the words left her mouth, she regretted them. No doubt it was rude to show skepticism for the woman's product.

"It works," Madame Rosa said simply, nodding. "It works."

That was enough of an endorsement for Delilah. "I'd like to purchase a bottle of it, please." She grasped her reticule, ready to hand over the money and take off with the elixir.

"Patience." Madame Rosa leaned back in her chair and smiled. Her grin revealed a set of uneven, darkened teeth, some of which were missing. "I cannot sell it to ye without ensuring ye understand the rules first."

A skitter of apprehension traced its way along Delilah's spine, as if a cool breeze had blown through the shop. Danielle must have felt it too because she rubbed her arms up and down.

"The rules?" Delilah asked, her voice cracking and uneven. She didn't want to listen to rules. She wanted to pay for the perfume and leave. Immediately.

Madame Rosa watched her down the length of her nose. "Yes. It's a powerful elixir, and I cannot sell it to just anyone. Ye must agree to abide by the rules or ye cannot have it."

"Very well." Delilah hadn't expected there to be rules involved, but now that she was here, she was willing to do whatever it took to earn the perfume. "What are the rules?" Too bad she'd never been good at following them. But she needn't tell Madame Rosa that. And she would do her best to abide by these.

Madame Rosa's bushy dark eyebrows descended over her captivating eyes. "First, ye can only use it during a night when the moon is full."

Delilah swallowed. That seemed . . . not impossible. She nodded.

"Second, ye must be the only person to use it. Ye cannot give it to another."

"That won't be a problem," Delilah said. Who else would believe her? Let alone want to borrow the elixir? Besides, she intended to keep it a secret, so no one would ask. Of course, that ruled out the possibility of her using it for future matchmaking assignments, but beggars should not be choosers. She wasn't about to disagree with Madame Rosa's rules.

"Third . . ." Madame Rosa paused. She leaned forward and peered at Delilah. "Ye must only use it once."

Delilah frowned. "Once? You mean if it doesn't work, I cannot try again?" That didn't seem like a particularly useful feature. Delilah was known to make mistakes. What if she missed Branville's eyes, for instance, and splashed it on his chin instead?

Madame Rosa's eyes narrowed to slits. "It will work, lass. It will work. But after ye've used it once, it's rendered impotent."

Apparently, the elixir called for perfection and precision. Normally, that would concern Delilah, but she would just have to ensure she didn't make a mistake with a magic potion called the Elixir of Cupid. Besides, she only needed to use it once. Once would be enough.

"Very well, I agree to all the rules." Delilah fumbled with her reticule. "How much does it cost?"

"Do ye have any other questions, lass?" Madame Rosa continued, ignoring her question.

Delilah's hands stilled on her reticule, and she thought for a moment. "Um, yes, I do. Will the person whose eyes are sprinkled fall in love with the first person they see? I mean . . . will I have to be the first person he sees in the morning? You see, that's how it works in *A Midsummer*

Night's Dream, and I can't help but think how much more difficult that will make the entire affair."

The old woman chuckled. "No, lass, that's only in the bard's play. The real Cupid's Elixir works differently. The person whose eyes are sprinkled will fall immediately in love with the person who sprinkled it, and no other, the next time he sees her."

Delilah nodded, swallowing the lump in her throat. This was real. At least it felt quite real at the moment. She would truly have the power at her disposal to make the Duke of Branville, or any man, fall madly in love with her.

"Very well, lass." Madame Rosa pulled a tiny heart-shaped vial out of her voluminous robes. The vial glowed a bright pink color.

A tiny gasp of joy escaped Delilah's lips. Oh, it had to be right. It was pink!

Madame Rosa pressed the vial into Delilah's palm and closed her fingers around it. "Cupid's Elixir is yours."

CHAPTER NINETEEN

"I'll have you know I've just come from the doctor, and he has declared me completely healthy. Fit as a fiddle, he said." Thomas sat next to Delilah in his new curricle. They were riding in the park.

Delilah was barely paying attention. Her thoughts were focused on the vial of elixir tucked inside her reticule. She'd had the stuff for nearly a day now, and she refused to let it out of her possession. It was silly, she knew. There was no guarantee that it would work. She may well have wasted her money.

As they'd left the shop yesterday with the elixir, Danielle had laughed and said, "What's the worst that could happen?" *That* had set Delilah's imagination into awful flights of fancy. She was keenly aware of the fact that all sorts of bad things could happen if she didn't do what she was told and follow the rules. But she *would* follow the rules. She would. It was true that catastrophes tended to trail her about, but not this time. Not when it was so important. She would keep the elixir, use it once on Branville, make no mistakes, and if they were meant to fall in love, it would work. She'd convinced herself of it. She'd even discovered that a full moon was predicted for the night of her birthday, when they'd all be asleep under the same roof at Lucy's estate. It was fate. It had to be. That was the last night she had left.

"Are you all right?" Thomas asked from the seat beside her. "You seem preoccupied. You aren't feeling faint after your head injury, are you? There are many trees on this route. I wouldn't want you to encounter another of the attack variety."

"Shut up," Delilah said primly. "And by the by, I cannot believe you made a jest about my needing to fend off attack trees in front of Branville at rehearsal last night."

Thomas frowned. "He didn't even laugh. I told you he wasn't funny."

Delilah fingered her reticule. She was trying to decide whether she should tell Thomas about the elixir. She'd promised Danielle to keep it a secret, but she'd absolutely burst if she didn't tell *someone*. Besides, she never kept secrets from Thomas. Surely Danielle wouldn't begrudge her having *one* confidant. Thomas was the perfect person to tell. He'd think it was madness. He was much more likely to scoff at it than ask to borrow it. Of course, he would relentlessly mock her, but she might need some mocking. Perhaps he would convince her to pour out the contents of the little vial and stop being ridiculous. Perhaps then this constant worry in her throat would go away.

She squeezed her eyes shut. "I . . . have something."

She opened one eye in time to see Thomas turn to her, a worried look on his face. "You mean like a fever?"

She expelled a half laugh. "No. No. Nothing like that. It's in my reticule."

Thomas glanced warily at the little pink satin bag that sat on the seat between them. "Is it alive? It's not another bird with a broken wing, is it?"

Delilah rolled her eyes. "No, it's not alive. Why would I keep an animal in my reticule?"

Thomas shrugged and grinned. He turned his attention back to the road in front of them. "I've known you to do more outlandish things than that."

The man had a point, but she wasn't about to admit it at the moment. Instead, she gathered up her reticule and opened it. She pulled out the little vial and cradled it in her palm, presenting it to Thomas.

He glanced at it looking entirely unimpressed. "What is that?"

"It's . . . perfume." How exactly could she explain this ridiculousness?

"What does it smell like?" he asked.

Delilah cocked her head to the side. "I don't know, actually."

His brow furrowed. "You bought perfume without smelling it?"

Delilah stuck her nose in the air. "The smell is not why I purchased it." She made a mental note to sniff it later.

Thomas frowned. "Are you certain you're feeling well? I'm not convinced you *don't* have a fever. Or a head injury."

She scowled at him. "It's . . . special perfume. An elixir, actually."

"A what?" Skepticism lined his features.

"Elixir," she repeated, doing her best to keep her voice perfectly calm and even. The more normal she pretended this was, the less mocking he might be. "It's called Cupid's Elixir."

Thomas took a long, deep breath. Then he rubbed one eye with his gloved palm. "Please tell me you didn't pay much for it."

She bit her lip and looked at him sidewise. "I'm afraid I did."

He took another breath, but kept his eyes on path ahead of them. "Delilah, I've told you, there are people out there who'll spin any tall tale to separate you from your money and—"

Delilah lifted her chin. "This wasn't a vendor on the street, Thomas. Danielle took me to see her."

"Her who?" His profile remained hard with suspicion.

Delilah stared straight ahead at the backs of the Thomas's perfectly matched horses. "A Roma lady. Madame Rosa."

Thomas closed his eyes briefly. He shook out the reins. "I can only imagine what she told you this *elixir* can do."

Now, Delilah was beginning to enjoy this. "Care to guess?"

He slowly shook his head. "No, actually. I don't care to guess."

She carefully tucked the little vial back into her reticule. "Very well, I'll tell you. You sprinkle it on the eyes of your true love while he sleeps, and the next time he sees you after he wakes, he'll realize he's in love with you."

Thomas closed his eyes for a longer period this time. Then he opened them, sighed, and shot her a dubious glance. "Really? A love potion?"

"That's right," Delilah replied with a firm nod. If he was going to turn mocking, she just might get defensive.

"I suppose you plan to use it on the poor, unsuspecting Duke of Branville."

"I don't *want* to use it on the Duke of Branville," she replied, tugging the strings of her reticule closed. "I'd much prefer our courtship to progress the normal way. But I will use it if I must."

Thomas shook out the reins again. "I'd no idea the lengths you'd go to in order to secure a match. What does Lucy say about this?"

Delilah bit her lip again. "I, er, haven't told Lucy."

Thomas frowned. "What? Why not?"

"Because Lucy prides herself on matchmaking the old-fashioned way. No doubt she'd scoff at this sort of thing. And I promised Cousin Danielle I wouldn't tell, which means you must keep the secret too."

He shook his head. "Feeling guilty, eh?"

Yes, that was it. Delilah hadn't been able to put her feelings into words yet, but guilt was the exact emotion she was experiencing. Once again, Thomas knew her best. Merely having the elixir in her possession made her feel as if she were cheating. She wasn't convinced her plan was fair to Branville.

"I only intend to use it if I have to." She repeated the words she'd mentally told herself a hundred times in the last day to Thomas.

"That makes it all right?"

"No, but . . . oh, I'm at my wits' end. I've done everything I can think of to attract Branville's attention, and none of it appears to be working."

Thomas barked a laugh. "I'd say your wits left around the time you thought buying a love potion from a Roma woman was a good idea. Do you really want a man whom you have to drug to fall in love with you?"

Tears sprang to Delilah's eyes. When he put it like

that, it sounded so . . . awful. "I haven't even decided if I'm going to use it yet," she replied primly, "but please promise me you won't say anything."

Thomas glanced at her and arched a brow. "Don't worry. I won't say anything. No one would believe me. In the meantime, I am going to hope you make the right decision and pour it out."

She straightened her shoulders as if trying to shrug off the guilt. It didn't work. "I may pour it out."

Thomas's eyes narrowed. "When did you plan to use this magic elixir, at any rate?"

She pulled a handkerchief from her reticule and dabbed at her sweating brow. "During the house party, of course. When else would I find Branville sleeping?"

"Ah, yes, the performance at Claringdon's estate. What's your plan? To sneak into the duke's bedchamber in the middle of the night?"

Delilah gulped. Thomas knew her too well. "That's precisely my plan."

CHAPTER TWENTY

"My lady?"

Delilah tore her gaze from the vial of elixir that sat on her dressing table to find Amandine blinking at her from the door to her bedchamber, an impish smile on her face. Delilah had been warring with her guilt all afternoon. Ever since her ride in the park yesterday with Thomas, she'd told herself a hundred times to pour out the elixir. And yet. There it sat. Sparkling and pink in its heart-shaped vial. She hadn't told Amandine about it. She hadn't told anyone else. After Thomas's reaction, she doubted she'd be tempted to tell anyone else ever again.

She grabbed the vial and set it carefully in the dressing table drawer. "Yes?" she called to Amandine.

"I just came from downstairs, and it seems you have a visitor." The smile remained firmly in place on the maid's lips.

"Who?" Delilah suspected it was Lucy or Cousin

Daphne. But she'd already seen Lucy earlier today, and Cousin Daphne usually called on Thursdays.

Amandine's eyes sparkled, and her smile widened. "The Duke of Branville."

"What?" Delilah nearly fell from her stool. If Amandine had just told her the king was waiting downstairs, she couldn't have been more surprised.

She wanted to jump up, rush out the door, and scurry down the steps immediately, but Lucy's voice sounded in her ear. *You must keep a man waiting, dear. You mustn't seem overly eager to see him.*

Lucy had a point. Besides, if Delilah rushed down to him, no doubt she'd trip and rip his shirt again. Or perhaps something worse. Like his breeches. Not to mention, waiting would increase the chances that her mother would discover he was visiting.

"Does *Mère* know he's here?" Delilah asked, a sly smile popping to her lips.

"But of course." Amandine waggled her eyebrows. "I *may* have gone out of my way to stop in the breakfast room and tell her."

"You didn't!" Delilah exclaimed with wide eyes and an even wider smile.

Amandine smoothed a hand over the front of her uniform. "Of course I did. It gave me great pleasure to see the look on her face too."

"Surprise?" Delilah asked.

"Shock!" Amandine replied in her heavy French accent. "I thought she might have a tiny apoplectic fit. Or at least I hoped she would."

The maid trotted over to touch up Delilah's hair and apply rouge to her cheeks, while Delilah forced herself to count to one hundred. She was wearing a light pink day dress that tightened at the waist with embroidered roses on the hem and matching slippers. It was a simple gown, but it would have to do. There was no time to change. When Amandine declared herself finished, Delilah stood and turned in a circle. "How do I look?"

The maid clasped her hands together next to her cheek. "*Très enchanté, mademoiselle.*"

"Wish me luck," Delilah whispered, as she forced herself to walk slowly from the room. An image of Thomas popped unexpectedly to her mind. She always said, *Wish me luck*, to Thomas.

As she warned herself to take the stairs down to the foyer one at a time, she forced thoughts of him from her mind. Amandine had recently told her London's gossip mills were also spouting the rumor that Thomas was courting Lady Emmaline. Of course, Delilah knew that wasn't true. Thomas's involvement with Emmaline had been entirely Lucy's creation. But the rumor bothered Delilah nonetheless. Thomas had admitted he was in love with someone. What if that someone was Lady Emmaline? What if the courtship wasn't a sham after all? Perhaps it had begun a sham, but then had turned quite real.

Oh, she'd think about Thomas another time. At the moment, she had another duke to worry about. The one waiting for her in the gold salon.

She entered the room and cleared her throat to catch his attention. The Duke of Branville stood near the window staring out at the road in front of the house. He wore impeccably tailored clothing as usual, black breeches, a blue overcoat, gray waistcoat, white shirtfront and cravat. He looked dashing and handsome, the epitome of what she'd always pictured a suitor would look like standing in the gold salon to visit her. A lump formed in her throat.

He turned with a wide smile on his handsome face. "Lady Delilah. Thank you for taking my call."

"But of course, Your Grace. Thank you for your visit."

"The mark on your forehead appears to be healing nicely," he said next.

She absently rubbed at the remnants of the scab. Then she snatched her hand away. "It's good to see you, Your Grace," she said in as stately a voice as she could muster. She'd already decided to stay far away from him. She was less likely to ruin any of his clothing that way. The scab had been a timely reminder.

Branville frowned. "Are you quite all right, my lady?"

"Yes, perfectly fine. Why?" Her voice remained high and prim, while her hands remained serenely folded in front of her.

"I don't know. You seem . . . unlike your usual self."

He probably meant calm. Good. Her usual self was too loud and too quick and too nervous and too everything. "Please, have a seat." She gestured to the settee. She lowered herself into a chair a comfortable distance away and concentrated on keeping her back ramrod straight and her eyes fixed on a spot above his head. Her back hurt and the fake smile she had plastered to her face was also painful. How did ladies like Emmaline Rochester manage to look this way all the time? Apparently, this is what it took to appear composed, to play the part of a well-behaved lady, one who would make a suitable future duchess. But it was uncomfortable, not to mention difficult.

"May I interest you in some tea, Your Grace?" she asked in the same pinched voice she'd affected since she'd first entered the room.

"No, thank you."

Merci à Dieu. She nearly sagged in relief. Pouring tea

while keeping one's back perfectly straight *and* not spilling it was a far more difficult task than it should be. She'd broken more than one teapot over the years while her governess had tried to teach her to do the thing properly. "Good," she breathed. "I, er, mean, very well."

Branville turned to face her, his hands braced upon his knees. "I've come to ask you something, Lady Delilah."

A trickle of sweat slid down her back. It tickled, and she tried not to squirm. Ask her something? Could it be? She held her breath. Was this the moment she would become engaged to a handsome, eligible duke? Good heavens, it had all been much simpler than she'd thought. She didn't need that silly elixir. Why, she would pour it out the window the minute she made it back to her bedchamber. How had she read the situation so incorrectly these past weeks? Branville wasn't put off by her. He liked her. Enough to come here and . . . ask her a question.

She tried to arrange her skirts perfectly so that she would be picturesque when accepting his proposal. But arranging skirts and keeping a straight back were incompatible tasks, and she quickly abandoned her efforts.

"Of course, Your Grace," she intoned.

"I hear you're a matchmaker, Lady Delilah," he began.

"Who told you that?" she blurted. Very well, *that* had been poorly done. She obviously needed more work on keeping her thoughts from springing from her mouth.

He smiled, and the dimple appeared in his cheek. "Lady Emmaline told me that you and Lucy are known for your penchant for matchmaking."

Of course, *Lady Emmaline* had told him, which only proved he'd been spending time with Lady Emmaline. The gossip mill was right. As usual. There was no use denying it. "Yes, it's true. I've made matches for several of my friends over the years."

He bit his lip, looking slightly guilty. "Yes, well, I was hoping you'd . . . help me."

She blinked. She had the awful suspicion that her face reflected her surprise. She was certain she looked as if she'd swallowed a bug.

"Help me . . . make a match," he continued, as if reading her mind.

Delilah swallowed hard. The fake smile on her face made her cheeks ache. She kept her voice as proper as ever, however. "A match? With whom?" Oh, *mon Dieu*. That was a stupid question. Of course he meant with Lady Emmaline. "It seems as if you and Lady Emmaline are already off to a fine start, Your Grace," she added, trying to keep the disappointment from sounding in her voice.

"Lady Emmaline? No." He shook his head, confusion marring his fine features. "She's not the lady upon whom I've set my sights."

The smile slid from her face. Her brow furrowed. "She's not?"

"No." He shook his head once more.

"Who then?" Delilah blurted.

"Lady Rebecca Abernathy," he said reverently, his eyes shining with obvious admiration.

"Lady Rebec—?"

"You two are friends, are you not?"

Delilah's chest ached with the effort to continue to act properly. "Yes, of course. I've known Rebecca since we were children. We danced the Maypole dance last year at the Penningtons' ball, and once we sneaked into Lord Abernathy's study and—" Now she was babbling. Babbling was never a good decision. She needed to stop.

Allow him to speak more. Not to mention the story about the time she and Rebecca had sneaked into Lord Abernathy's study and imbibed brandy didn't serve to portray either lady in a good light.

Thankfully, Branville didn't seem to hear any of that. "I'd hoped you might be able to tell me what sort of flowers she likes, and . . ."

Delilah barely heard another word. The duke continued to talk, but her mind was spinning. The Duke of Branville fancied Rebecca? All her well-laid plans were ruined. How had this happened? She'd been prepared to fight Lady Emmaline for him. She was completely unprepared to battle Rebecca. As far as she knew, Rebecca wasn't even interested in him.

"So, as you can tell," the duke was saying when Delilah began to listen again, "I hoped you'd put in a good word for me with Lady Rebecca."

"Put in a good word? You are aware that you're a duke, aren't you?" It was a crass thing to say, but it was also the first thing that sprang to her mind. With the shock she'd just received, Delilah had obviously returned to saying the first thing that came to her mind. Her back was no longer ramrod straight either, and it felt heavenly.

"Yes, but I . . . I believe . . ." Branville blushed and looked away.

Delilah narrowed her eyes on him. What was he trying to say? Why was the duke being so vague? She much preferred men like Thomas, who came right out with what they meant. It made them far easier to deal with. She'd never been particularly adept at guessing at subtleties. "Yes?" she prodded.

Branville cleared his throat. "I'm trying to say that unless I mistake my guess, I believe Lady Rebecca may be more interested in Huntley than me."

Oh. That.

Thankfully, Delilah caught herself before saying, *You're right*. She pressed her lips together and counted to ten to afford herself important moments to gather her thoughts and say something more . . . helpful.

"Rebecca *has* been asking after Thomas," she finally said. There. That was both true and vague enough to afford her more time to think.

"I've seen her dancing with him at a few parties," Branville said. "I've hardly had a chance to ask her to dance."

He'd hardly had a chance to ask Rebecca to dance because he'd allowed Lady Emmaline to occupy all of his time. But pointing that out would not be helpful. Instead, she inclined her head and said, "Perhaps if you made it a *priority* to ask Lady Rebecca to dance?"

"Yes, you're right. I know you're right." He leaned closer and lowered his voice to a conspiratorial whisper. "See? I need your help. Please agree to help me with your matchmaking advice."

"You do know I haven't successfully made my *own* match yet?" Clearly the man needed the obvious pointed out to him.

"Yes, but Lady Emmaline said it's because you've been busy making other matches. She said she had every faith you'd find true love one day and make the best match of all."

Delilah's mouth formed an *O*. "Lady Emmaline said that?" She pointed to herself. "About me?"

Branville nodded. "Yes, she said she greatly admires your skill, and says you and Lucy Hunt are thick as thieves."

"We are." Delilah smiled, but she was preoccupied by the notion that Lady Emmaline had been so complimentary. Here she'd been shooting daggers at Emmaline every chance she got, and Emmaline had done nothing but pay her compliments to the duke. Delilah felt petty and small.

A tug of sympathy for Lady Emmaline shot through her chest. Apparently, Branville didn't want her any more than he wanted Delilah. There were both in the same unwanted little boat.

"Will you consider it, then?" the duke asked. "Helping me catch Lady Rebecca's attention, I mean."

Delilah blew out a breath that ruffled the curls on her forehead. She certainly hadn't expected this when she'd come down here today, but she saw no point in turning the duke away empty-handed. "Lucy and I are quite busy this Season." It was true. She'd lost count of how many people they were trying to pair.

"I see." Branville looked positively crestfallen.

"But with the play rehearsals, we've been able to keep a close eye on things," she continued. "I don't see why we couldn't help you too."

A smile spread across his face. "Thank you, Lady Delilah."

"I cannot make any promises, of course. We don't have much more time, and this Season has been rife with the wrong people taking a fancy to each other."

Another frown lowered his brow.

"But I do promise to put in a good word for you with Lady Rebecca and ensure you two spend more time together. The rest is up to you, however."

"Yes." He nodded fervently. "Yes, of course."

Delilah stood and made her way toward the door. She needed time to think about all of this, to readjust her plans.

"I'll see you in the country," she said. "At Claringdon's estate."

"Thank you again, Lady Delilah. You're a true friend."

She forced a smile to her lips. *Friend*. Lovely. "Good day, Your Grace."

Branville exited the room, and Delilah shut the door behind him and leaned back against it. What in heaven's name was she to do now? All of her plans had evaporated in the space of a quarter hour. She should be sad. She expected tears to spring to her eyes at any moment. She blinked and blinked again, but there was . . . nothing. She wasn't sad. She had to admit that to herself. She wasn't. She'd coveted Branville as a prize to be won, and the rivalry with Lady Emmaline had brought out her competitive nature, but now that she realized she'd been sparring with the wrong lady the entire time, she felt nothing but a vague sense of dissatisfaction. Delilah wasn't in love with the Duke of Branville. It was that simple.

Certainly, she'd been hoping to *fall* in love with him. She'd been expecting to, even. But it hadn't happened yet, and his announcing that his affections lay with Lady Rebecca did nothing but make Delilah wonder if Rebecca might abandon her pursuit of Thomas and return Branville's affections instead.

Delilah shook her head. It had been a mad, mad Season. None of the people she and Lucy had attempted to pair off were cooperating. It was obvious they would be forced to come up with an entirely new set of plans. Starting with Branville and Lady Rebecca, perhaps. Delilah wasn't certain why she'd agreed to help Branville with his pursuit of Rebecca. Perhaps she'd done it because the duke had been nothing but kind to her. Perhaps she'd done it because she felt she owed him a favor after ripping his shirt in front of half the *ton*.

Perhaps she'd done it because deep down she relished

the idea of giving Rebecca someone to pine for other than Thomas.

A knock on the wood near her ear startled her. She jumped and turned to open the door. Her mother stood on the other side. She was dressed in purple satin, her arms crossed over her chest, a heavily interested look on her face for once. *Mon Dieu*. Her mother had seen Branville leave.

Delilah opened the door wider, and Mother slinked into the room. "So? Did he offer for you, then?"

Delilah gulped. How had she forgotten about her declaration to her mother when she was promising Branville to help him with Lady Rebecca? If she gave up Branville, she'd be giving up her chance to show her mother once and for all that she wasn't a complete failure. Her mind raced. Perhaps she could ask Branville if he would pretend to be engaged to her for a sennight or two, to appease her mother. Then she could cry off, or pretend to. She quickly discarded the notion. That seemed like quite a lot to ask of the man. Not to mention, it might ruin his chances with Rebecca.

"Not yet," she replied to her mother, still desperately sifting through all the thoughts that blurred her reason.

Guilt sliced through her. There was always the elixir. If it worked, her problems might be solved. She didn't want to marry a man who didn't love her, of course. And she didn't necessarily want to marry one whom she didn't love, but securing an offer from him and actually marrying him were two different things. If she could secure an offer from Branville, a real one, it would afford her precious time to decide what to do next without her mother insisting she marry hideous Clarence Hilton. Yes, it was ludicrous, but Delilah couldn't give up. For all she knew, the elixir didn't even work, but she had to try.

"But you *do* expect an offer?" Mother prodded.

"Yes," Delilah lied. She lifted her chin and straightened her shoulders. "An offer is forthcoming."

The smug look on her mother's face faded, and she arched a brow. "Really?"

Delilah nodded. She'd had no idea how good it would feel to see her mother's smugness drain from her features. "Yes."

"Good, because your birthday is in a few days, and if there is no offer from Branville, Lord Hilton and I intend to post the first banns for your wedding with Clarence next Sunday."

Delilah swallowed. "Don't worry, Mother," she said, thinking of nothing but the vial of elixir hidden upstairs in her bedchamber. The elixir that now was all that stood between her and an unwanted marriage to a man who made her shudder. "I intend to be betrothed by the time I return from Lucy's house party on Sunday."

CHAPTER TWENTY-ONE

The ride to Lucy and Derek's country house was long and bumpy, but Delilah couldn't leave town fast enough. If she had been feeling guilty about using the potion on Branville instead of helping him win Lady Rebecca's affection, her guilt had faded after her mother's renewed threat to marry her off to Clarence. Delilah set out for the countryside, more determined than ever to wring an offer out of Branville by the end of the house party, magic potion packed securely in her trunk.

During the long, guilty trip to the estate, she'd decided exactly what she would do. First, she would see if the elixir worked. If so, all her problems would be solved. Hadn't Madame Rosa said the elixir made the person whose eyes you sprinkled it upon fall madly in love with you? If that were true, then Branville would truly love her. He wouldn't just *think* he did. It wasn't such a bad thing she was doing, was it? After all, she had no indication that Lady Rebecca felt any affection toward Branville. It wasn't as if she'd be splitting up a couple in love. Now that would be odious.

Besides, she reasoned, what if the elixir was fake? No doubt it had been a ludicrous notion to believe it would work in the first place. That was one reason why she hadn't informed Lucy of its existence. Thomas had scoffed at it too. The odds of it working were actually quite low when one stopped and truly considered it. She may have done nothing but waste her money that day when she'd handed over nearly five pounds to Madame Rosa. Likely the woman had been secretly laughing at her the entire time.

If the elixir was fake, Delilah had already determined how she would handle it. She would ask Branville for a favor, to pretend to be engaged to her for, say, a fortnight, so she might inform her mother. Then she would cry off. It might cause a tiny scandal, but better a scandal than a lifetime shackled to Clarence Hilton. She just couldn't live with her mother's censure and disappointment. As for Branville, he had to agree. Delilah had something he wanted, didn't she? She would offer him her services as matchmaker to Rebecca. Only this time, there would be a slight catch. She'd tell him that Rebecca would be there to comfort him after Delilah cruelly cried off. Yes. That would do the trick. It had to. Only it didn't sound like something Branville was likely to relish doing, which was why the elixir was her first choice.

If the elixir did work, she'd thought of another way to absolve her guilt. She would use it as planned to secure an offer from Branville, then, after she'd had sufficient time to decide what to do next and how to avoid a marriage to Clarence, she would tell Rebecca about both Branville's affections and the potion. If Rebecca returned Branville's regard, she could go purchase some of the elixir for herself, and Delilah would help her use it any way she chose. There. That would solve the entire problem.

She expelled a deep breath and shook her head. Either the elixir would work, and she and Branville would be engaged by the end of the house party, or she'd beg Branville to play along temporarily. That was her plan.

In the meantime, Delilah only hoped her mother wouldn't discover she was acting in the play. She'd have to face Mother's wrath if she found out. *Mère* knew she'd gone to Lucy's country house for the performance, and she'd had plenty to say about that alone, but she had no idea Delilah was one of the actors, and she wanted to keep it that way as long as possible. After that? Delilah planned on doing what she normally did when she behaved in a way her mother disapproved of: Ask for forgiveness instead of permission.

By the time Delilah's coach arrived at the front of Lucy's estate on Friday afternoon, she'd convinced herself everything would work out perfectly. And if she kept repeating that to herself, she might begin to believe it was true.

The company rehearsed the play twice that day at Lucy's country house, once in the morning and once that evening. A few lines were flubbed or outright missed, but for a play for charity with a company of actors who'd never before been on stage, Jane Upton had declared their performance, "Not half-bad."

That evening, Delilah retired to her bedchamber, where Amandine helped her remove the costume she'd worn at the dress rehearsal. Delilah had already dismissed the maid and was about to climb into bed when a knock on her bedchamber door startled her. She hurried over to her wardrobe and wrapped her dressing gown around her. "Come in."

The door opened, and Lavinia Hobbs strolled inside. She looked around the bedchamber as if she were judging its contents. She eyed Delilah up and down.

"Lavinia? What are you doing here?" Delilah asked, hoping she could usher the older woman out sooner than later. She was exhausted. Tomorrow was her birthday, and not only would she have to give the performance again in front of a real audience, she'd have to stay up late and tiptoe around in the darkness to sprinkle magic elixir on the duke's eyes. Such subterfuge was exhausting, it turned out. She hoped to get plenty of sleep tonight.

"I've come to ask for your help," Lavinia said, crossing her arms over her chest.

Delilah didn't want to turn her back to the lady. She didn't trust her. She shuffled over to her wardrobe. "I told you, Lucy and I are doing our best to put Lord Berwick in your path, but—"

"Putting him in my path isn't good enough," Lavinia shot back.

"I'm not certain I know what you mean," Delilah replied.

"Don't you?" Lavinia drawled. A slow smile spread across her face, a smile that looked partially evil.

"No." Delilah frowned. What in heaven's name was Lavinia getting at?

The smile dropped from the other woman's face, and she narrowed her eyes. "Don't play dumb, Delilah. It doesn't suit you. I'm talking about the potion you've got."

"P-potion?" Delilah sucked in her breath. How in heaven's name had Lavinia, of all people, found out about the potion?

"Yes, the magic perfume," Lavinia continued. "The one you and Danielle bought."

Delilah swallowed hard. "Why do you think I have a ma-ma-magic potion?" She was a horrible liar. She tended to stutter when she lied.

Lavinia drummed her fingertips along the sides of her folded arms. "I overheard Danielle telling you about it at one of the rehearsals in London."

So Lavinia had been eavesdropping that day? Leave it to her to do something so underhanded. Delilah eyed the older woman. Lavinia was clever, and she obviously knew about the elixir. Was there any use denying it any longer? Very well. They might as well have it out. This was certain to be unpleasant. How in the world had Thomas and his lovely sister Alexandra come from the same parents as this awful woman?

"You want to try it on Lord Berwick?" Delilah asked.

Lavinia's smile was tight and fake. "Of course, I want to try it on Lord Berwick."

Delilah moved to position herself between Lavinia and her trunk where the perfume was hidden, as if Lavinia might jump into action and attempt to steal it from her. Truthfully, Delilah wouldn't put that past her. "I've no idea if it even works, you know?" She would at least *attempt* to reason with the woman.

"It cannot hurt, though, now can it?" Lavinia opened her hand to reveal a small empty glass vial. She handed it to Delilah. "I'm willing to try. Give me some."

Delilah expelled her breath. This was going to be even more difficult than she'd originally thought. "I cannot give it to you."

Lavinia's eyes narrowed even more. "Why not?"

Delilah tightened the dressing gown's belt around her

waist, pulling hard on both ends. "Because I promised Madame Rosa."

"Who is Madame Rosa?" Lavinia asked in a bored voice that indicated she didn't give one whit who Madame Rosa was.

"The woman who sold me the perfume," Delilah replied. "She made me promise to follow the rules."

Lavinia's eyes were barely opened slits. "Rules? What rules?"

"One of them is not to share the elixir with anyone else."

Lavinia dropped one hand to her hip. "Do you think me a fool? You're obviously making that up to keep it from me."

Delilah shook her head. "I swear I'm not."

Lavinia took a step closer and searched her face. "What does it matter if you share it?"

"I don't know." Delilah shrugged. "But I promised I wouldn't."

Lavinia raised her chin. "Fine, then, you can either give it to me or share it with me. The choice is yours."

Delilah pursed her lips for a moment as if in actual thought. "I choose neither."

Lavinia turned on her heel and marched toward the door. "Then I shall tell the Duke of Branville what you're planning."

Delilah dropped the belt and clenched her fist, a fist that itched to pummel Thomas's sister at the moment. "If you do that, you won't be able to use it on Berwick either, because I won't give it to you." *Mon Dieu,* this woman was difficult.

"Perhaps, but *you* won't be able to use it either."

Delilah glared at her. "You'd be that spiteful? To render it useless to both of us?"

Lavinia moved back toward Delilah. Her voice turned cajoling. "Share it. Who knows why that was a rule to begin with? No doubt it was simply because the woman wanted your friends to come and buy a vial of their own so she could make more money."

Why was awful Lavinia suddenly making sense?

"Besides," she continued, "at this point, either we both use it or neither of us use it. The choice is yours."

Delilah eyed the older woman carefully. She supposed she had no choice. Even if breaking the rule rendered the elixir useless, she at least wanted the opportunity to try it. Besides, Lavinia might actually be right about Madame Rosa's reason for the rule to begin with. Either way, Delilah couldn't let Branville find out that she'd intended to sneak into his room and sprinkle magic perfume on his eyes. She'd end up in Bedlam if anyone else found out.

The guilt that had been riding her since she'd purchased the perfume multiplied tenfold as she opened her empty palm and presented it to Lavinia. "Fine. Give me your vial. I'll share my elixir."

CHAPTER TWENTY-TWO

The next morning dawned bright and beautiful, the sky a cloudless blue. A slight breeze in the air kept it from being too hot, and both the day and night promised to be lovely. Coaches began arriving from London, filled with playgoers who'd paid a hefty sum to attend the private performance.

Thomas had awakened with the sun. He'd gone for a long ride about Claringdon's property. A long ride in which he'd had plenty of time to think.

Delilah's magic potion scheme was madness. It was probably the most insane thing he'd ever known her to get up to, and that list included a great many insane things. But the scheme also posed the perfect solution to his dilemma. He'd been waiting for the opportunity to tell her how he felt about her. But he'd been worried that if she didn't feel the same, the entire plan would fail and he'd be left without his friend.

Today was her birthday. He'd intended to tell her how

he felt about her after the performance tonight. He'd intended to ask to speak with her alone and confess his feelings, to ask her if she thought she might be able to return them.

Instead, he decided to use her deuced elixir plot to gain what he wanted. He reasoned that he'd be doing her a favor. If Delilah did end up tiptoeing about the Duke of Branville's bedchamber tonight, not only might it cause a huge scandal—one from which she'd never be able to extract herself—but lovable, clumsy Delilah also might trip and fall on the bed, wake the duke, and horrify him with her forwardness. That would cause her no end of embarrassment. More importantly, Thomas loved her and always had, so the silly fairy dust might just be the perfect way to show her his true feelings.

It was finally time to ask one of the gentlemen for assistance.

Thomas returned from his ride, went to his bedchamber to change his clothing, and met a group of similarly early risers in the breakfast room. After finishing his meal, he waited until Claringdon left the room before he excused himself and followed Derek out into the corridor.

"A moment of your time, Your Grace," Thomas said.

Derek turned and inclined his head. "Of course. My study is around the corner."

The older man led Thomas to the large room and closed the door behind them. Thomas took a seat in the leather chair that sat in front of Claringdon's desk. Claringdon made his way behind the desk and took his own seat.

"What did you want to speak to me about, Huntley?" Derek asked, as soon as he was settled.

Thomas leaned back in his chair. He could only hope

Claringdon was an understanding man. "I need your help."

Claringdon's astute eyes searched Thomas's face. He nodded. "Name it."

Thomas took a deep breath. "First, I must warn you, it's going to sound . . . unconventional and perhaps . . . odd. Even ludicrous."

Derek grinned at him. "I've spent many years with Lucy, my friend. I'm an expert in the unconventional and odd. And I'm well-acquainted with ludicrous."

Thomas threw back his head and laughed. Perhaps this would go better than he'd hoped. "Excellent. Then perhaps you won't be shocked when I ask for you to help me switch bedchambers with the Duke of Branville to-night."

Derek narrowed his eyes. "Branville?"

Thomas nodded. "Yes, but Lucy mustn't know. None of the ladies must know."

Derek drummed his fingers on the desk. "Out of curiosity, why do you want to switch rooms?"

"Here comes the ludicrous part." Thomas bit the inside of his cheek. "Delilah purchased a vial of perfume that she intends to . . . sprinkle on Branville's eyes because . . ." He choked a little. "It's, err, purported to make him fall in love with her."

Derek's eyebrows shot up. "You're right. Even after all the schemes I've known Lucy to get up to, including the invention of an entirely fictional chaperone named Mrs. Bunbury, *that* does sound ludicrous."

Thomas tugged at his cravat. It had sounded even more ludicrous when he'd said it aloud. "Nevertheless, it's true."

Derek resumed drumming his fingers. "I assume you

want to switch rooms because *you* want to be the one who falls in love."

"I'm already in love," Thomas admitted with a sigh. "I merely want an opportunity to let her know it."

"Switching bedchambers, eh?" Claringdon said, smiling a little. "This sounds like something my wife and her friends would do, you know."

"Is that a no?" Thomas asked, his gut clenching.

"On the contrary," Claringdon replied. "I'm happy to prove that my wife is not the only one who can matchmake if need be. I'll make the arrangements."

"Thank you, Your Grace." Thomas stood and all but fled the room. He made it into the corridor before he leaned back against the wall and expelled his breath. He grinned to himself. That had gone better than expected. He'd known Claringdon was a good man, but Thomas hadn't been entirely certain the duke would agree to such mischief. Derek had a point, however. Being married to Lucy Hunt all these years had to have upped the man's tolerance for the absurd. Lucy was always up to something.

A slight twinge of guilt pinged Thomas's conscience. The deception he intended to play upon Delilah wasn't right. But, he reminded himself, it also wasn't as if love potion truly existed. Delilah had always been fanciful, and sometimes too easily convinced. If she sprinkled the elixir on Branville, all she would receive was bitter disappointment. This unfortunate way, however, Thomas would get his chance to show her how he truly felt about her.

He'd spent all these weeks showing her he possessed the qualities she wanted in a husband. She needed to see him in a different light. Not as a friend. If he could wake up tomorrow morning and confess he was in love with her, perhaps she'd change her mind. Perhaps she'd finally realize they were made for each other. That damned potion was the perfect excuse.

His plan was simple. He would switch rooms with Branville, and when Delilah came to sprinkle the elixir, he'd ensure she couldn't see his face until after she'd done it. Then he would have to make certain she saw him so she'd know he was the one who was enchanted. It was as easy and as absurd as that.

He shoved his hands in his pockets, made his way to the foyer, and bounded up the stairs to his bedchamber. By this time tomorrow, he would finally be able to tell Delilah how he truly felt about her.

CHAPTER TWENTY-THREE

The gown Delilah wore to play Helena was a simple white one, gathered at the waist and shoulders with a deeply rounded collar and no sleeves. Danielle Cavendish and her maids had worked endless hours to make all the costumes, and Cousin Daphne had been in charge of ensuring all of the players had enough cosmetics on their faces to be seen from the audience. Daphne had applied rouge and powder to Delilah's face and lips, and used soot mixed with oil to outline her eyebrows and eyelashes. She finished the look with lip salve made from the attar of roses that gave a decided pink hue to Delilah's mouth. The effect was quite startling when Delilah saw herself in the looking glass. But Daphne had assured her that all players wore such substances on their faces. Apparently, her cousin had gone to the Drury Lane Theatre and discussed it with them at length.

Before the play began, all of the players met in the corridor outside the library, where the sets and stage had been set up. The small audience faced the stage in five rows of seats, separated by an aisle. There were approximately fifty people who'd come for the play, but it might as well have been five hundred for the amount of nerves in Delilah's belly.

Lucy's library had been transformed into a woodland copse at night. Trees and vines covered every space, and twinkling stars hung from the ceiling. Cass's lovely paintings of trees graced the room. The moss and leaves and all of the other items they'd spent the last few months collecting had been artfully arranged by Cass and Danielle to make the room look like one had stumbled into the forest.

Out in the corridor next to the library's side entrance, excitement bubbled in the air. The players spoke in hushed and anxious voices, all of them ready to finally put their hard work to use. Delilah's slipper tapped against the floor like a jackrabbit's foot while Lady Rothwell from the Royal Society for the Human Treatment of Animals made a speech to the crowd about how kind and generous the players were to take on such a feat for the assistance of the animals. The audience clapped. Then Jane Upton sailed into the library, climbed onstage, and announced the performance.

The last of her words floated out into the corridor, making Delilah's stomach flip. "And so we give you William Shakespeare's *A Midsummer Night's Dream*."

More applause followed before Rafe Cavendish's voice began the play as Duke Theseus with Lavinia as his Hippolyta.

"Nervous?" Thomas asked, sliding into the space next to Delilah as they waited by the library doors.

His part came before hers so there was little time to answer before he winked at her and entered the library.

Lucy, dressed as Titania, the fairy queen, was a sight

to behold. She had sparkles all over her face and arms and neck, and her hair was entwined with leaves, twigs, and berries. She wore a golden gown that looked like a robe a Roman goddess would have owned. She winked at Delilah in passing.

Scene after scene was executed if not flawlessly, then at least as good as could be expected. Delilah recited her lines in each of her scenes, barely aware of them. Thank goodness her memory was accurate because her mind was elsewhere. It resided firmly in the plot to sprinkle elixir on Branville's eyes later. The sane, reasonable part of herself argued that she should pour out the elixir and stop the madness, while the mad, desperate part of herself kept whispering that it would all work out perfectly if only she stuck to her plan.

They'd made it all the way to the part where the lovers wake up in the glade the next morning before Delilah even realized how much time had passed. After Thomas as Demetrius delivered his line, "Why, then, we are awake. Let's follow him. And by the way let us recount our dreams." He turned, pulled Delilah into his arms and . . . kissed her.

For the first time all evening, Delilah was catapulted into the present moment. Thomas's lips on hers shocked her into reality. Her head fell back, and her lips parted as the kiss seemed to go on forever. Her toes curled in her slippers, and her body went hot and feverish. Her knees nearly buckled. The audience stood and clapped, and Delilah was vaguely aware that Jane and Garrett as Lysander and Hermia must be kissing too, before Thomas's mouth pulled away from hers, and he whispered in her ear, "Happy birthday, my dearest friend."

She could barely stand. He had to help steady her as they made their way back into the corridor.

The rest of the performance was over in a blur as Delilah recited her lines as best she could while trying to make sense of the kiss Thomas had given her. It hadn't been a play kiss. Nothing they'd rehearsed. It had been more like a . . . real kiss. Like the one he'd given her in the Hillards' garden. The one that had stolen her breath and made her knees weak too. Yes, that was it. Her knees had been weak again. But it all made no sense because it was *Thomas* who'd kissed her. Not the Duke of Branville, but Thomas. And she'd been caught up in it. She'd looked up into his eyes and had a moment of wanting to wrap her arms around his neck, kiss him again, and never stop kissing him. What was the meaning of that?

It felt like only minutes had passed before Cade Cavendish gave his final speech to the audience as Puck, resounding applause followed, and then Delilah and the other players were whisked out of the corridor, back into the library, and onto the stage to take their final bow.

And then it was over. The play they'd all worked so diligently on all summer was complete. Relief flooded her, along with a sense of melancholy. No more rehearsals. No more costumes. No more reason to see her friends three times a week. At least she would no longer have to sneak about and lie to her mother. No doubt the fact that she'd kissed Thomas would make its way back to the London gossip mills, and therefore back to *Mère*, but Delilah would worry about that later.

Tonight, she had a secret operation to carry out. But first, there would be a party where all of the playgoers would mingle with the players. She could only hope Lavinia wouldn't give away their secret.

The party was well underway in the estate's giant ballroom when Delilah made her way over to Lucy's side.

All of the players had gone up to their bedchambers to remove their cosmetics and change out of their costumes. By the time the ballroom was filled with the partygoers and players enjoying drinks carried on silver salvers by footmen, it was well past midnight. *Mon Dieu*. Delilah had officially failed to secure an offer from Branville by her birthday. But no matter. She intended to get one in the morning at her earliest convenience. Besides, as long as she had the offer before she returned to London, Mother would hardly quibble over that minor detail.

"We did it!" Lucy declared when Delilah stepped into place next to her. Lucy reached out and squeezed her hand.

"We certainly did," Delilah replied. She leaned over and hugged Cass and Jane, who were drinking glasses of champagne nearby. They handed one to Delilah.

"Lucy," she whispered, "I need to speak to you."

Lucy nodded and excused herself from the group. She and Delilah made their way over to the wall near a potted palm, where Lucy turned to face her. "What is it?" Her two different colored eyes searched Delilah's face.

Delilah clasped her hands together and squeezed them hard. "I kissed Thomas tonight."

The hint of a smile played across Lucy's lips. "I know, dear. We all saw. It was quite convincing. Well done."

"No, I mean, we *kissed*. It wasn't an act. I promise." Delilah tried to keep the panic from her voice, but she feared she hadn't done a good job of it.

Lucy's tilted her head to the side and narrowed her eyes. "What exactly are you trying to say, dear?"

"I'm trying to say I *kissed* Thomas, and I . . . liked it." Now that the admission was out, it felt good. She breathed a sigh of relief.

Lucy shook her head and squelched a smile. "Delilah

dear, there's absolutely no harm in enjoying a kiss with a handsome young man. Why, you're only human, after all."

"I know, but it makes me feel so . . . confused." Confused wasn't the precise word she wanted, but it would do.

Lucy rubbed her friend's shoulder. "Because of your pursuit of Branville, dear?" Sympathy shone in her eyes.

"Yes. Meanwhile, I don't think Branville has spoken two words to me all evening." Delilah bit her lip.

She hadn't told Lucy that Branville had asked for her help with Rebecca. Her reasoning being that once she used the elixir—if she used the elixir—how would she explain Branville's abandoning Rebecca so suddenly? She glanced over to where Branville sipped champagne at Rebecca's side.

Guilt sliced through Delilah again. Not only did she intend to drastically alter Branville's life tonight, she would also be altering Rebecca's. Only Rebecca was still glancing longingly at Thomas, she noted. Meanwhile, Thomas seemed to be deep in conversation with Lady Emmaline, whose attention was obviously fully attuned to Branville.

The entire thing had become so terribly complicated, and it wasn't helping anything that when Delilah closed her eyes, all she could think about was Thomas's kiss.

"Go speak to Branville, dear," Lucy said. "He's not going to notice you if you're all the way over here."

Delilah nodded, and Lucy folded back into the crowd, but instead of going to speak to the Duke of Branville, Delilah made her way over to the Duke of Claringdon's side. She tapped Derek's arm and the tall, formidable man turned.

"Delilah?"

With a nod, she motioned for him to follow her.

Derek walked behind her until they were several paces away from the others. "What is it?"

Delilah pressed a hand to her chest to slow the painful pounding of her heart. "I need a favor, Derek, but I must also request that you ask me no questions about why I want to know."

He frowned. "I'm afraid I don't follow."

"I need to know where the Duke of Branville's guest bedchamber is, but I cannot tell you why I want to know. I will say, however, that my intentions are entirely honorable. Well, my intentions are not indecent, I mean."

Derek shook his head. "I'm certain I don't want to know," he replied dryly. "But I trust you, Delilah. I would warn you, however, whatever you're up to, be careful."

"I will be, Your Grace. I promise."

CHAPTER TWENTY-FOUR

Delilah glanced up and down the dim hallway. It was well past three in the morning, she was still dressed in the pink ball gown she'd worn to the party, and she clutched the small vial of Cupid's Elixir in her sweaty, guilty palm. She pressed her back against the shadowed wall not far from the Duke of Branville's bedchamber. She could do this. More importantly, she *would* do this. She'd come this far, hadn't she? What did a little sneaking about in the middle of the night matter?

She'd got detailed instructions to Branville's room from Derek, who thankfully hadn't asked any questions about why she wanted to know. According to him, the room was four doors to the right, just past the staircase on the third floor. The third floor was where all the bachelor gentlemen were sleeping. It would be a complete scandal if she was found lurking about alone at this time of night, but she'd waited until the household seemed quite asleep and then waited a bit longer for good measure.

Anyone who saw her now would be skulking about themselves, which meant they would hardly be in a position to judge her. She briefly wondered if she'd run into Lavinia.

It was not as if she was out to do anything particularly scandalous. It was more silly and frivolous than anything else. She'd simply die, however, if Branville woke up and asked her what she was doing sprinkling pixie water in his eyes. She'd already decided to pretend as if she were dreaming, thinking she was Puck in the play. Sleepwalking. That would make all the sense in the world. Wouldn't it? She swallowed hard. Probably not, but she wasn't about to let the fear of being caught stop her. Besides, all of her and Lucy's matchmaking had turned into a colossal mess. If a spray of perfume could sort it out, so be it. Of course, Delilah's conscience reminded her that she hadn't offered any of the perfume to Rebecca to use on Thomas. She didn't want to even contemplate that. She'd already shared it with one other person, and that made her guilty enough. The image of Madame Rosa's disapproving, craggy face had haunted her all evening.

Delilah shook off the thought and turned her attention back to the matter at hand. Pressing her empty palm against the darkened wall, she inched her way along until she came to Branville's door. She felt like a spy. This was how professional spies did such things, wasn't it? Too bad she was too embarrassed by her actions to ask the veritable house full of professional spies who happened to be asleep behind other doors right now.

She transferred the vial into her opposite hand and slowly reached to grasp the door handle. The metal was cold in her bare hand. She'd discarded her gloves, deciding that they would make her actions more clumsy. The last thing she needed tonight was to be more clumsy than usual. Decidedly, she needed to be less so.

She clutched the door handle like a lifeline and closed her eyes, steadying her shaking fingers on the knob. She was close, so close. Praying that the door wouldn't squeak, she turned the handle slowly. The only sound was the thumping of her own heart in her ears.

When the handle was turned as far as it would go, she pushed it, praying fervently that it wasn't locked. It took a moment before she realized the door was opening. Its hinges silent, *merci a Dieu*. Completely silent.

She slipped inside the cool, dark room. Steady, deep breathing came from the bed. Thank goodness, she hadn't woken the duke with her entrance. She could barely see a thing, but she didn't dare light a candle. A tiny stream of moonlight filtered into the room through a small opening in the curtains on the far window. She used that to identify the hulking bed in the center of the room. She tiptoed over to it slowly, taking care in case there was anything to trip over. No doubt she would find it if there was.

She made it to the foot of the bed without incident and paused, trying to quell her nerves and dispel her guilt. She clutched the vial more tightly in her palm, shaking with fear and anxiety. Now that she was here, she had no earthly idea how to drop liquid on a man's eyes without awakening him. Besides, how much of it was she supposed to use? Surely not much. She would employ the tiniest drops possible so as not to disturb him, but she also needed to ensure the perfume touched his eyelids. Tricky business, this being a fairy. She had a sudden appreciation for Puck.

Holding her breath, she lifted her skirts with her free hand and tiptoed to the right side of the bed. Because it was summer, the bed curtains weren't drawn. The window was open, and a slight breeze blew through the crack in the curtains.

The outline of the duke's body was barely visible in the moonlight. He was turned away on his side, his back to her, his face toward the window. She would have to lean over his body to sprinkle the elixir on his eyes. The bed was tall. She must carefully climb up to do this task properly. She only hoped she didn't jostle the mattress enough to wake him.

She waited in silence for a few moments to ensure his breathing remained steady, then she carefully lifted first one knee and then the other, bracing them on the mattress and pulling herself up, still clutching the vial. She winced as he moved slightly in his sleep, but he kept his face turned away. Blast it.

Once she was fully atop the bed, she paused and hoped the hammering of her heart didn't wake him. He smelled good, a combination of soap and maleness that she wanted to breathe in. There was something vaguely familiar about his scent.

Shaking away that unhelpful thought, she moved gingerly across the mattress on her knees until she came to a stop at his side. His shirt was off. The beam of moonlight hit his smooth, muscled arm. She swallowed. The man's chest was positively swoon-worthy. She took a deep breath to calm her nerves and uncorked the vial. Then she carefully leaned over as far as she could to locate his eyes. They remained shrouded in the dark, but she took a guess as to their general direction and tipped the little vial as slowly and carefully as she could. He turned then, and she was afforded enough light to see that the first tiny drop of liquid did indeed fall directly onto his eyelid.

He blinked, and she held her breath. When he settled back into sleep, she closed her eyes and said a brief prayer that she would get away with it a second time before tipping the vial once more to allow another tiny drop to fall on his other eyelid.

He blinked and rubbed at his eyes while Delilah held her breath again, paralyzed with fear. Soon, he settled back into his pillow and his breathing returned to its steady pace.

She pressed a hand to her throat. It was over. She was done. All she had to do was extract herself from the bed and the room without being seen or heard. The difficult part was behind her.

Still praying he wouldn't stir, she backed away from the duke. Slowly. Slowly. She'd nearly made it to the edge of the bed when he flipped over to face her. A beam of moonlight slid over his sleeping features.

Delilah gasped.

CHAPTER TWENTY-FIVE

Delilah had no idea how she'd managed to get out of the bedchamber without waking Thomas. The volume of her gasp alone should have brought half the house running, but she managed to make it to the corridor with him still sleeping in the bed. The moment she shut his bedchamber door behind her, she raced across the darkened corridor, flew down the stairs to Lucy's room on the second floor, and pounded on the door. Moments later, a none-too-amused Derek opened the door, wearing only his breeches. He stepped behind the portal when he realized who it was. "Delilah, what is it?"

"Delilah?" came Lucy's sleepy voice from behind her husband.

Delilah was too beside herself to even care that she was clearly being inappropriate coming to a married couple's door in the middle of the night.

"What's happened?" Lucy materialized and pulled her into the room.

Derek had vanished into his adjoining bedchamber. He returned moments later, properly robed. "Are you all right?" he asked, concern etching his brow.

Delilah's eyes were wide. She couldn't catch her breath. Aunt Willie had told her once she must take shallow breaths and not try to speak when she was like this, but Lucy and Derek clearly wanted an explanation for her late-night arrival, and she owed them one.

"I need you to tell me which room Danielle and Cade are in," she choked out.

Lucy searched Delilah's face. "What? Why?"

"I . . . I . . . I must talk to Danielle immediately."

Lucy squeezed her shoulders. "Calm down, dear. Tell me. What's happened?" She put her arm around Delilah and led her to a small sitting area on the other side of the bed. She forced her friend to sit.

Delilah lowered herself to a green velvet chair and let her head drop into her hands. "It's going to sound mad."

Derek chuckled. "Remember who you're talking to."

Lucy lifted a brow toward her husband before turning back to Delilah. "Derek is correct, dear. I've heard and done many mad things."

Delilah still couldn't breathe. A thousand thoughts whirled through her mind. What had she done? *What had she done*? "I need Danielle. I must speak with Danielle."

Lucy nodded. "What if Derek goes to fetch her while you tell me what happened? Would you like that?"

Delilah nodded. When Lucy inclined her head toward the door, Derek gave a nod and left. Lucy lowered herself to kneel on the thick rug in front of Delilah's chair and grasped her hands. "Your fingers are freezing, dear. If didn't know any better, I'd think you saw a ghost."

Delilah shook her head. "It was worse than a ghost! Much worse. It's *real*!"

"What's real, dear? Did you have a bad dream?"

"I . . ." Delilah bit her lip. How would she ever explain herself? She'd promised not to tell Lucy anything about this, but how else would she find Danielle in the middle of the night? And now, after what had happened, Danielle couldn't possibly blame her for enlisting Lucy's aid.

"Dear, whatever it is, it'll be all right. I promise. Just tell me so I can help you."

"Lucy, I made a mistake. A large one."

Lucy gave her a matter-of-fact look. "What did you do?"

The door swung open, and Danielle hurried in with Derek at her heels. The French woman wore her night rail and a dressing gown. "Delilah, darling, what is it?" She hurried over to kneel next to Lucy in front of Delilah.

Delilah stood from her chair and paced across the room to the fireplace, where she rubbed her freezing hands together in front of the flames. "Danielle, I made a terrible mistake."

"What happened?" came her cousin's worried voice from behind her. The two women remained sitting on the rug, facing her.

Delilah braced one hand against the mantelpiece and pressed the other to her middle, certain she would cast up her accounts at any moment. "I went into the wrong room," she moaned.

"What?" Danielle's voice was filled with alarm.

Delilah whirled to face all three of them. Derek and Lucy exchanged a worried glance.

She wrung her hands. "I went to the wrong room. I thought I was going to the Duke of Branville's room, but I went to Thomas's room instead."

Danielle hurried over to her, grabbed her shoulders,

and searched her face. "Are you certain, Delilah? Can you be sure?"

"I'm sure. I thought I followed the instructions precisely. But it was so dark. I must have chosen the wrong door. Only I didn't know it until it was too late."

"Tell me exactly what happened," Danielle prompted.

Delilah nodded. "I tiptoed over to the bed, and I—"

Derek cleared his throat. "Perhaps I shouldn't be hearing this."

She reached a hand toward the duke. "No, Derek, please stay. It's not what you think."

"What is it?" Lucy asked, clearly thinking the same thing Derek had.

"Go on," Danielle said.

Delilah forced herself to take a deep breath. "I climbed up to the top of the mattress, leaned over, and tipped the vial."

"What vial?" Lucy asked, frowning.

Delilah ignored her. "I let one drop fall on each eye. At least I thought it was his eyes. It was difficult to tell in the darkness."

"You tried to blind someone?" Derek scratched his head.

"If it was so dark, how did you discover it was the wrong room?" Danielle prompted, worry lines creasing the sides of her mouth.

"Because after I did it, he rolled over into the moonlight and . . . it was Thomas," Delilah finished miserably.

"You tried to blind Thomas?" Lucy chimed.

"She didn't try to blind anyone," Danielle replied, as if the entire story made perfect sense. "She was applying the Elixir of Cupid to his eyes."

"Elixir of Cupid?" Lucy dropped to her backside and blinked at the fireplace.

Danielle nodded and turned to face Lucy. "Yes, it's a special perfume that's purported to make the person you use it on fall in love with you."

"Love potion," Lucy breathed, a wondrous expression on her face. "Why didn't you tell me, Delilah?"

Delilah rushed back over to where Lucy sat, kneeled down, and grasped the duchess's hand. "I assumed you'd think I was mad."

"I don't think that at all," Lucy said, climbing to her feet with Delilah's help. "I've heard talk of the potion before. I just didn't know it actually existed."

"I got it from a Roma woman in London who Danielle knows," Delilah explained.

Lucy sighed. "Danielle knows all the most interesting people."

Derek eyed the lot of them as if they'd lost their minds.

Delilah turned to Danielle. "I'm sorry. I know you wanted me to keep all of this a secret, but it spiraled out of control."

Danielle stood too and hugged Delilah. "It's all right. I understand. You need help now that you've made a mistake. I can only guess how frightened you were when you discovered you were in the wrong room."

Lucy gave Danielle an accusing glare before placing her fists on her hips. "If you knew there was a love potion out there all these years, why didn't you tell me?"

The hint of a smile touched Danielle's lips. "I thought you'd think I was mad too. Delilah seemed interested and open to it."

"You're all missing the point!" Delilah raised her voice. "The deed is done, and I've administered the potion to the wrong duke."

"Did Thomas wake up?" Danielle asked.

"No." Delilah shook her head. "As soon as I realized it was him, I left the room as quickly as I could."

"And you're certain the potion touched his eyes?" Danielle added.

"As certain as I can be." Delilah slumped back down on the chair. "What am I supposed to do? Please tell me the potion has an antidote."

Danielle bit the tip of her fingernail and winced. "The truth is I don't know. I never asked Madame Rosa about an antidote. I never thought of anyone needing such a thing."

Delilah groaned and slapped her palm against her forehead. "Leave it to me to botch something as simple as magic."

"Don't worry, dear." Lucy patted her arm. "I've little doubt magic is exceedingly complicated."

Danielle paced away. "We'll have to go back to London and speak with Madame Rosa."

Delilah nodded resolutely. "Fine, but in the meantime, what am I supposed to do if Thomas sees me in the morning and is madly in love with me?"

CHAPTER TWENTY-SIX

Delilah tiptoed to the entrance of the breakfast room early the next morning. Despite her anxiety, she was hungry, and she'd been told by a reliable source, namely Cade, that Danielle was in the room. She couldn't risk running into Thomas, however, so she was hovering outside the door, trying to work up the nerve to peek inside, when Lucy's voice rang out from within. "It's all right, Delilah. He's not here."

Delilah expelled her pent-up breath and made her way into the room, where she took a seat next to her friend. The only people in the breakfast room at the moment were Lucy, Cass, Jane, and Danielle. A servant rushed to place a napkin on Delilah's lap and pour her some tea.

"Who's not here?" Cass asked, blinking interestedly at Delilah.

"Thomas." Lucy took a sip of her heavily sugared tea.

Cass furrowed her brow. "Why does Delilah not want Thomas to be here?"

Lucy waved a hand in the air. "It's an excessively long story."

"Excellent." Jane grabbed a teacake from the plate in the center of the table. "I love excessively long stories. The excessively longer, the better. As long as they're entertaining, of course."

Delilah glanced around the room at the sparse company.

"Most of the men have gone off on a ride together," Lucy explained as if she'd read Delilah's mind. "Thomas went too."

Delilah let out a sigh of relief. She picked up her teacup and took a sip.

"So who is going to tell me this excessively long story?" Jane pushed up her spectacles on her nose.

Delilah gave Lucy an apprehensive glance.

"It's more complicated than you know," Lucy said to Delilah.

Dread swam in Delilah's belly. "How so?"

Danielle crossed her arms over her chest and looked at Delilah. "You didn't mention you gave some of the potion to Lavinia."

Delilah winced. "She told you?"

"You don't understand," Lucy continued, buttering a slice of thick, brown toast. "Apparently all hell broke loose in this house last night."

Delilah set down her cup. "What do you mean?" The dread was swimming faster now.

Lucy finished buttering her toast and set down the knife. "Apparently Lavinia tried to use the elixir on Lord Berwick, and while she was at it, Branville found her gallivanting around the bachelor's quarters in the middle of the night. He demanded to know what she was doing there, and she gave him some of the potion to keep him quiet. He wanted to use it on Lady Rebecca."

Delilah gasped. "No!" In her wildest imaginings, she hadn't guessed *Lavinia* would have given some of it away. She cursed herself for the thousandth time for not following Madame Rosa's rules.

"Yes," Lucy replied, taking a bite of toast.

"You're not making any sense," Jane said, nibbling on her teacake. "What potion are you talking about?"

"Care to explain?" Lucy said to Delilah.

"I really don't care to, no." Delilah took a piece of toast from the plate in the center of the table, but she just stared at it. She couldn't eat. She was no longer hungry.

Danielle took a deep breath. "I'll do it, then. Delilah and I purchased some perfume from a Roma woman in London. It's purported to make the person whose eyes you sprinkle it upon fall madly in love with you the next time they see you."

Jane snorted. One dark eyebrow arched over the rim of her silver spectacles. "You're not serious?"

"I'm entirely serious," Danielle replied, taking a sip from her teacup.

"You paid *money* for this?" Jane continued, directing her remarks to Delilah. "Real money?"

Delilah wanted to curl into a ball and disappear. She turned to Lucy. "Did you say Branville got some of the potion too?"

"Yes," Lucy continued. "Lavinia bought his silence with two drops of it."

"If he was supposed to keep silent about it," Jane said flatly, "how do you know about it, Lucy?"

"That was my next question as well," Cass said softly.

"I'm not finished with my story yet," Lucy declared.

"Unfortunately, last night's antics didn't end with that particular transaction."

Jane rested her chin on her propped-up elbow. "Oh, please, do continue."

A headache pounded in Delilah's skull, but she forced herself to listen as Lucy continued.

Lucy folded her hands in front of her on the tabletop. "So as I said, Lavinia was sneaking around, trying to use the potion on Berwick when Branville found her. Then Branville attempted to use some of it on Lady Rebecca, who woke up in the middle of the thing and demanded to know what Branville was doing in her bedchamber."

"Oh, no! I don't blame her." Cass shook her head. "That must have been terribly frightening for her."

"Yes, well," Lucy continued, "Branville apologized profusely and told her what he was about. She told him she'd keep quiet about the incident if he gave her the potion so she might try to use it on Thomas."

"No," Delilah whimpered. Had the entire household gone mad? At one time, she'd thought no one would believe her if she claimed to have a love potion. Now, she realized half the company had been eager to use it without so much as a whit of proof that it actually worked.

"Yes," Lucy replied gravely. "However, when Rebecca asked one of the maids the location of Thomas's room, she ended up finding the Duke of Branville again instead, a fact which still baffles me. Then she came in search of me to ask the location of Thomas's room, and I was the one who put an end to the entire debacle."

"That has to be one of the most ridiculous tales I've ever heard." Jane pushed her spectacles up her nose again. "And I've heard a great many."

"I agree," Cass added. "But it is ever so entertaining."

"When did this happen, Lucy?" The sinking feeling in the pit of Delilah's stomach hadn't abated.

"Not an hour after I sent you back to your room after your own debacle," Lucy replied, taking another bite of toast.

"I wish I'd never heard of that potion," Delilah said miserably. "Did any of it appear to work on any of them?"

"We're not entirely certain any of them actually had a chance to use it," Lucy replied.

"And Madame Rosa warned that it could only be used once, by one person," Danielle added.

"I assume none of them knew that, or they wouldn't have been gallivanting around the house last night," Jane pointed out.

"I tried to tell Lavinia," Delilah replied. "She seemed to think Madame Rosa only said that to increase her sales."

Danielle placed a hand on Delilah's shoulder. "I'm sorry, Delilah. I never would have mentioned the perfume to you had I known this much trouble would result."

Delilah smiled and patted the Frenchwoman's hand. "It's not your fault, Danielle. I should have followed the rules. Not doing so was bound to cause trouble. I simply had no idea it would be like this."

"Wait a moment," Jane said, munching on a teacake. "So *no one* actually managed to administer the potion to anyone else's eyelids?"

"One person did," Lucy replied with a nod. "Our Delilah here."

"You sprinkled it on Branville?" Cass asked. "But I thought he found Lavinia and—"

"No." Delilah squeezed her eyes shut. "I didn't sprinkle it on Branville. I *meant* to sprinkle it on Branville."

Jane's eyes went wide. She slapped her palm against her cheek. "If you didn't sprinkle it on Branville, then who—"

"Thomas," Lucy finished. "She accidentally sprinkled it on Thomas."

Danielle stood. "Which is why Delilah and I must leave for London immediately. We need to find Madame Rosa and ask after the antidote."

"Wait another moment," Jane said. "How do you even know that it worked? It all may be just a lot of nonsense with no need for an antidote."

Delilah had never wished she'd wasted money before in her life. But now she did. She not only hoped for it, she prayed for it. "I do hope it's just a bunch of nonsense, but it's not a chance I'm willing to take. If Thomas sees me and falls madly in love with me, I . . . couldn't stand it."

Jane glanced back and forth between Delilah and Danielle. "You're telling me that you intend to run off to London and presumably pay even more money for an antidote to a thing that may well have never worked in the first place on the chance it's not a scheme?"

Delilah pressed her fingertips to her pounding temples. "I know quite well the entire thing may be ludicrous, but this is one situation in which I'd much rather be safe than sorry."

"I say you at least wait and see if Thomas loves you," Jane replied. "If he does, then you can go ahead and look for the antidote."

The mere thought of waiting made Delilah's heart pound. The notion of Thomas declaring his love for her, his false love, made her skin clammy. She glanced at Danielle.

"It's up to you, Delilah," Danielle said.

"What do you think, Lucy?" Delilah fixed her frightened gaze on her dear friend.

Lucy took another sip of tea as she contemplated the matter. "I *want* to believe there is a magic love potion that works, dear, I truly do. But even I must admit that it may be more prudent to wait and see if Thomas seems to be any more partial to you today than he was yesterday."

Delilah swallowed the lump in her throat. "Cass?"

"Oh, dear," Cass said softly. "I understand how tempting it must have been to believe in a potion, but I agree with Lucy and Jane. I wouldn't run off in search of an antidote without speaking to Thomas first."

Delilah nodded. The ache in her chest was real and painful. The thought of having Thomas tell her he loved her and not mean it, was excruciating, but she supposed it would be ridiculous of her to run off to London before ensuring the stuff had worked in the first place. "Very well," she murmured. "I'll find Thomas as soon as he returns."

CHAPTER TWENTY-SEVEN

Delilah's slipper tapped against the marble floor in Lucy's green drawing room at an alarming speed. She'd gone upstairs after breakfast and forced herself to sit still while Amandine fixed her hair in a chignon with a few dark tendrils floating around her face. Then she dressed in a lavender gown with a tight waist and embroidered violets on the hem, and dabbed her lily-scented perfume—not the enchanted kind—behind both ears. A pearl necklace and matching earbobs completed the ensemble. Amandine hadn't bothered putting rouge on Delilah's cheeks today. She didn't need it. She was already bright red with worry.

Delilah had arranged with Lucy to have one of the footmen deliver a note to Thomas's bedchamber asking him to meet her in the green salon before luncheon. It felt as if an eternity had passed before a slight knock sounded on the door.

"Come in," she managed to call through her suddenly

dry throat. She should have accepted Lucy's offer of tea, but given her nerves, Delilah had been convinced she would spill the stuff all over herself.

Thomas stepped through the door, looking as handsome as ever. His dark hair was slicked back. His blue eyes were sparkling. He wore buff-colored, skin-hugging trousers, a blue coat, a white shirt with a crisp white cravat, and perfectly shined black boots.

The moment their eyes met, she knew something was different. She knew it the way she'd known something awful had happened to her father the day he'd died. Without even being told, she'd felt in her gut that something had changed her life forever.

The look on Thomas's face was earnest and . . . different. His long strides ate up the space between the door and her spot on the settee. He kneeled down in front of her, took her hands, and stared up into her face as if he'd never seen it before.

"Delilah," he breathed. "You wanted to see me."

She'd spent the better part of the morning practicing what she would say to him. He knew she'd purchased the elixir. She'd shown it to him, for God's sake. But now that the moment was here to tell him what she'd done, the words were too mad to make it past her lips.

Very well. She didn't have to admit to him that she'd sprinkled the potion on his eyes. All she had to do was ask him how he felt about her. Then she'd know. Perhaps he'd guess that she'd used it on him. How else would he explain going from being her friend to being madly in love with her overnight? If he even *was* madly in love with her. *Mon Dieu.* This entire charade was ridiculous. For the hundredth time, she wished she'd never purchased the blasted elixir.

She searched Thomas's handsome face. The memory

of their kiss during the play the night before swept through her mind. She memorized the lines on either side of his eyes, the small scar above his eyebrow. For a long, mad moment she wished he was actually in love with her.

"I must ask you something," she whispered.

"Anything." He rubbed the backs of her hands with his thumbs.

She sucked in her breath. "How do you . . . feel about me?"

The corners of his eyes crinkled and his gaze swept her face. He was going to say something sarcastic and wonderful and Thomas-like and all would be well. She nearly sagged against him in relief.

"Delilah," he murmured. "The truth is . . . I love you."

Time stopped. Her breath caught in her throat. It was as if the room and all its contents froze. "No," she whispered, shaking her head emphatically. "You don't."

He nodded. His gaze didn't falter. "Yes, I do."

She pulled her hands from his grasp. "You mean you love me like a friend, correct?"

"No. I love you, Delilah. Truly."

She stood and pushed away from him and paced toward the fireplace. "Think what you're saying, Thomas. It's me, Delilah."

"I know it's you, and you're beautiful and wonderful and smart and funny and perfect, and I love you." His voice was husky, but there was a tone deep in it, one she'd never heard from him before. Gone was the laughing, playful Thomas. He was entirely serious. He thought he loved her. He was telling the truth.

She whirled to face him. "Remember the elixir I bought?"

"Yes, the ridiculous elixir that doesn't work. I know all about it."

"But it does work. I—"

"No, Delilah. It doesn't. You weren't meant to marry Branville. He doesn't love you. I do."

"But Thomas, I—"

He was beside her then, and her words were silenced as he pulled her into his arms and kissed her. And instead of pushing him away, she, awful person that she was, rose on her tiptoes and kissed him back. She wound her arms around his neck and let her fingers thread through his soft hair. His tongue darted past her lips and she sucked on it. She was mindless from the kiss. She could go on like this all day. Their first kisses had been surprising, but this one, this one was purposeful and delightful. She didn't want it to end.

She was *such* a bad person. She was kissing someone she'd duped into loving her. She was obviously a harlot too, because she let the kiss go on for nearly another minute before finally taking a step back. "Thomas, no! We must stop." But she was saying the words more to herself than to him.

He grasped her hands and held them to his chest, where his pounding heart thumped beneath his vest. "Think about it, Delilah. Is it so mad, really? You and I? We've been friends for an age. Why not us? Why can't we be in love?"

She couldn't breathe, couldn't think. She had to get away from here. She'd done an awful thing to him. She had to make it right. First, she had to get to London and find Madame Rosa.

She pulled from his grasp and rushed toward the door, fighting back tears. "I'm sorry, Thomas. I never meant for this to happen. Don't worry. I will find a way to fix this."

She flew from the room and was halfway down the corridor before she heard Thomas's voice calling after her. "Wait, Delilah. You must listen to me. I really do love you!"

CHAPTER TWENTY-EIGHT

Delilah and Amandine had never packed her trunk so quickly. They tossed everything inside with nary a thought about the condition of the clothing and shoes and underthings. Two of Lucy's footmen came to cart the trunk off to the coach, and Delilah and Danielle left for London that same afternoon. With Lucy's assistance, Delilah ensured that she didn't see Thomas again before she left. He'd sent a note to her room begging her to come back and finish their conversation, but of course, she refused.

As Danielle's coach rattled away from the Claringdon estate, Delilah sat curled in a ball in one corner, tracing a fingertip against the velvet squabs. What in heaven's name had she done? She'd ruined her friendship with Thomas, that's what. She'd toyed with a blameless person's emotions. She had no business playing God the way she had. She realized that now. Even her plan to make Branville fall in love with her had been awful and selfish. Who was she to dispense emotions to other people? She hated herself for the idiotic way she'd behaved, and for the fact that she'd introduced the elixir into the lives of so many people who didn't deserve such trouble.

The entire ride back to London, all she could think about was Thomas and the wrong she'd done him. They were nearly to Mayfair before she even had a chance to think about the other implications of the elixir plot going so horribly awry. Namely that the Duke of Branville was hardly in danger of falling madly in love with her anytime soon, and she had not secured an offer from him by the appointed time. Her mother would be looking for her. She'd gloat when she discovered that Delilah had failed. She'd gloat, and she'd demand Delilah marry Clarence Hilton.

But none of that mattered at the moment. All Delilah cared about was ensuring that she did right by Thomas. She'd changed him, her closest friend, her confidant, the person who was always there for her and always would be. She'd done something to him that she shouldn't have, and she hadn't even been brave enough to admit it. Instead, she'd run away like a coward in search of a quick solution. The antidote.

Oh, she would explain it all to him. Eventually. She'd confess and beg his forgiveness, but first, first, she had to find a way to make him Thomas again. To make him her friend. Not some love-addled fool who thought she was perfect. He'd even said it. Those words tore at her heart. She was none of those things. She never had been, and she never would be. The elixir had made him say them. Tears stung her eyes, but she dashed them away with her fingers.

It didn't matter if she was forced to become engaged

to Clarence. Nothing mattered but making things right with Thomas. She had to find Madame Rosa. She had to discover how to clean up the mess she'd made.

They didn't stop at Delilah's house or at Danielle's. Instead, Danielle instructed the coachman to drive directly to Lombard Street. It was dark by the time the coach pulled to a halt. Delilah flew from the carriage, Danielle close on her heels. They made their way down the street to the little gate they'd entered the last time. The footman accompanied them like before, but unlike before, when they reached the entrance, Delilah didn't knock. She pushed opened the green wooden door and barged inside.

"Madame Rosa?" she called, desperation making her voice thin. "Madame?"

A strange, cold wind blew through the little shop and slammed the door behind them. Danielle jumped.

"Who's there?" came Madame Rosa's strained voice. A few moments later, the old woman hobbled out of the back of the shop, leaning heavily upon a cane. When she saw Delilah, her eyes lit with concern.

She tottered over to the same table where she'd sat the first time and took a seat, leaning on her cane and breathing heavily.

"Something bad has happened," Madame Rosa said in an eerie, matter-of-fact voice.

Delilah swallowed and nodded. She approached the table and sat on the edge of one of the chairs in front of it. "Yes. Yes. We've come for the antidote."

The old lady's eyes crinkled in a frown. "Antidote?" She pronounced the word as if she didn't know what it meant.

"Yes, we need it immediately," Delilah breathed, searching the old woman's face.

"Settle down, lass," the old lady said. "First ye must remind me what potion I sold ye."

Panic clawed at Delilah's insides. Madame Rosa didn't remember her. Delilah forced herself to take three deep breaths. Of course the old woman wouldn't remember her. Madame sold potions to ladies every day. Madame Rosa was memorable to Delilah, not the other way around.

"I'm Lady Delilah Montebank, and this is my cousin Danielle. You sold us a vial of Cupid's Elixir." Danielle had come to sit on the other chair in front of Madame Rosa's table.

"Oh. Yes." The old woman pursed her lips and shook her head. "I'm afraid I cannot help ye then."

"What?" Delilah's voice went up an octave. "What are you talking about? You must help us. There must be an antidote."

"Antidote," the woman repeated strangely as if she'd heard the word for the first time. "Do ye know what antidote means, lass?"

Delilah clasped her shaking hands in her lap. Madame Rosa wanted to talk about the meaning of words at a time like this? "It means it will fix what happened. Do the opposite, perhaps?"

"It comes from Latin," the old lady replied. "*Antidotum*. Meaning remedy against poison."

"Yes, that's what I want," Delilah replied. "The remedy against it."

"No." Madame Rosa shook her head. "Ye see, Cupid's Elixir isn't a poison, lass. There is no *antidotum* for it."

A chill spread through Delilah's body. "There must be some way to fix it. To reverse what it's done."

"Did it do its work?" Madame Rosa asked. "Did it bring true love to the heart of the one whose eyes were touched by its essence?"

"Yes," Delilah said flatly, "but I accidentally put it on the eyes of the *wrong* man."

Madame Rosa's soft laughter filled the stale air of the room. The Roma woman was laughing. This had to be the worst moment of Delilah's life, and the woman was actually laughing at her. Delilah hung her head.

"There's nothing funny about this," she whispered. "I've made an awful mistake. I've ruined someone's life."

"No, no, lass," Madame Rosa said, shaking her head again. "I'm afraid that's not possible."

Delilah pulled her handkerchief from her reticule. She wanted to rip the thing in half. "I'm afraid it is. You don't understand the situation."

Madame Rosa smiled up at her, exposing her mostly toothless grin. She reached over and patted Delilah's face with a papery hand. "There is nothing I can do," she said. "*Verus amor nullum facit errata.*"

Delilah stood. The room seemed to be closing in around her. She'd no idea what the old woman had just said. She barely paid any attention in her Latin studies—the subject had bored her senseless. Something about *the mistakes of love.* But whatever the lady had said, Delilah was clear on one thing: Madame Rosa obviously had no intention of helping her. She spun toward the door. "Let's go, Danielle. We'll find no assistance here."

Danielle nodded, stood, and quietly followed Delilah out of the shop.

CHAPTER TWENTY-NINE

Delilah spent the ride to her mother's town house staring blankly out the window. "I cannot believe she wouldn't help me," she said to Danielle, who sat beside her and patted her hand.

"She said there was nothing she could do," Danielle offered.

"*Absurdité*. There had to be *something* she could do. If the Roma have a potion that can make a person fall in love, why in heaven's name do they not have a potion that can reverse the effect?"

"I'm not certain these things work that way," Danielle replied softly.

Delilah sighed. "Obviously not. I've been such a fool. How am I going to explain this to Thomas?"

The coach pulled to a stop in front of her mother's house.

"Don't worry about it tonight, dear," Danielle said. "Get some rest. Things may look better in the morning. Sleep tends to fix many problems."

Delilah gave a vague nod. Sleep sounded good. She could only hope her mother had already retired for the evening. She couldn't face the woman tonight.

The footman helped her down from the coach and delivered her trunk, and the conveyance remained in the street until she made it safely up the steps and entered the front door.

The moment she stepped inside, her mother's voice rang out from the gold salon. Delilah closed her eyes as misery washed over her.

"There you are!" Mother marched into the foyer, her eyes blazing with anger.

"I cannot talk right now, Mother. I'll speak with you in the morning." Delilah tried to turn toward the staircase, but her mother caught her arm and whirled her around to face her.

"How dare you lie to me?" Mother raised a hand and slapped Delilah across the face. Delilah's ears rang and tears filled her eyes, but she'd barely felt the blow, and her tears weren't for her mother.

She did her best to focus on the woman's enraged face. "Lie to you about what?" she asked calmly.

Another backhanded slap across the face sent Delilah to her knees. She stayed there, staring at the marble floor. Her mother could beat her to death for all she cared at the moment.

"Don't feign ignorance with me. Half the town is talking about the *play* you were in. The play at the Duchess of Claringdon's country home. The one in which you *kissed* a man."

So Mother was angry about the play. Delilah had expected this moment. It was still worth it to have raised the money for animals.

Delilah slowly raised herself to her feet and took a step

away from her mother. "It was only Thomas I kissed, and the play was for charity," she said in a voice devoid of all emotion.

"You think that makes it acceptable?" Her mother raised her hand to slap her again.

"Vanessa, we talked about this."

The Earl of Hilton stepped out of the gold salon, and instantly Delilah's mother dropped her hand.

"Yes, but I had no idea she'd be so insolent, Edgar," Mother replied, her eyes still blazing.

Delilah cradled her rapidly swelling cheek in her palm. "I'm not being insolent. I was telling the truth."

Her mother's jaw was clenched so tightly the muscle in her cheek jumped. "The truth? Please. You've been lying to me for weeks. I had to be informed that my daughter had turned into an *actress* by a woman at church this morning. Do you have any idea how humiliating that was for me?"

"I'm not an actress. It was only one performance, and it wasn't as if it was in public."

"Public or not, I—"

"The damage is done, Vanessa," came Hilton's clipped voice behind her. "We should turn our attention to the *future*. Don't you agree?"

"Ah, yes, the future," Mother spat. "I'm certain the Duke of Branville won't be pleased when he finds out you kissed Huntley in front of half the *ton*. Tell me, are you betrothed or not?"

"No." Delilah slowly rose to her feet. "I'm not."

Her mother's nostrils flared. "I knew it. You've always been nothing but a disappointment. Why I even entertained the notion that Branville would offer for you, I'll never know."

"I just want to go to bed now," Delilah said, staring longingly toward the staircase.

"No, you don't." Her mother's hands clenched in fists at her sides. "You may not have become betrothed, but I have. Edgar and I intend to marry, and we won't have you hovering around our new home like the unwanted little spinster you are. We're going to see to it that you're married. As soon as possible."

Delilah lifted her skirts and made her way toward the staircase. "I don't care. Do what you like."

"Fine, then. We'll post the first banns for your marriage to Clarence next Sunday."

CHAPTER THIRTY

The next morning, Delilah sat in the gold salon, hugging a sapphire throw pillow to her chest while her mother flitted around the room with two of the maids and discussed the plans for both of their weddings.

"We'll need appointments at the dressmakers, the flower shop, and we must plan a wedding breakfast." She turned toward Delilah. "Now that I think on it, I don't see why we don't all get married at once. It will save quite a lot of trouble and expense." The woman seemed completely oblivious to both her daughter's red, swollen cheek and her complete lack of interest in her words.

Delilah stared unseeing at the wall. "Whatever you like."

She had spent the night tossing and turning. Now, she was pretending to listen as her mother spoke. Meanwhile, her mind raced with thoughts of Thomas. Where was he? What did he think? By now, he must have guessed she'd used the potion on him. What else could explain his thinking she was his friend one day, and declaring his love for her the next?

But every time she had that thought, the memory of their kiss on the stage flitted through her mind. At the time it had felt quite . . . real. Real enough to curl her toes. Real enough to make her knees weak. It had been the first moment she'd truly thought about Thomas as someone other than just her friend. Well, that wasn't entirely true. The *first* moment she had that thought had been when he'd kissed her in the Hillards' gardens. Or actually, *perhaps* it had been when Rebecca had informed her that Thomas was the most eligible bachelor of the Season at the Penningtons' ball.

"You're fortunate that Clarence is willing to overlook the scandal your kiss with Huntley caused," Mother said, jolting Delilah from her thoughts.

"Is there a scandal?" Delilah asked uninterestedly. Of course, Clarence was willing to overlook it. No one else would marry him.

"I'm *certain* there will be a scandal," Mother continued. "You know as well as I do that a young, unmarried lady cannot go about kissing a young, unmarried gentleman in front of others without causing a scandal. Why, I've half a mind to ask Edgar to call out Huntley. He had no right to touch you."

Delilah tentatively fingered her bruised cheek. "We were *acting*, Mother."

"Still, it's completely inappropriate and—"

A knock on the salon door interrupted her mother's diatribe. Goodfellow stepped into the room. "The Duke of Huntley is here to see you, my lady."

Delilah's heart thundered in her chest. Thomas was here? This was certain to be awkward with Mother present.

"I'll bet he is," Lady Vanessa said, arching a brow.

"Show him in. I refuse to allow him to be alone with you," she said to Delilah.

Delilah squelched her smile. At least Mother would allow her to see him.

Moments later, Thomas strolled through the door to the salon. He looked so handsome. Delilah wanted to rush into his arms.

He took in the scene with Delilah and her mother. "Good morning, Lady Vanessa," he said in his most polite drawing-room voice. "You're looking well."

"Huntley," Mother intoned. "I'm surprised you'd show your face here after what you've done."

He blinked. "I'm not certain what you mean."

"Must you both be liars?" Mother said, sighing. "Are you honestly going to pretend that you didn't kiss Delilah in front of half the *ton* at the Duchess of Claringdon's play the other night?"

The familiar grin spread across Thomas's face. It made butterflies scatter in Delilah's stomach. "Oh, yes, well, I did do that. But it was in front of only about fifty people, and have you not read today's paper? Delilah and I were praised for our performances."

Mother's face drained of color. "My daughter is in the paper as an acknowledged actress?"

"No, nothing like that." Thomas stuck his head outside the door and called to Goodfellow for a copy of the *Times*. "The play was lauded as a lark for charity, which is precisely what it was. All of the players were applauded for their generosity."

When Goodfellow returned with the paper, Thomas quickly opened it to the correct page and handed it to Mother. Mother, of course, never read anything. In their house, the paper was mostly used to wrap old food after Delilah finished reading it.

Mother's eyes scanned the page. Thomas gazed at Delilah while her mother was momentarily distracted. "Why is your cheek red, Delilah?" Suspicion laced his words as he eyed her mother. Delilah shook her head and glanced away.

Mother was still studying the paper. "Well," she said haughtily. "If that's not the most ridiculous thing I've ever seen."

"Nothing ridiculous about it," Thomas replied, an edge to his voice. "Lady Rothwell and the others at the Royal Society are quite pleased with the money we raised."

Mother tossed the paper to the tabletop. Her nostrils flared. "Why exactly are you here, Your Grace?"

The look on Thomas's face turned completely serious. He stood up straighter and cleared his throat. "I'm here, my lady, to ask you formally if I may court your daughter."

Mother's face went from white to mottled purple in a matter of seconds. She looked as if she was about to have an apoplectic fit. "Court my . . . Delilah?"

Thomas nodded. "Do you have any other daughters?"

Delilah winced. He shouldn't have said that, but she admired him for it. If only she could say such things to Mother. Delilah held her breath. *Mon Dieu.* How would Mother react if Thomas blurted out that he thought he was madly in love with her? Delilah could only guess her mother would be nothing but pleased with a proposal from a duke. It was Delilah who didn't want to marry a man she'd tricked into it.

It took the better part of a minute for Mother to regain control of her features and for her face to return to a normal color. When she did, she pressed her thin lips together tightly, turned to Thomas and said, "I'm afraid that's impossible, Your Grace. I've already accepted an offer for Delilah's hand from Lord Clarence Hilton."

CHAPTER THIRTY-ONE

"*Mon Dieu*, Lucy, you should have seen the look on *Mère*'s face when Thomas asked to court me. Then you should have seen the look on Thomas's face when *Mère* told him that she'd already promised me to Clarence. If my life wasn't such a disaster at the moment, I'd laugh about it."

It was later that same afternoon and the two friends were sitting in the gold salon. Lucy had returned from the country, and her first order of business had been to find Delilah and ask what had happened with Madame Rosa and the elixir. Mother, *merci a Dieu*, had gone out to shop for the weddings, but not before rebuking Lucy for allowing her daughter to be part of a common play.

"It was not common at all, Lady Vanessa," Lucy had replied, tucking an errant curl back into her coiffure. "It was extraordinary, if I do say so myself."

"To ensure you never do anything like that again," Mother said, narrowing her eyes on Lucy, "I intend to hire a new chaperone for Delilah. One who will keep a close eye on her until her wedding." Mother had never cared much that Lucy was a duchess and far above her in social standing.

"Wedding?" Lucy asked, her eyes wide.

"Yes, Delilah is going to be Lord Clarence Hilton's bride."

"Egad," Lucy had replied, eliciting an angry glare from Mother before she quit the room, leaving Delilah and Lucy alone. Delilah had just finished telling the duchess the entire tale.

Lucy shook her head. "Dear, it's no laughing matter. This is all quite serious. I cannot think of a reason in the world why your mother would prefer Clarence Hilton to Thomas. It makes no sense."

"My guess is that she doesn't want to disappoint her new fiancé, Lord Hilton."

"Yes, dear, but even Lord Hilton should understand why a mother would choose a wealthy duke over a future earl who may be a bit light in the pockets." At Delilah's questioning look, Lucy continued, "I've heard rumors. Now, we must think of a way to convince your mother to allow Thomas to court you, at least."

Delilah sat up straight. Had she heard Lucy correctly? "Thomas cannot court me."

Lucy took a sip of her heavily sugared tea. "Whatever do you mean? Of course he can."

"I mean, he only thinks he's in love with me because he's been enchanted by a perfume. It's utterly ridiculous. Meanwhile, I'm betrothed to a man who makes me shudder every time I'm in the same room with him. I'd toss myself off a cliff, but I fear that's too dramatic."

"It's far too dramatic, dear. There are much simpler and less gruesome ways to deal with problems. But I don't understand why you don't want Thomas to court you. You cannot mean you'd rather marry Clarence?"

"Of course not," Delilah replied, "but I'm not about to trick Thomas into marriage only to save myself from Clarence. I've done enough damage to Thomas. I won't use him to save my own skin."

Lucy blinked at her. "I suppose that's somewhat noble of you, dear, but I'm not certain how I can be of any help. What would you like me to do?"

Delilah thought for a moment. "While I don't want Thomas to court me, I do need to be alone with him so I can explain what happened. With the perfume, I mean. I owe it to him to tell him the truth. Perhaps he'll be able to overcome the spell if he knows the potion is what's making him think he loves me."

Lucy shook her head and took another sip of tea. "I seriously doubt that, dear. If it were that simple, Madame Rosa would have told you."

Delilah hugged a throw pillow to her chest. "I know, but I have to try, and Thomas deserves the truth."

"Very well," Lucy replied. "I'll help you get alone with him." A slow smile curved her friend's lips. "Your mother mentioned she's in the market for a new chaperone for you, didn't she? I happen to know the perfect candidate. Her name is Mrs. Bunbury."

CHAPTER THIRTY-TWO

The next morning, Lucy took Delilah riding in the park. Ostensibly, the trip was to meet the elusive Mrs. Bunbury, so Mother allowed Delilah to go. It didn't hurt that Mother was entirely preoccupied with the wedding planning. That, and Lucy had spent a considerable amount of time picking discreet friends who hurried over to Delilah's house and told Lady Vanessa that Mrs. Bunbury was the most strict, rigid chaperone who ever drew a breath. The plan had worked perfectly, and Lucy had arrived later, claiming a connection to the woman in question and promising to take Delilah to meet her posthaste.

They pulled up in Lucy's coach to a secluded area behind Rotten Row. Thomas's curricle was stopped behind a large hedgerow. Thomas sat in the driver's seat, an inscrutable expression on his face. Delilah jumped down and rushed over to him. Thomas grinned at her. He looked as handsome as always, and Delilah's heart gave a little flip as he reached to help her up into the curricle.

"Don't be more than an hour, loves," Lucy called, waving her gloved hand. "Mrs. Bunbury has plans this afternoon." She threw back her head and laughed as her coach took off toward the entrance to the park.

"I'm glad you could get away," Thomas said as soon as Delilah had settled herself and her skirts on the seat next to him.

She turned to face him and put her hand on his sleeve. "Listen, Thomas, I need to tell you something. Something important."

"Very well, but first I have to ask you . . ." His smile faded a little. "Why are you engaged to Clarence Hilton? How did that happen?"

Delilah sighed. "It's my own fault. When I came home from the house party without an engagement to Branville, Mother insisted I marry Clarence."

Thomas cocked his head to the side. "I hear Branville is courting Lady Rebecca."

Delilah nodded. "I'm not surprised. He told me he fancied her, but I thought she was set on you."

"After the performance at Lucy's estate, I told Lady Rebecca that I didn't return her affections," Thomas continued.

Delilah stared unseeing at her lap. "I truly wish you hadn't done that."

"It would be cruel to lead her on." He curled a finger under Delilah's chin and lifted it to meet her eyes. "Look, Delilah, there are other choices, you know? Besides Branville and Clarence. Like me, perhaps." He searched her face, all the humor gone from his expression.

Delilah's eyes filled with tears. She reached up and placed her palm against his warm, familiar cheek. "Oh, Thomas. I wish I could pick you."

He pressed her hand against his cheek. "Why can't you?"

She pulled away and plucked absently at her skirts. "Because I . . . I know you'll laugh at me, but . . . remember that potion I bought to use on Branville?"

Thomas nodded. "Given his courtship of Lady Rebecca, I'm assuming it didn't work on him." The hint of a smile passed over his face.

"It didn't," she breathed, "because I didn't use it on him."

"Thought better of it?" Thomas prompted.

"No. I tried. But I . . ." Oh, she couldn't tell him. It was too ridiculous, and she was too guilty. Besides, she knew he wouldn't believe her. He'd always thought the potion was silly. She normally told Thomas all manner of ridiculous things, but she couldn't bring herself to tell him this. It was too painful. It was the difference between Thomas loving her or not, and that made her heart wrench.

"Delilah, listen, forget about the potion," he said urgently. "The potion doesn't matter. It was madness to begin with."

"You're right about that. I wish I'd never even heard about Cupid's Elixir."

"Will you let me court you?" he asked. "Your mother doesn't have to know."

She furrowed her brow. "I don't understand. What good will that do?"

"You deserve a proper courtship and . . . I love you."

Her breath caught. "No. You don't." She glanced away from his handsome, beloved face. *Mon Dieu*. Her heart was in a vise.

"Let's not argue about it. Spend time with me. I

promise we'll have fun. You cannot tell me you'd rather be courted by Clarence Hilton."

She shook her head and managed a smile. "You're right. I'd much rather be in your company."

"Excellent. We won't call it courting. It'll merely be . . . two friends spending time with each other."

That seemed perfectly reasonable. She brightened. "Very well. What will we do first?"

He grabbed the reins and shook them out. "Go for a ride in the park, of course."

Thomas couldn't sleep. He slid out of bed and made his way to the window, where he nudged open the curtain and stared down into the darkened gardens behind his town house. After spending a delightful hour in the park with Delilah today, he'd returned her to the meeting spot with Lucy and gone about his regular business the remainder of the afternoon, but he'd been entirely unable to concentrate.

He still hadn't told Delilah that he'd switched rooms with Branville. What would be the use? There was no value in trying to reason with her about the elixir. The elixir was ludicrous, and any discussion about it would only be a fool's argument. The point was that he loved her, he'd told her he loved her, and he'd meant for her to realize that she loved him too. Instead, the plan had failed, and she was preoccupied by the notion that the damned elixir was the reason he loved her. He should have seen this coming.

Now, he was in a bind. He could tell her he'd changed rooms on purpose, but that wouldn't prove to her that the elixir didn't work. If anything, she might just be angry with him for thwarting her plans. He had to get her to stop thinking about the elixir and focus on him and their feelings for each other. To that end, Thomas intended to court her. Properly.

When Delilah was a girl, she'd been filled with dreams of courtship. He remembered her talking about it longingly, heavily interspersed with the word *j'adore*. Something had happened to make her stop believing in that dream for herself. Most likely something her mother had said. But he wanted to give that dream back to her. The Duke of Branville hadn't courted her, and Clarence Hilton surely wouldn't. Delilah deserved a proper courtship— one with flowers and chocolates and rides in the park— and by God, Thomas was going to give it to her.

CHAPTER THIRTY-THREE

The first thing Thomas did was to take her on a picnic in the park the next day. Lucy arranged it courtesy of the ever-available Mrs. Bunbury. When Delilah arrived at the assigned spot—a grassy knoll in a secluded part of the park—she found a veritable feast had been spread out along a wide quilt on the soft grass. Pink roses lined the perimeter of the blanket, filling the air with their sweet scent. Thomas stood in front of the spread, smiling his irresistible, and oh-so-familiar smile.

"What is all this?" she asked, stopping short and blinking tears from her eyes.

He bowed. "For you, my love."

A thrill shot through her when he called her *my love*. It wasn't real, of course, but she could pretend. And she desperately wanted to.

Thomas jogged over to her, took her hand, and brought it to his mouth for a kiss. Then he tugged her gently behind him as he led her toward the picnic arrangements.

He waited until she was settled upon the quilt, her skirts billowing out around her, before he took a seat beside her. He discarded his coat and hat before he began serving her the cheese, bread, grapes, olives, and slices of meat that were spread out before them. Delilah removed her bonnet too. Then she slipped off her shoes and rubbed her stockinged feet along the pillowy softness of the quilt. It felt completely decadent, and she adored it.

Thomas grinned at her and handed her a full plate. She ate tentatively at first. But then she realized she was in the company of the person she'd always felt the most at ease with, and that hadn't changed, despite the mistake she'd made with the elixir.

They spent the next hour talking and laughing about all manner of things just as they always had, and Delilah was able to forget for a while that she had caused a significant change between them.

Setting her empty plate aside, she leaned back and braced her arms behind her, palms down. She closed her eyes and tilted back her head to allow the sunlight to bathe her face. "It's so lovely being with someone who isn't constantly criticizing me."

Thomas was silent until Delilah finally raised her head and looked at him. His jaw was tightly clenched, and anger lined his features. "Your mother struck you, didn't she?"

Delilah tilted her head back again, suddenly self-conscious about her cheek that was still slightly bruised.

"Tell me the truth, Delilah." His voice was a low growl.

"I shouldn't have been in that play. I knew it would make her angry."

Thomas cursed under his breath. "Damn it, Delilah.

Stop making excuses for her. She had no right to strike you, no matter what you did. And while we're on the subject, I cannot fathom why she would discard my suit so quickly in favor of Clarence Hilton, of all people. At the risk of sounding like a braggart, I *must* be more eligible than he is."

Delilah sat up straight again and plucked one of the pink roses from the side of the blanket. She twirled the thornless stem between her fingers. "I wondered about it too," she admitted. "Mother must hold a grudge against you from when we were children. Perhaps the pebbles on the window were more vexing than we thought." She tried to smile, but Thomas did not join her.

"It makes little sense," he replied. "I hate to say it, but my guess is that she's doing it purely to spite you."

Delilah blinked. "Surely not—"

"I can think of no other explanation. Can you?"

Delilah lifted the rose to her lips and inhaled its light fragrance. "As I told Lucy, perhaps she doesn't want to disappoint Lord Hilton. He is her fiancé now, you know."

A look of mild disgust crossed Thomas's features. "You give her more credit than I do."

Wanting to change the difficult subject, Delilah moved closer to him and grabbed his hat from the quilt beside him. She placed it atop her head and pulled it down to cover her eyes then tilted up her chin to give him a coquettish stare. "How do I look? Like a snobbish duke?"

Thomas laughed and leaned over to snatch the hat from her head, but Delilah lunged backward and he followed, toppling over onto her.

Catching her breath, she glanced up into his face. It immediately turned serious. The hat had rolled away from her head, and Thomas braced both of his forearms on either side of her shoulders, searching her face intently.

Her heart pounding madly, Delilah reached up to pull him down atop her more fully. She wanted to feel every inch of his hard body against hers. His mouth swooped down to capture hers, and she threaded her fingers through his hair, clutching him against her.

"Delilah," he breathed against her mouth.

She lifted her chin again, and he kissed her throat and her neck before moving lower to her décolletage. He showered kisses along the tender flesh above her bodice, and his hand came up to rub against her breast on the outside of her gown.

"Can I touch you here, Delilah?" he asked. "With my mouth?"

Heat exploded between her legs, and she nodded eagerly. "Yes," she breathed.

He gently tugged down her bodice, and his lips moved to cover one nipple, gradually sucking it into his mouth. His tongue lavished the tip, and she sobbed in the back of her throat. It felt so good. So amazingly good. And shameless wanton that she was, she didn't want him to stop.

Her hands clutched his shoulders, and her legs moved fitfully against the soft blanket. It was a dream come true. She was lying in the sunlight, surrounded by pink roses, while the man of her dreams made love to her.

She moved her hand down to touch the outline of his manhood beneath his breeches, and Thomas swiveled his hips away. He pulled his mouth from her breast and pressed his forehead hard against hers, giving a shaky laugh.

"Why won't you let me touch you?" she asked, disappointment lacing her words.

"Love, I'd like nothing more, but this is for you." He gingerly wiped a curl from her forehead, before reclaiming her lips in another captivating kiss.

Minutes later, Thomas gently pulled up her bodice and rolled away from her. "We must stop before we get carried away."

"I'm already quite carried away," Delilah replied with a laugh. She stared up into the blue afternoon sky and stretched like a cat. Then she gathered more of the pink roses and let them fall atop her.

"Have you enjoyed our picnic?" Thomas asked, sitting up next to her and tracing the edge of her cheek.

"So much," she replied, rubbing her cheek against his hand.

"I'm glad," he replied. "This is the type of courtship you deserve."

She pushed herself up on one elbow. "Oh, but we're not—"

"Will you go to the theater with me tomorrow night? Lucy will accompany us."

Delilah didn't want to stop pretending, so instead of finishing her sentence, she nodded and said, "I would love to go to theater with you tomorrow night."

"Excellent." Thomas stood, pulled her to her feet, and helped to right her clothing. He leaned down and grabbed her bonnet from the quilt and placed it atop her head and tied the ribbon beneath her chin. "You're beautiful," he said, stroking the tip of her nose with the end of his finger.

"No, I'm not." She nudged at the roses with her foot.

He stopped, lifted her chin with his finger, and stared deeply into her eyes. "Delilah, listen to me. You're beautiful and always have been . . . inside and out."

Tears stung her eyes. She turned away, pretending to be occupied helping him clear away their picnic. Thomas had always loved her as a best friend should, but now, now things were different between them, and she couldn't help but wish they were real. What she'd done here today had been nothing short of shameless. She'd allowed him to kiss her and touch her, knowing he was only doing it because he was enchanted. She'd selfishly wanted it and allowed him to continue. How would she ever explain this to him when he realized the truth?

She blinked away the tears. "I should get home. Mother will be waiting for me."

CHAPTER THIRTY-FOUR

The next night, Delilah accompanied Thomas to the theater with a group of friends including Lucy and Derek, Cass and Julian, and Jane and Garrett. When they arrived and situated themselves into Claringdon's box, a small group of the theatergoers who'd attended the performance in the country gave them a standing ovation.

They stood and bowed and blushed appropriately before settling in to watch a performance of *Much Ado About Nothing*.

When the play was over, Jane and Garrett launched into an argument about whether Beatrice or Benedick was the more clever of the two main characters in the play. Lucy rolled her eyes and exclaimed, "Neither of them ever wins this argument. They've been having it for years."

Thomas excused them from the others and escorted Delilah out to the waiting coach.

She stopped short when she saw Clarence Hilton standing in front of their conveyance.

The robust man dabbed a handkerchief at his wet bottom lip and glared at Thomas. "Good evening, Lady Delilah," Clarence said, as Thomas took a protective step in front of her.

This was the first time Delilah had seen Clarence since their supposed engagement. She certainly hadn't spoken to him. He hadn't bothered to so much as pay her a visit, let alone formally ask for her hand. He'd allowed his father and her mother to arrange the entire thing.

Clarence was nearly five and twenty, but he rarely left his father's home. From what Mother had told her, he preferred instead to stay in his bedchamber playing Patience with an old deck of cards, drinking port, and eating sweets. Lord Hilton had been trying for years to get his son to leave the house and find a bride to produce an heir, but Clarence had refused. Apparently, the earl had found another way to accomplish that task.

"Lord Clarence," she said woodenly, inclining her head to him. She had to wonder what had made the short man leave the comfort of his bedchamber this evening. His clothing was too small for him, and he looked exceedingly uncomfortable in it, as if his cravat was choking him.

"What are you doing here with *him*?" Clarence asked, nodding toward Thomas.

"*Him* has a name," Thomas declared. "I'm the Duke of Huntley, but you may refer to me as *Your Grace*."

Thomas was angry. He would never behave this way otherwise, lording his title over someone else. At the moment, Delilah couldn't blame him.

"Very well, *Your Grace*," Clarence sneered the honorific. "I'll thank you to unhand *my bride*." He glared at Thomas, whose hand lay on the small of Delilah's back.

"She's not your bride yet," Thomas retorted.

"We're to be married in a fortnight," Clarence replied.

"If she were *my* bride, she wouldn't be out with another man." Thomas narrowed his eyes on Clarence.

Clarence clenched his fat little fist, but he was obviously too intimidated by Thomas to do anything else. Instead, he glared at Delilah. "I want you to stop spending time with him." He jabbed a round finger toward Thomas. "I demand it." He stomped his foot.

"People in Hades want iced water," Thomas replied quickly.

"We'll speak of this later," Clarence said to Delilah. He gave Thomas one last glare before turning on his heel and walking away.

Delilah stared at his back as he ambled off. "Clarence," she called, after a moment's thought.

The man stopped and turned around.

"Why are you here? At the theater tonight?" she asked.

His eyes shifted back and forth, and he tugged at the cravat that covered nearly half of his squat face. "Father made me. He wanted me to tell you that we're to have dinner tomorrow evening at your mother's house." He sniffled and wiped at his nose with his bare hand. "I'm going home now." He turned and meandered away.

"That coward," Thomas said through clenched teeth. He shook his head. "I cannot believe your mother would have you marry *him*. A stump post would be a better choice."

Delilah laid her gloved hand on his to calm him, nausea roiling in her belly. She was beginning to agree with Thomas. Had her mother picked Clarence merely to

cause Delilah distress? She didn't want to believe it, but
she suspected it was true. Not that it changed the fact that
Thomas was courting her only because she'd tricked
him into it. She couldn't marry Thomas, and she wouldn't
marry Clarence. In the meantime, however, apparently,
she would have to spend an evening with the awful little
man. Tomorrow.

If the dinner with the Hiltons could be described in one
word, that word was *excruciating.* Delilah sat at her
mother's dining table the next evening to the right of Lord
Hilton who resided at the head. She was forced to look
directly across at Clarence, who was the only person of
her acquaintance who managed to spill more of his food
on his clothing than she did. Perhaps that's why Mother
believed they would suit, she thought to herself with a
snort. She wished Thomas were there to share the comment with. Instead, she was forced to swallow her laughter under her mother's penetrating stare.

"The wedding plans are coming along nicely," Mother
said, taking a ladylike sip from her soup spoon.

The last thing Delilah wanted to do was talk about the
weddings. "I heard that Parliament took a vote on the latest Corn Law, Lord Hilton. How did you vote?"

"Good heavens," Mother said, forcing a fake smile to
her lips. "I'm certain Lord Hilton doesn't want to talk
about men's business at the dinner table with ladies
present." She gave Delilah a condemning glare, clearly
meant to quell her from asking such bluestocking-like
questions in the future.

"Yes," Lord Hilton boomed. "I daresay it would be too
complicated for you to understand, my dear." He gave her
a condescending smile.

"Oh, I doubt it," Delilah replied, before her mother kicked her under the table.

Fine. If she couldn't discuss politics with Lord Hilton, she'd attempt to make conversation with his son. The man must have *something* to say. Delilah turned her attention to Clarence. "I hear the poet William Blake is ill. What do you think of his views on the church, Lord Clarence?"

Another swift jab from her mother's foot made Delilah yelp. She reached down and rubbed her sore ankle, frowning at her mother.

"William Blake?" Clarence blinked at her, while he dripped more soup down his stained shirtfront.

Delilah glanced back and forth between Lord Hilton and his son. Surely they knew the famous William Blake. The Corn Laws and Blake were both subjects she'd spoken about upon many occasions with Thomas. She'd had no idea these two men would seem so affronted by the topics. What in heaven's name did dull men like to speak about then?

"I've chosen white lilies for the ceremony," Mother interjected.

"White lilies? Aren't those the flowers of death?" Delilah asked, blinking innocently at her mother. This time, she was quick enough to move her leg before Mother could execute her next kick.

"Pink roses have always been my favorite," Delilah continued, sighing. Her cheeks heated as she recalled her picnic with Thomas. Of course, she had no intention of marrying Clarence Hilton with or without pink roses present, but she might as well say something to lighten up this horribly dull dinner conversation.

"Yes, well, pink roses are costly," Mother said, nodding toward Lord Hilton.

Delilah frowned again. Since when had Mother worried about the price of anything?

"Are flowers entirely necessary?" Lord Hilton asked, his face pinched.

"No, not at all," Mother replied. "We'll make do without them."

The next two courses were served while the occupants of the table barely spoke a handful of words to each other. Mother occasionally made a comment about the weddings, Lord Hilton occasionally asked a question about the cost, and Clarence continued to eat at an alarming pace.

Delilah was about to ask him if he wanted another helping of salmon when he groaned and clutched his belly.

"Are you all right, Clarence?" his father asked with obvious annoyance.

"No, I'm not." Clarence continued to groan. "My belly aches."

"You shouldn't have eaten so quickly. I've warned you about that a dozen times," Lord Hilton snapped.

Delilah hid her smile behind her wine glass. Oh, dear. She could commiserate with poor Clarence Hilton. The young man was clearly as harassed by his father as she was by her mother.

"I feel quite ill," Clarence moaned. His forehead was sweating profusely, and he was rapidly turning an unfortunate shade of green.

"Get yourself together, Clarence," Lord Hilton commanded, his nostrils flaring.

Delilah pushed back her chair and stood. She hurried around to Clarence's side of the table and placed a hand on his forehead. "He feels quite hot," she announced. "Perhaps he should rest in the salon."

"Yes, thank you," Clarence said. He clutched Delilah's arm as she and one of the footmen escorted him out of the dining room.

She helped to settle him in the salon, before turning back toward the door. "I'll inform your father you're all right," she said.

"Please ask him if we may go home," Clarence said, and Delilah realized then that he was as uncomfortable as she had been, perhaps more so. Clarence didn't want to marry her any more than she wanted to marry him.

"I'll do better than that," she said with a friendly smile. "I'll tell him you must go."

She turned to leave. "Thank you, Lady Delilah." Relief was apparent in Clarence's voice. "Thank you very much."

"May I ask you a question, Lord Clarence?"

He nodded, rubbing his belly and groaning.

"When you saw me at the theater with the Duke of Huntley, did you truly care that we were together?"

Clarence blinked his eyes open. "Father said I should tell you to stop spending time with Huntley. He said it was unseemly."

"I see," was all Delilah replied before she quit the room. But it made sense. Poor Clarence Hilton had never had a thought of his own. His father told him everything to do. Delilah shook her head. She couldn't help but feel sorry for him. Not sorry enough to want to marry him, but sorry nonetheless.

A quarter hour later, Lord Hilton and his son had taken their leave. Delilah and her mother had seen them to the door.

"I do hope Clarence recovers," Delilah said, as she started toward the staircase to retire.

"Beginning to care about him, are you?" her mother said snidely.

"Why?" Delilah asked. "Would that make you wish you hadn't picked him for me?" She didn't turn back to allow her mother to see the smile that rested on her face as she mounted the stairs.

CHAPTER THIRTY-FIVE

The next evening, Thomas took Delilah to Vauxhall Gardens to see the fireworks. The gardens were dark, the perfect place for a rendezvous if one didn't want to be seen. They'd found a secluded spot in the trees where he spread out a blanket for them to sit on.

"How did your dinner with the Hiltons go?" Thomas was watching her profile. He often watched her profile of late. It was a distinctively unfriend-like thing to do. She tried to pretend she didn't notice. She also tried to pretend as if she didn't want to kiss him—and do more—a task that was becoming increasingly difficult.

Delilah sighed and leaned back on her palms to stare up at the inky night sky. "Exactly as you might expect. Clarence refused to speak unless prompted by his father. My mother talked of nothing but the weddings, and I was a complete failure at my attempts to change the subject. Fortunately, Clarence declared a stomachache halfway through the meal, and he and Lord Hilton were forced to take their leave."

Thomas glanced away. He shrugged out of his coat and tossed it to the edge of the blanket. This time, she had the opportunity to stare at *his* profile.

"I can't believe you're still acting as if you're truly going to marry him," he said.

"I have no intention of marrying him, but I haven't yet thought of how I shall avoid it. I suppose I could run off and elope." Belatedly she realized she shouldn't have said that. She tried to force a laugh, but the humorless sound that emerged from her lips was unconvincing.

"Say the word," Thomas clipped.

Silence fell between them, a heavy silence in which the reality of their situation weighed upon them. Thomas had no idea how much she'd love to ask him to take her to Gretna Green to save her from Clarence Hilton. But ever since the night his father died, Thomas had turned into a knight in shining armor. He wanted to save everyone, especially his friends. He deserved a woman whom he truly loved and who truly loved him. Not his desperate friend who was in need of a timely rescue. It wouldn't be fair to Thomas to let him save her.

She was about to tell him so when he turned to her. "Delilah," he murmured. "Your mother doesn't deserve you. You are a breath of fresh air, a light in the darkness. You're everything she's not, and if she was half the mother you deserve, she wouldn't waste you on a man like Clarence Hilton."

Delilah opened her mouth to respond, but words failed her. How could she answer to such a thing? Her mother was her mother. One didn't get to choose one's parents. She highly doubted anything she did at this stage in her life would change her mother's opinion of her.

"Thomas," she whispered. "I don't think you understand."

He leaned toward her until his lips were only inches from hers. He smelled like soap and spice, and she wanted to wrap her arms around his neck and never let go.

"I understand far more than you realize," he breathed, just before his lips descended to hers.

The kiss was gentle at first. Then, as seemed to be their habit, it turned into something completely different. Pure, raw emotion and need infused it as their tongues met and clashed. He gently pushed her down onto her back and rolled atop her.

"Yes," she whispered, pulling him hard against her. Her hands tangled in his hair, and she let her head fall back as he rained kisses down her neck.

His hand skimmed down her ribcage, and he hoisted up her skirts on one side, before his fingers brushed against the side of her bare hip. A gasp escaped her. No one had ever touched her this way. He'd moved her shift aside. As if guided by some inner female knowing, she opened for him, spreading her legs as his hand found the juncture between her thighs. She wanted this. Wanted his touch. Shamelessly begged for it.

"Delilah," he said in a low, warning tone that thrilled her to her toes, "I'm about to take this from improper to purely sinful. But not without your permission. Shall I—"

"Please, yes," she whispered against his ear.

His finger moved along the seam of her sex—impossibly sinful, perfect—and she shuddered and closed her eyes. Then he dipped one finger inside of her. He slid it in, so slowly and deeply. She bit her lip and called his name against his ear.

He withdrew his touch and slowly moved his finger along her seam again until he found some magical point of pleasure between her thighs. He nudged it again and again with his fingertip while Delilah thought she might go mad from pure longing. She'd never felt such need before. An intense sensation built in her loins, and she tossed her head back and forth fitfully against the blanket, unsure of what she wanted, but desperate for it.

His hand left her momentarily and she gasped, "No."

His fingers trailed up to her décolletage, where he slid her gown off her shoulder and tugged it down gently, freeing one breast from her shift and stays. "You're beautiful," he whispered reverently, before his lips descended to her nipple. He sucked the little bud between his teeth, and Delilah's eyes rolled back into her head. She clenched her jaw against the raw emotion as his hand descended once more to torture the tender flesh between her thighs.

He sucked her nipple hard into his mouth and lavished it with his tongue while his finger continued its insistent circling between her legs. Her thighs tensed and shook. Sweat beaded down her back. She clutched at his muscled arms, her fingers digging into the fine fabric of his shirt. He tugged at her nipple and then laved it while her breathing came in short little pants against his shoulder. Her eyes couldn't focus on the night sky. It was all a blur of velvet blue, the stars pinpricks sprinkled across it.

When Thomas's finger stopped for what felt like an eternity but was probably only seconds, she clutched at his shoulders. "Don't stop, Thomas. Please," she nearly sobbed. He started again, simultaneously sucking her nipple into his mouth once more, and the combination of sensations sent her over the edge into some kind of trembling, shattering pleasure she could never have imagined existed. She closed her eyes and saw the stars on the insides of her lids as wave after wave of pure bliss rocked her body.

His breath came in hard pants too, as though he had experienced her pleasure vicariously. He pressed gentle kisses to her cheeks, her damp forehead, her eyelids, and then a single, parting one to her lips. "Delilah. My Delilah."

Yes, she thought. *His*. Heart, body, and soul.

CHAPTER THIRTY-SIX

"I'm falling in love with Thomas!" Delilah exclaimed the next afternoon over tea in Lucy's drawing room. Delilah paced in front of the fireplace, her hands pressed against her cheeks, while Lucy, as usual, administered an inordinate amount of sugar into her teacup.

The duchess barely glanced up. "Is that a bad thing?"

Delilah's eyes widened. "Are you quite serious? *Yes*, it's a bad thing."

Lucy's brow furrowed. "Why? You said he told you he loves you too."

"It's a bad thing because he doesn't *really* love me. He only *thinks* he loves me because of the potion. I've ruined everything. And now he's . . . he's . . ."

She couldn't bring herself to tell Lucy what Thomas had done to her last night at Vauxhall with his hands and mouth. She still didn't know what to make of it herself. She only knew it was the most extraordinary thing that had ever happened to her body, and she wanted to do it again with him at the earliest opportunity. Which was part of the problem. She couldn't allow Thomas to continue to believe he was in love with her and do things for her like *that* with his tongue and hands. Not when she'd duped him into loving her to begin with. It was all quite wrong. Even if it felt absolutely right.

Lucy took a tentative sip of tea, no doubt to test its sugar content. "I don't think you've ruined everything, dear. Complicated it, perhaps. But isn't that what we do best? We are only mortal." She fluttered a hand in the air.

Delilah continued her pacing. "Thomas said it himself. The day I told him I'd purchased the potion. He said, 'Do you really want a man whom you have to drug to fall in love with you?' The answer is no. No, I don't want a man whom I have to drug to fall in love with me."

Lucy scrunched up her nose. "But you wanted the Duke of Branville. And you intended to drug him."

Delilah groaned. "That was a mistake, and honestly, I don't think I ever really wanted Branville. I want Thomas, but I can't have Thomas because he's . . . Thomas. But more importantly because I tricked him into loving me."

Lucy added another lump of sugar to her cup and stirred it daintily with a tiny silver spoon. "You cannot possibly think you should marry Clarence Hilton."

Delilah paused and slid her slippers against the floor. "No, of course not, but that doesn't mean I *should* marry Thomas. There are more than two men in this world."

Lucy tapped her cheek. "I don't see what the problem is, dear. I suppose we could try to find a third man, but it seems quite a tight schedule, given your marriage is planned for less than a fortnight from now."

Delilah made her way to the settee where her friend sat and lowered herself to sit beside her. "I don't want another man. I want Thomas. At least I think I want Thomas." She cradled her head in her hands. "Oh, why is this all so confusing?"

Lucy pulled the silver spoon from her teacup and set it on a nearby napkin. "You're making no sense, dear, and that's coming from someone who is often told by others that she's making no sense. If you want Thomas, I don't see why you shouldn't have him."

"Haven't you been listening? Thomas doesn't truly love me."

Lucy arched a brow and expelled a long breath. "Wait. I admit it's not usually my way, dear, but perhaps we should look at this predicament logically. Does Thomas meet your criteria? Your list, I mean."

Delilah froze and blinked. "I've never considered it before."

Lucy nodded. "What are the qualities, dear? Remind me."

In all the confusion over the past weeks, Delilah had completely forgotten about her list of future-husband qualities. But Lucy was entirely right. She could indeed apply the list to Thomas. She ticked them off on her fingers. "Thomas is eligible, kind, intelligent, funny, healthy." She cleared her throat. "And I've recently discovered he's quite handsome and kissable."

Lucy lifted her teacup to her lips. "Sounds perfect to me. He's also fiercely loyal to those in his inner circle, dear. You are both quite alike that way."

"But he loves me because I drugged him," Delilah answered miserably.

Lucy tilted her head to the side. "Perhaps."

Delilah winced. "There's one more quality on my list that I didn't mention."

Lucy pointed her nose in the air. "What is it, dear?"

Delilah swallowed. "Forgiving."

Lucy took a sip of tea. "You know what I always say, dear."

"Be bold," Delilah said in a voice that was anything but.

"That's right. So what do you intend to do?"

Delilah smoothed her skirts and rose from her seat. "I need to make this right."

CHAPTER THIRTY-SEVEN

The carriage pulled to a stop on Lombard Street in the pouring rain. The coachman opened the door for Delilah, but she didn't wait for him to pull down the stairs. She nearly jumped into his arms, forcing him to lower her to the muddy ground. She lifted her skirts and rushed down the street, mud splattering her stockings and gown. Her hair melted into her eyes, and she swiped it away with one hand, but she kept running until she made it past the little white gate and stood before the green front door to Madame Rosa's shop.

She knocked heavily, but didn't wait for an answer. She pushed open the door and lunged inside, breathing heavily, heart hammering, hair plastered to her head. She glanced around the darkened, sweet-smelling shop. A few candles burned here and there, illuminating the space enough for her to see that Madame Rosa sat at the little table in front of her perfume vials. The old woman looked up at Delilah, but didn't appear to think anything out of the ordinary about a young lady arriving wet and muddy on her doorstep.

"Madame Rosa," Delilah called.

"Come and sit, lass," the old lady said. "I'll get ye some tea."

She stood slowly and, using her cane, shuffled off behind a curtain in the back of the shop. When she returned, she held a teacup in her free hand and had a shawl slung over her shoulder. She resumed her seat and propped her cane against the side of the table before handing the teacup and the shawl to Delilah, who had settled onto one of the rickety wooden chairs in front of Madame's table.

"Ye've come again," Madame Rosa said, her eyes searching Delilah's face.

Delilah pulled the shawl around her shoulders to keep herself from shivering and took a tentative sip of the strong herbal tea. "You remember me?"

"Of course I remember ye, lass. Ye wanted ta reverse the effects of Cupid's Elixir."

Delilah nodded. "You told me it couldn't be done."

"And so it cannot," the old woman replied.

"There must be something, Madame Rosa. Some way to fix it." Tears choked Delilah's voice. "Something I can do."

Madame Rosa's eyes filled with sympathy. She reached out and patted Delilah's hand. "Tell me, lass. What happened?"

Delilah forced herself to take another calming sip of tea. "I sprinkled the potion on the wrong man's eyes. When he awoke, he told me he was in love with me. Since then, I've come to love him too. Only I refuse to marry him if he only loves me because of the potion. I cannot live a lie."

Madame Rosa's eyes narrowed, and she reached out one hand. "Let me see yer palm again, lass."

Delilah pulled off her glove and offered her hand. Madame Rosa extracted the looking glass from the drawer as she had the first time Delilah visited. She cradled Delilah's hand and examined her palm carefully. "Ah, yes, I remember this hand."

"You said true love was in my future."

"And so it is. That is why I sold ye the elixir to begin with . . . because ye were worthy of it. Yer palm told me so."

"What does that mean?" Delilah shook her head. "What can I do to fix this?"

Madame sighed heavily and stared off into the darkness. "I suppose in this instance, there is one thing ye can do."

Delilah lurched forward, desperate hope clawing at her insides. "What? Tell me."

"Ye're not going to like it, lass."

Delilah grasped both of Madame Rosa's warm hands. "I'll do anything. Tell me. Please."

"If ye truly love him," the old woman said, meeting her gaze with steady eyes that seemed to blaze with the fire of truth, "ye must let him go."

CHAPTER THIRTY-EIGHT

Thomas threw a pebble at her window like he had a hundred times before. And like he had a hundred times before, he waited with bated breath to see if Delilah had heard him and would lift the pane.

He was about to toss another pebble when her shadow appeared in front of the glass. She pulled open the window and stared down at him, her shoulders filling the space. She was wearing her night rail, and her hair streamed past her shoulders. Worry lined her features. "Thomas. Shh. *Mère*'s still awake." She glanced back over her shoulder.

"Can you come down?" He cupped his hands over his mouth so she might hear his whispered words.

She glanced behind her again. "Give me a minute."

The window closed again before it reopened a few minutes later, and Delilah, wearing a dressing gown over her night rail and her hair hastily made into a bun on the back of her head, stuck out her foot and began climbing down the trellis as she'd done a hundred times before. Her bedchamber's window faced the back of the house and the darkened gardens, so they wouldn't be seen from the street. Thankfully, Lady Vanessa's bedchamber was on the other side of the house, a fact that had always been conducive to their late-night talks.

Delilah nimbly climbed all the way down and hopped off into the grass, and Thomas was filled with nostalgia for a girl who was always game to do things like climb trellises regardless of the way she tended to rip her stockings in the process.

"How are your stockings?" he asked with a grin.

"I'm not wearing any at the moment," she admitted before her face turned serious and she eyed him warily. "What are you doing here?"

"I had to see you." The fact was he'd nearly gone mad these past nights without her. After their trip to Vauxhall Gardens, he'd taken her home. They'd barely spoken two words to each other on the journey. He had no idea if she was angry with him for what they'd done. Did she regret it? How did she feel? He had to know. That had been over a sennight ago. Each time he'd asked to see her since, she'd made some excuse about how busy she was. Tonight, he'd had enough of her putting him off. They needed to have this out, once and for all. There was no time left.

"I'm supposed to be getting married the morning after next," Delilah said, her voice devoid of all emotion.

"That's why I'm here." He grasped both of her hands and found them chilled. "Run away with me, Delilah. It's our last chance."

Her eyes filled with tears as she gazed up into his face. "Run away with you?" she echoed.

"Yes. To Scotland. We'll go to Gretna Green. Your

mother won't fight us after she knows we're married. She won't want the scandal."

Delilah glanced back up at the looming town house. She gently pulled her hands from his and crossed her arms over her chest. "*Mère* won't let me go that easily."

"She will when I tell her that I'll settle twice the sum of your dowry on her if she does," he replied resolutely.

Delilah sucked in her breath. She suspected that might do it, actually. Perhaps Mother would be swayed by the figure. Lord Hilton no doubt would be. Her throat ached. Thomas would do that for her? He'd pay a fortune to have her. Because she'd drugged him. That's what made it so wrong.

But even if she told her mother that she would *not* marry Clarence, it didn't matter because Delilah couldn't marry Thomas either. She wanted him, but only if he met her at the altar with a heart full of love born of years of friendship and natural, life-given adoration. Madame Rosa's words rang in her ears. *If you truly love him, you must let him go.*

She would do it. She owed it to him. But first, she had to tell him the truth.

She sought his hand and curled her fingers around it, even now unable to keep from touching him in this, the last moments before everything changed between them forever. "Thomas, you must listen to me. The night at Lucy's country house. The night of my birthday. I told you I didn't use the potion on Branville."

Thomas searched her face. "Yes, I know."

"But I did use it." She paused to take a breath. "On you."

He rubbed a hand across his brow and shook his head. "The blasted potion? Is that what this is all still about?

Who cares about the potion? I love you, Delilah, and my love for you has nothing to do with that idiotic potion. Run away with me."

If you truly love him, you must let him go.

"I can't, Thomas." Tears gathered on her lashes. "I cannot. Please don't ask me to again."

"This isn't about my feelings anymore, is it?" He clenched a fist and braced his arm against the brick wall behind her. "Is it because you don't love me? Is that it?" His voice was accusatory, harsh, a tone she'd rarely heard from him, even at the worst of times.

If you truly love him, you must let him go.

"I love you as a friend, Thomas. I always will." There. That would have to do because she couldn't say more than that. It nearly broke her to say those words. She couldn't even look him in the eye.

"You don't want to marry me? You'd rather marry *Clarence Hilton*?" He spat the words.

She clenched her jaw. This was excruciating. But it was also what she deserved after what she'd done. "I won't marry Clarence," she said. "But I also won't marry you. I cannot allow you to save me. It wouldn't be fair to you."

He turned from her, facing the darkness as if he could no longer bear the sight of her. "Don't do this to us, Delilah," he said through clenched teeth.

"I'm sorry, Thomas. Please. Go." And then she could speak no more. Grief had stolen her words. When she managed to swallow the sobs shaking through her and dashed the tears from her eyes, Thomas was gone. And Delilah had never been more alone.

CHAPTER THIRTY-NINE

Delilah had been waiting in Lucy's salon for the better part of half an hour when Derek entered the room alone. She blinked at him and started. "Is Lucy all right?"

She had expected to spend the afternoon before her supposed wedding discussing with Lucy what she should do. She intended to cry off, of course, but it was certain to be a difficult feat, and Delilah expected both her mother and Lord Hilton to take the news very, very poorly. She would need a place to stay if her mother forced her from her home.

"Lucy is well," Derek replied. "But she's not here at the moment."

Delilah frowned. "I don't understand. I received a message asking me to meet her here."

"I know," Derek said. "I sent the message."

Delilah crossed her arms over her chest and stared at the duke. None of it made any sense.

"Please," he said, gesturing to her to follow him. "Come with me."

She followed him out into the corridor, across the foyer, and down another corridor until they came to two large doors. Derek opened them, revealing his spacious wood-lined study.

The moment she entered the room, Delilah sucked in her breath. They were not alone. Julian Swift was there. And Garrett Upton. Christian Berkeley and Rafe and Cade Cavendish. The men all stood or sat around the room in various states of relaxation. Most of them had drinks in their hands. Delilah's startled gaze flew back to Derek.

"Usually we do this at the Curious Goat Inn," he began, "and unfortunately for us, it's usually a man we're having to talk sense into. But in this case, Huntley seems to have his head on perfectly correctly. It's *you* we're worried about."

Delilah turned in a wide circle and nodded at each of them. "What do you mean?"

Derek walked over to his desk and offered her one of the seats in front of it. She stiffly perched on its edge, while he took his seat behind the desk. "Our wives are known for their matchmaking skills, but it seems their husbands aren't too bad at it either. We're here to tell you that you need to admit to Huntley you love him."

Delilah's gaze trailed about the room, stopping on each of the handsome, friendly male faces of her friends. "How do all of you know I love Thomas?" She blinked at them.

Julian inclined his head. "It's obvious, Delilah. We've all known you and Thomas were meant for each other for years. You're never happier than when you're together, and you make an adorable couple, I might add."

Delilah shook her head. "You don't understand. There are other things to consider. My mother—"

Garrett cleared his throat. "With all due respect, your mother is a wasp."

"She's worse than a wasp. She's a shrew," Rafe replied.

"I think that's an insult to shrews," Cade added.

"Whatever she is," Derek continued, "she doesn't deserve you as a daughter, and she never has. Lucy has told me the things she's said and done to you over the years."

Tears filled Delilah eyes. These men, these kind, loyal men, all cared enough about her to come here, to tell her how they felt, to make her see reason.

"We understand the importance of family," Julian said, "but when family treats you as poorly as your mother has treated you, you owe her no loyalty."

Confused, Delilah glanced at Derek.

"It's true," Derek replied. "I hate to tell you something so awful, but your mother wants to marry you to Clarence so that she and Hilton can keep your dowry for themselves."

"If that's not a horrible thing for a mother to do, I don't know what is," Garrett breathed.

"It's true," Rafe added, and Delilah's confused gaze flew to her cousin's face.

Rafe took a deep breath. "I sent my friends Mark Grimaldi and Daffin Oakleaf to Hilton's club the other night. They bought him a few drinks and asked a few questions. Hilton admitted it to them. Seems he's been hurting for money lately after a series of poor business ventures. I did some investigating on my own and apparently, the money your father set aside for your mother would return to the estate upon her marriage."

Delilah took a long shaky breath. The truth was painful to hear, but it didn't entirely surprise her. She'd wondered why Mother had been so adamant for a match with Clarence when Thomas had a better title and more money. She had suspected Mother wanted to keep her dowry, but she hadn't allowed herself to fully believe it until this moment. She could just imagine Hilton, imbibing too much and bragging about the small fortune he stood to inherit once he was married to her mother and Delilah was married to his son. It made her sick.

"But that's not the only problem," she said miserably. "Thomas doesn't love me that way. He only thinks he does."

"No, *you* don't understand." Derek leaned forward to meet her eyes. "Huntley switched rooms with Branville the night of the play. He knew you had that ridiculous elixir, and he knew you intended to use it. He wanted you to use it on *him*."

Delilah hand fell to her lap. She felt as if she'd swallowed a brick. "What?"

"That's right." Derek nodded.

"But why?" She searched the duke's face, wildly confused. The blood drained from her cheeks only to fill anew with heat.

"Because he was already madly in love with you, you daft girl," Derek said with a smile that belied his words. "He only needed a reason to be able to tell you."

Delilah clapped a hand over her mouth. "No." She shook her head. This couldn't be true. Could it?

"I'm afraid so," Derek continued. "Huntley asked me personally to ensure he and Branville traded rooms. I obliged. Don't you remember that you asked me where Branville's room was that night? Did you ever wonder why Huntley was there instead of Branville?"

Delilah pressed her fingertips to her lips. "I thought I'd mixed up the directions. I had no idea."

"You didn't make a mistake." Derek sat back in his massive chair, the satisfied smile still lingering on his lips. "I sent you there. On purpose. Of course, if I'd known I was the one you'd ask, he wouldn't have needed to change rooms to begin with, but it worked out exactly as Huntley planned. All's well that ends well, I suppose."

"You sent me to Thomas's room?" she breathed, in complete awe of the information that was slowly sinking into her dazed mind. That night, she'd thought she was the one being sneaky. She'd had no idea. A slow smile spread across her face.

"Yes," Derek replied, "and at the risk of sounding too much like my lovely wife, I must tell you that you were so preoccupied with trying to manipulate true love that you failed to see it right in front of your face."

"That does sound like Lucy," Christian replied. "But I daresay, it's true." He gave Delilah a sympathetic grin.

Tears filled her eyes. She swallowed hard. "I've been a fool."

"Yes, you've been a fool," Julian agreed, "but we've all been fools for love at one time or another. The good news is, it's easily corrected. The man is madly in love with you, after all." He grinned.

"As for your mother," Derek continued, "I wouldn't give her or Lord Hilton a second thought."

"Say the word," Cade Cavendish added, "and I'll send Miss Adeline over to bite them both."

Delilah nipped the inside of her cheek to keep from laughing at the offer, but the men were right. Her mother was awful to her and had been all her life. Thomas had tried to tell her gently on more than one occasion. All these years, she'd made excuse after excuse, but she refused to allow one more day to pass without setting things to right.

She stood and rushed to the door. When she grabbed the handle, she paused and turned back to the group. "Thank you. Thank you, all. You've no idea how much you've helped me. Truly."

"It's our pleasure," Derek said, with a nod of acknowledgment. "What are you going to do?"

"I'm going to find Thomas, of course, but first I have one stop to make."

CHAPTER FORTY

Delilah flew up the stairs to the front door of her mother's town house. As soon as Goodfellow opened door, she dashed inside. "Where is my mother?"

"She's in the gold salon with Lord Hilton, my lady."

Of course she was. Good, they both could hear this together.

Delilah didn't bother to deposit her bonnet and pelisse with Goodfellow. She wouldn't be staying long. She didn't bother taking three deep breaths either. Instead, she marched directly to the gold salon and shoved open the door hard enough to send it cracking against the far wall.

Her mother glanced up. "Delilah, there you are. Good. We were just discussing what time we should all awake tomorrow morning. We want to be refreshed, but we mustn't linger abed. We have much to do. What do you think?"

"Decide for yourself, *Mère*. You always do. Though

it's cunning of you to pretend as if you care about my opinion in front of Lord Hilton."

Her mother's eyes briefly flared. She pursed her lips. "I'll thank you not to speak to me in that tone of voice, young lady."

Delilah crossed her arms over her chest and strode toward her mother. "I'd like to thank you too. I'd like to thank you for all the times you let me cry without a comforting hand. I'd like to thank you for all the occasions you pointed out my flaws and told me I wasn't good enough to be your daughter. I'd like to thank you for all the nasty names you've called me and all the instances when you made me feel small. Most of all, I'd like to thank you for telling me that it was a good thing Papa died so he wouldn't have to live to see what a disappointment I've been."

Mother straightened her shoulders and glanced at Lord Hilton uneasily. "Delilah, once again, you're being dramatic."

She gave the other woman the same cold, hard stare that Delilah had suffered countless times from her mother. "Am I, *Mère*? Am I being dramatic? Are any of the things I said untrue?"

"They may be true," Mother replied, "but you're making far too much of them, as usual."

Delilah turned her attention to Lord Hilton, who was watching with a hard look in his eye. "What do you think, Lord Hilton? Do you think I'm making too much of my mother's words?"

Lord Hilton tugged on his lapels and glanced away. "I'm not about to insert myself in a difference of opinion between a mother and her daughter."

"Delilah," Mother snapped. "Stop calling me *mère*.

Take off your wrinkled bonnet and your dirty gloves and sit down. We have wedding details to discuss."

Delilah lingered close to the door, refusing the old habit to escape. "There's not going to be any wedding, *Mère*. At least not for me. I wouldn't marry Clarence if he were the last man in London."

Her mother's eyes flared. "He may just be the last man in London who'll have *you*."

Delilah clenched her jaw and lifted her chin. "See, that's exactly what I'm speaking of. I never thought I was worthy of love before. You taught me that from an early age. As long as I wasn't perfect—and I will *never* be perfect—then I didn't deserve your love or your attention. Or anyone's attention, for that matter. But I know better now. I'm perfectly right, exactly as I am. Thomas loves me and I love him."

Her mother's sharp bark of laughter followed, shattering the room's thick atmosphere. "Huntley? Are you mad? He might be amused with you, but he'll never *marry* you."

"He is going to marry me. And I'm going to marry him. But you'll never see your grandchildren, and you won't be welcome in our home. I'm leaving this house now, and I won't be back. You'll have to take out your vitriol on someone else. Perhaps Lord Hilton will put up with it."

Lord Hilton gave her mother a sideways stare that clearly indicated he was concerned by that statement.

Mother lifted her chin. Her voice was filled with ice. "Delilah Montebank, if you leave now, you'll never be welcome under this roof again."

"I can only hope that's a promise," Delilah tossed over her shoulder as she marched into the foyer and said good-bye to Goodfellow.

CHAPTER FORTY-ONE

Delilah pounded on the door to Thomas's town house. The butler opened it and his jaw fell.

She'd never arrived alone at Thomas's door before. It was improper. She'd been here for parties before, of course, but always accompanied by a chaperone. Either Lucy or her mother.

"My lady?" the butler said as she moved past him and strode into the foyer.

Voices sounded in the nearest salon, and she rushed inside to see Lavinia and Lord Stanley sitting together on the settee, sipping tea. "My apologies," she said, blushing and trying to back out of the room as quickly and gracefully as possible.

Lavinia had a smile on her face, a genuine smile. "You might as well be the first to know, Lady Delilah. Lord Stanley has proposed, and I have accepted."

Delilah smiled too. This was a surprise, but they both looked so happy. "Best wishes to both of you," she said. "I'm trying to find your brother to ask him the same question."

She didn't pause long enough to explain that loaded statement. Instead, she turned and hurried through the foyer and down the corridor in search of Thomas's study. When she arrived, she pushed open the door and stepped inside. Thomas sat behind a large wooden desk in the center of the room, bent over some paperwork. He started when he saw her.

"Delilah?" His jaw was clenched and his expression hard. "What are you doing here?"

She quickly made her way over to the side of the desk and fell to one knee beside him, tears in her eyes, blurring her vision. She grasped his hand in hers. "Thomas Marcus Devon Peabody Hobbs, will you and all of your ridiculous names marry me?"

"What?" His brow furrowed and confusion played across his handsome features.

"Madame Rosa told me I had to let you go. I think she meant you'd have to come back to me, but now I realize that I always needed to come to you. I've been a fool for a long time, Thomas, but I promise I see everything clearly now. And I love you too."

His gaze searched her face for a breathless, heart-pounding moment, and then, to her abject relief, the hint of a smile played at the corner of his mouth. He pulled her into his lap and kissed her cheek. "Why do you love me?"

She gave him a half-grin. "Because you're kind, intelligent, funny, and extremely handsome and kissable. I can only hope you're also forgiving."

"You forgot healthy." He nudged her temple with his nose.

"That too." She wrapped an arm around his shoulders

and trailed a finger along his jaw. "I think I've always loved you. Only I didn't realize what love felt like until now."

"What about your engagement to Clarence?" he asked, his expression turning thunderous.

"I *may* have told my mother I wouldn't marry Clarence if he was the last man in London."

Thomas's eyebrows rose. "You didn't."

"I did." She nodded and laughed.

"What about the elixir?" he asked.

She winced. "Derek told me you knew about that all along."

His fingers played with the satin lining of her bodice. "Yes, I was awake that night. I switched rooms with Branville. I knew what you were going to do."

"You did it on purpose," she said. "But you didn't need to."

"I've loved you for years, Delilah," he admitted. "Only I couldn't figure out a way to show you that would make you believe. Your silly potion gave me the perfect excuse."

"If you knew, I suppose that means . . ."

"The potion doesn't work?" He grinned. "I suppose we'll never really know, will we? Because I am madly in love with you, and you did sprinkle it on me."

She threw back her head and laughed. "Whether it worked or not, Madame Rosa was right about one thing."

"What's that?"

"She told me true love was in my future."

"Indeed."

"But I don't understand." She brushed the hair back from his temple. "If you were in love with me all these years, why did you constantly say you had no interest in marriage?"

"So you and your meddling friend Lucy wouldn't matchmake me, of course. I needed an excuse to remain a bachelor until you were ready to find a match. Only, I had no idea you'd set your sights on someone so quickly and without warning."

She pressed her nose to his neck and breathed in his familiar scent. "I suppose I was impetuous."

"Impetuous and determined. It gave me quite the conundrum."

Delilah laughed and hugged him harder. "Do you know I tried to find an antidote to that silly elixir? Madame Rosa refused. She said, *'Verus amor nullum facit errata.'*"

Thomas sat up straighter and blinked at her. "What did she say?"

"*'Verus amor nullum facit errata,'*" Delilah repeated more slowly. "Or something like that." She waved a hand in the air.

"You know what that means, don't you?"

She shook her head. "You know I didn't pay attention in my Latin classes. Or any classes, for that matter."

He gently tugged at one of the curls that had come loose from her coiffure. "It means: True love makes no mistakes." He brushed his fingertips along her cheek.

Tears filled Delilah's eyes, and she leaned her head against his. "It's true. Madame Rosa was right all along. My mother never truly loved me. She's been nothing but awful to me my whole life."

Thomas nodded. "It's unfortunate, but it's true," he said softly. "But you have friends who love you dearly. And you're about to have a husband who couldn't love you more."

A sly smile curled Delilah's lips. "I also may have told

Mother that I intend to marry you, and that she'll never see our children or be welcome in our home."

His eyes widened. "Truly?"

"Yes, you and Lucy tried to tell me for years how awful Mother was to me. I didn't want to believe it. But now I see you were right. You were always right, Thomas, and you and Lucy are the ones who've always been there for me. Family isn't always the people who you were born with."

He tipped up her chin with a finger and kissed her. "I'm glad you've finally realized that. You've been *my* family for years. Now we're simply going to make it official." His lips descended to hers again and the kiss deepened.

"Thomas?" she asked a few moments later, breathing heavily.

"Yes?"

She hid her smile against his shoulder. "If Miss Adeline lives in a duke's household and belongs to a duchess, does that make him a lady?"

Thomas rolled his eyes. "I suppose this means Miss Adeline is coming to live here eventually."

"Of course he is," Delilah replied brightly.

"You're going to have to tell him he's not allowed to bite me."

"On the contrary." She wagged a finger in the air. "You're going to have to have a talk with him. Perhaps you can convince him that your intentions toward me are honorable."

He trailed kisses along the side of her neck, sending gooseflesh scattering across her skin. "But what if my intentions aren't honorable? I can take you straight to Gretna Green if you like," he murmured against her ear.

Delilah tipped back her head and smiled. "Oh, no. I think we should make Mother and Lord Hilton pay for an elaborate wedding worthy of a duchess. Derek told me they wanted me to marry Clarence so they could keep my dowry."

Thomas cursed under his breath. "Don't give them another thought. I'll marry you whenever and wherever and however you'd like. And money is no object."

She sat up straight and faced him again, both arms wrapped over his wide shoulders. "There is someplace I'd like to go now, however."

He pulled her hand to his lips and kissed the back of it. "Your wish is my command, my lady. Where to?"

She bit her lip and glanced up at him from beneath her lashes. "Your bed."

His brows shot up. "Truly?"

"Yes, truly," she whispered. "Can you make that happen?"

"With all due haste."

CHAPTER FORTY-TWO

Thankfully, Lord Stanley had taken Lavinia and her maid riding in the park, while Thomas's mother was out shopping for the afternoon. They only had to dodge the servants to make it upstairs to Thomas's bedchamber.

They peeked their heads out of the study and looked both ways in the corridor before sneaking toward the foyer. They hid against the wall while the butler walked through the foyer, then they dashed across the marble floor for the staircase. Thomas grabbed Delilah's hand and led her up the stairs to the second floor and down the long corridor to his bedchamber at the end of the row of doors.

He closed the door behind them and locked it while Delilah turned in a wide circle taking it all in. His bedchamber was as unfussy as he was. The space consisted of a large bed in the center with dark blue linens atop it. It was decorated in hues of blue and gray with a painting of a hunting dog on the wall. Blue-and-white curtains adorned the windows, and two comfortable-looking leather chairs rested in front of the fireplace. It smelled like him too, soap and spice. She closed her eyes and breathed it in.

Thomas lit two candles on either side of the bed, then went to the windows and pulled the curtains closed. The room descended into mostly darkness, and a thrill shot through Delilah's middle and settled in her core. She'd wanted to do this with him at least since the night at Vauxhall, and perhaps even since their first kiss. She had no trepidation. No confusion. This was exactly how it was meant to be.

He turned back to her and pulled her into his arms.

"I've . . . never done this before," she murmured. That was her only apprehension. She would die if he was disappointed in her performance.

"Neither have I," he admitted, kissing her again.

"What?" She pulled back to search his face, not certain he was serious.

"It's true," he said with a small laugh.

"Why?" The word flew from her mouth, and she clapped her hand over it. "I'm sorry. Perhaps that's none of my business."

"I told you once. I've been saving myself for the woman I'm madly in love with."

Tears rushed to her eyes. "Me?"

He rubbed the underside of her chin with his finger. "Of course you, Delilah. It's always been you."

"Then I feel as if we need an instruction manual or something," she said with a nervous laugh.

"I am confident I can manage without one. For instance, I'm almost certain the first thing we should do is take off our clothes."

Delilah nodded amiably. "I agree. That sounds right to me. You go first."

He laughed. "With pleasure."

She kicked off her slippers and sat on the bed, watching while Thomas sat next to her and removed his boots and stockings. Then he stood in front of her and began unraveling his cravat. She held her breath, mesmerized by the sultry look in his eyes. She swallowed. They were truly going to do this. Make love. Be each other's first lovers. She'd never wanted anything more.

"You can help if you'd like," he offered, stepping closer to her so she could touch him.

Delilah tentatively reached up and helped him with the cravat. Once it was free of his neck, he tossed it to the floor. Then he shrugged out of his coat. His waistcoat was next, and she helped him unbutton the thing. Next, he pulled his shirt over his head with two hands. All that was left were his breeches. Delilah helped with those buttons too. Her fingers nimbly opened them while her eyes never left his. When the breeches were completely unbuttoned, she held her breath.

Thomas slid a hand over her mildly disheveled hair. "Why don't you take off some of your clothes too?"

With a nod, she stood and offered her back so he could undo the buttons on her gown. When they were undone, she turned and pulled it down and over her hips. She stepped out of it, wearing only her stays, stockings, and shift.

"Now your breeches," she breathed.

Without taking his eyes from hers, Thomas slowly pushed down the fall of his breeches. Delilah watched, entranced, as he lowered the breeches over his hips and to the floor. When he straightened, his manhood jutted out from the patch of hair between his legs.

It was . . . big. Her married friends had shared with her a bit about what to expect on her wedding night, but seeing the size of him sent a skitter of apprehension through her.

He stepped toward her and she turned and allowed him to undo the laces of her stays, then he pushed the straps of her shift over her shoulders. She shimmied it over her hips, and the loose garment fell away. Fnally, she faced him, naked except for her stockings.

"You're beautiful, Delilah," he murmured, leaning down to press his face against her neck and breathing in the scent of her hair.

"So are you," she said solemnly.

He scooped her into his arms and laid her on the bed. Then he hovered over her, softly pushing the hair away from her face.

She reached up and plucked pin after pin from her coiffure. She handed him the pins, and he dutifully set them on the bedside table. When she finally leaned up on her wrists and shook out her hair, the dark tresses streamed over her shoulders and breasts and down her back.

"You're gorgeous. I love you so much," Thomas said.

"Kiss me," she breathed. And he did.

She reached her arms around his neck and pulled him down atop her. His warm, muscled body felt so foreign against her softness, so delicious.

His mouth nibbled at hers, played with her, and then his tongue pushed her lips open and the kiss became wild. There was no need for propriety or restraint, for he was hers, and she, his. She lifted a knee and wrapped a leg around his backside, drawing him to her, flesh to flesh, and when he uttered a groan, she felt a surge of feminine power that was wholly foreign, wholly intoxicating.

She spread her legs and clamped her eyes shut.

Thomas went still above her. "What are you doing?"

Her eyes opened. "Eleanor Rothschild told me it will hurt. I was hoping we could get it over with quickly."

To her surprise, he actually gave a soft chuckle. "I may not have much experience, but I'm quite certain it's not supposed to be over with quickly, and when it's done correctly, there shouldn't be much pain—if any."

"Is that true?" Delilah asked, searching his eyes.

"I've read about it," he assured her. "I wanted to make certain it was good for you."

Delilah's heart wrenched. Thomas had always regretted the fact that he hadn't been able to finish his schooling. She knew he'd privately tutored himself over the years, read scores of books, talked to his friends at Oxford on their breaks and asked what they were studying so that he might keep up with them. But the fact that he had taken time to read about this intimate subject because he wanted it to be good for her, made tears well in her eyes. She loved him. She loved him completely with her heart, mind, and soul. Her family, her home, was wherever this man was.

"Remember what we did at Vauxhall?" Thomas asked.

"Yes." Delilah was thankful for the relative darkness in the room because she was certain she was blushing.

"That didn't hurt, did it?"

"No." She firmly shook her head. "The exact opposite, actually. It was magnificent." She sighed with the memory of that particular, exquisite pleasure.

A smile of masculine pride curved Thomas's mouth. "I don't intend for this to hurt either. Relax," he added, a little breathless. "Let me touch you."

Delilah exhaled and allowed the tension to drain from her arms and legs. She trusted Thomas completely, and if he only wanted to touch her, she would allow it.

Especially if it was anything like what he'd done to her body at Vauxhall. More of that was nothing but welcome.

He kissed her lips and trailed his mouth down to her neck, to her collarbone, and then to her breasts. He cupped them in his hands and lavished attention on each one of them, first one, then the other. By the time he was done, all the tension had fled Delilah's body. She felt like a cat stretching in the sun.

Thomas's dark head moved lower, and he rained kisses along her belly. The odd one tickled, but she remained dutifully splayed beneath him, resisting the urge to squirm with pleasure, unsure of what a lover should do, but praying none of it ever stopped. When his head moved down even farther, and he positioned his mouth between her legs, he clamped his hands around her wrists, pinioning them to the mattress next to her hips.

In the next moment, she realized why he'd done that, because the second Thomas's hot, wet tongue slid between the folds of her sex, she tried to move her hands to push him away and found them trapped.

"Let me," he breathed against her intimate flesh. "I won't hurt you."

Both mortified and delighted, she struggled for only a moment before another deep lick made her groan and her thighs fell apart on their own wicked volition. She had no idea which book Thomas had read that had taught him about what he was presently doing to her, but she made a mental note to borrow it later. What a sinful, impossibly improper, and wildly delicious assault. Her thighs tensed, and she drew up her knees while his tongue licked her in deeper and deeper strokes, owning her, making her so wet she thought she'd melt into a pool of need.

Her head moved back and forth fitfully on the sheets. "Thomas," she called, not entirely certain what she was asking for, but knowing she didn't want him to stop.

His tongue moved up to gingerly touch the small flash-point of delight between her thighs, the same nub that had made her cry out while a rush of pure emotion flooded through her at Vauxhall. She caught her breath. *Mon Dieu.* Thomas was going to do it again, only this time he was going to do it with his tongue.

She whimpered in the back of her throat as the tip of his tongue played with her, his hands still trapping her wrists. He licked the perfect little spot, again and again, circling it, brushing it with the flat part of his tongue and then teasing it with the tip over and over until her thighs clenched. He brushed against her trembling warmth one last time as she tumbled over the edge of sensation that tore a scream from her throat.

Her body was not her own. It shivered and quaked, even after he moved back up and cradled her against his chest. Eventually, though, her breathing steadied. It took her several moments before the haze cleared from her mind, and then it zeroed in on Thomas, on the heat radiating from his hard body, on the way it strained against hers.

"Tell me," she breathed. "Tell me how to touch you."

Delilah pushed him down on his back and leaned over him. Her dark hair falling over her shoulders and skimming her nipples had to be the most erotic thing he'd ever seen. He'd dreamed about this moment a thousand times, but the reality of having her in his bed was far better than any of his dreams.

She'd asked him to show her how to touch him. *With pleasure.* He couldn't wait another moment. He gently took her hand and moved it down to his cock. Her fingers quickly encircled his hard flesh, and he showed her how to stroke him.

Damn. She was a fast learner. Too fast. Her hand on his flesh was unholy torture. He'd spill his seed in her palm if he let her go on much longer. But he bit the inside of his cheek and forced himself to endure the sweet agony for another long minute before he pulled her hand away and settled it safely on his shoulder. Then he flipped her onto her back and moved atop her, pushing her legs apart with his knee. His body was shaking with the need to plunge inside her, but he tempered himself, caught her mouth in a deep, distracting kiss, and when her body arched in fresh need against him, only then did he slowly slide his cock inside her. When he reached her maidenhead, he paused, lifted his head to meet her sleepy eyes, and found no reticence there—only love. With a surge of joy, he pushed all the way inside her, and they were as one.

"Oh," was all Delilah said.

"Are you in pain?" he asked, wishing he could take away any discomfort she might feel.

"No," she said, confusion marring her brow. "I don't think so. It only felt like a little pinch."

"I won't move until you say it's all right," he breathed against her neck, despite the fact that the need to thrust inside of her was an unholy ache in his loins.

"I want you to," she whispered.

Those were the only words Thomas needed to hear. He pulled his hips back slowly and plunged into her again. He searched her face for any sign of pain. She nodded to him, and he continued, pulling back his hips and thrusting again and again, going faster each time until he was mindless with the need to spend himself, and

Delilah was clinging to him, soft little moans sounding in the back of her throat, driving him mad.

"It feels so . . . good," she whispered, her eyes tightly closed, her head thrown back. She wrapped her legs around his thighs, and Thomas thought he would die of pleasure. Bracing his hands against the mattress on either side of her head, he thrust into her again, again, and one last time before she cried out his name, and his own release jolted through him.

In the aftermath of their lovemaking, Thomas held Delilah in his arms, his hands filtering through her long, dark hair. He couldn't stop touching her, didn't want to, at any rate.

"If you've never done that before, how in heaven's name did you know how to do it like *that*?" she asked in awe.

Thomas chuckled. "In addition to my reading, I have many male friends whose lips are loosened when they're deep in their cups. I stayed sober and took notes."

"Not really?" she asked, her mouth open in shock.

"Not literally," he allowed, smiling. "But mentally, for certain." He winked at her.

Delilah giggled. "I'm only sorry it took me so long to realize I love you," she murmured.

"I'm sorry I didn't tell you how I felt the day you announced your intention to marry Branville."

She smiled against his shoulder. "That wouldn't have worked. I was certain and determined, and you know you cannot talk me out of anything once my mind is made up. Unfortunately, I have to learn everything the difficult way . . . for myself."

He kissed the top of her head. "Which is precisely why I didn't tell you, and why I set about trying to convince you instead, by playing along with your ridiculous elixir scheme. But I'm not entirely blameless either."

She traced the edge of his ear with a fingertip. "What do you mean?"

"I thought about what you said, about my need to rescue everyone. You're right. Part of me wanted to make everything right. I wanted you desperately, but only if you came to me out of love, not out of need."

She nodded against his chest. "Precisely as Madame Rosa said." She lifted her head to look at him. "Perhaps it wasn't a complete mistake to purchase that elixir. She helped me realize that I couldn't have you unless I came to you from my own free will."

He gazed back at her, his eyes filled with love. "I'm only thankful we didn't make a complete mess of things before they were irretrievably broken. I love you, Delilah. I never want to lose you again."

Looking at him now—so earnest, so handsome, so completely mussed and undone from their lovemaking—she thought her heart might burst. She swallowed the lump in her throat and joked, "In fifty years, you'll be begging to get away from me."

"Fifty years is quite a long time," he replied with a chuckle.

"Yes, well." She gave the curve of his shoulder a playful nip. "I suppose we should begin the next fifty years by planning our wedding. Cousin Daphne will be beside herself with glee. And Aunt Willie and Aunt Lenore will too. I'm certain of it."

"You shall have a wedding fit for a duchess, my darling," he said, and rolled atop her again, kissing her deeply.

CHAPTER FORTY-THREE
London, April 1828

The wedding of Lady Delilah Montebank to Lord Thomas, Duke of Huntley, was the grandest affair London had seen in an age. It was held at St. Paul's and attended by no less than five hundred members of the Quality, and some common folk as well, including Madame Rosa, Amandine, and Will, the valet.

The bride had insisted upon delaying the wedding till spring in order to wear a pink wedding gown. The dress was made of light pink satin with pink bows and pink slippers. She even had pink flowers twined in her hair. Her mother would never have approved of the amount of pink Delilah chose to have at her wedding, which made it all the more delightful that she had it. But Lucy and Daphne and Aunt Willie and Aunt Lenore had all ensured that she had as much pink as she desired. And Delilah felt like nothing so much as a fairy princess.

Delilah's mother and new stepfather, Lord Hilton,

attended the ceremony, but they sat conspicuously in the back of the church. Clarence was not with them. No doubt he was otherwise engaged in his room. Lady Vanessa and Lord Hilton were not invited to the wedding breakfast or the festivities later that night at Huntley Park.

The reception at Huntley Park was another grand affair. Pink roses covered nearly every inch of the manor house, including the ballroom, where a grand ball was held that evening to celebrate the marriage.

All of their friends were there. They gathered round the newly married couple to wish them well.

"Just think," Thomas said to Jane Upton. "If it weren't for you adding that kiss to the script last summer, we might not be here today."

Jane frowned. "I didn't add that kiss. I thought you all did that on your own."

Lucy winked at them just before she raised her glass for a toast. "Another match well made, and I might as well finally admit that this was a match I had been planning for quite some time."

Derek nearly spit his drink. "Pardon, my love?"

"Delilah and Thomas," she continued. "I'd hoped for years they would fall in love. Only I couldn't let on. Delilah can be quite stubborn when she wants to be. I had to ensure it seemed like it was her idea."

Delilah smiled and tipped her glass of champagne to her lips. She and Lucy had already had this discussion, and she'd properly thanked the duchess for the role she'd played in helping her find true love.

"Are you quite serious?" Derek replied to his wife. "You think *you* planned this?"

Lucy blinked and pressed a hand to her chest. "Didn't I?"

"On the contrary, *we* planned it all along." He rolled his finger in a circle, indicating the group of his male friends who stood nearby.

"Who?" Lucy blinked at him, her brow furrowed in confusion.

"The gentlemen." Derek inclined his head, gave his wife a smug smile, and took a drink from his champagne flute.

Lucy, Cass, and Jane glanced around at the men, who all wore the same self-satisfied grins. They clinked their champagne glasses together as if in salute to one another.

"Unbelievable," Jane Upton breathed.

"Yes, well, you should believe it," Garrett Upton replied. "It's true."

"It is true," Julian Swift added.

Delilah laughed. "They did give me a much-needed talk, and they conspired with Thomas to ensure the elixir was administered to the right man. Meanwhile, I think my matchmaking days are behind me now."

Lucy gasped. "What? Delilah, why would you say such a thing?"

Delilah laughed again. "I'm a matchmaker who was completely oblivious to my own match. I daresay that is a reason enough to retire."

Lucy shook her head. "Nonsense. It's like a maid who has a messy room. It's often difficult to see your own circumstances correctly."

"Yes, well, there is one more match I'm intent upon making before I completely abandon the profession altogether," Delilah said.

"Ooh, who?" Cass asked, leaning forward to better hear.

"Amandine and Will seem to have an affinity for one another."

"That is the most romantic thing I've ever heard," Cass said with a sigh.

"It is, isn't it?" Delilah replied, a dreamy look on her face.

"Yes, and it's a helpful alliance as well," Thomas added. "Amandine has already taught Will how to properly tie a cravat."

Alex and Owen Monroe, along with Christian Forester, Viscount Berkeley, and his wife, Sarah, joined the group.

"Delilah," Alex said. "I'm so happy you're finally my sister. And the wedding was gorgeous. I daresay the Duke of Branville's wedding to Lady Rebecca Abernathy last autumn wasn't half as grand."

Delilah smiled. "Yes, well, Rebecca told me she didn't want a large wedding. But it was lovely just the same."

"Lavinia's wedding last Christmastide was certainly grand," Thomas said.

"Yes, and we even managed to plan it quickly," Delilah replied to her new husband. "I hadn't forgotten how you told me she threatened to make your married life miserable."

He kissed the top of her head. "Never with you, darling. She adores you. You helped her find Lord Stanley, after all."

Sarah asked. "I admit I was surprised when the engagement was announced. I thought Lavinia wanted Lord Berwick."

"She did want Lord Berwick, until after the play," Thomas replied. "Lord Stanley began coming round day after day, and if there's one thing Lavinia cannot resist, it's someone who thinks she is as wonderful as she finds herself."

"Yes, well, I'm just happy she's married," Alex said. "Now Devon and baby Elizabeth may have cousins from both of you."

"Never fear. I shall get started at my earliest opportunity," Thomas replied with a roguish grin.

"What about Lady Emmaline? Has she found a match yet?" Lucy asked.

"Lady Emmaline and Lord Berwick were courting, last I heard," Cass interjected.

Derek closed his eyes in mock agony. "No more matchmaking, my love. I swear you'll send me to an early grave."

"That's interesting, coming from you," Lucy retorted. "After you were just bragging about your part in Thomas's plans."

Derek threw back his head and laughed. "Yes, well, seems I've learned from the best too."

Cass reached out and patted Delilah's arm. "I saw your mother in the church this morning. Are you sad she isn't here?"

"No." Delilah shook her head. "I think it's best if I limit her role in my life."

"Your mother should be nothing but happy, dear," Lucy replied. "After all, you did end up marrying a duke, just as you said you would."

"I suppose you're right," Delilah replied with a sigh. "I never really considered it."

"Yes, but you're forgetting that at first, you wanted to marry the Duke of Branville," Thomas pointed out.

She turned to him, put her arms around his neck, and kissed him thoroughly and indecently. "The Duke of Branville? Who is that? As far as I'm concerned, my darling, there is no other duke but you."

EPILOGUE

Cade Cavendish sat on the settee in the library at Huntley's estate. Thomas and Delilah's wedding festivities were winding down, but the children, who had been allowed to stay up late, had all come out to sit in a semicircle around his knees and stare up at him. They liked him to tell them tall tales about his daring former life at sea.

"Uncle Cade, Uncle Cade, give your speech, the one we like," Devon Monroe insisted.

"The one about fairies that rhymes," Bella Swift added.

"What are they talking about?" Danielle said to her husband. She stood behind him smiling and shaking her head.

Cade threw back his head and laughed. "They want me to recite the speech I memorized when I played Puck."

"Which one?" Danielle asked.

"This one," Cade said, before clearing his throat. He

turned to the children. "If we shadows have offended, think but this and all is mended. That you have but slumbered here. While these visions did appear. And this weak and idle theme. No more yielding but a dream. Gentles, do not reprehend. If you pardon, we will mend. And, as I am an honest Puck. If we have unearned luck. Now to 'scape the serpent's tongue. We will make amends ere long. Else the Puck a liar call. So good night unto you all. Give me your hands if we be friends, and Robin shall restore amends."

Thank you for reading *No Other Duke but You*. Delilah has been one of my favorite characters from the moment she stepped on the page in *The Irresistible Rogue*, and when Thomas appeared in *The Untamed Earl*, I knew they should be together. I sincerely hope you've enjoyed their story. I'd be delighted if you'd email me and tell me how you liked the book.

I'd love to keep in touch.

- Visit my website for information about upcoming books, excerpts, and to sign up for my email newsletter: www.ValerieBowmanBooks.com or at www.ValerieBowmanBooks.com/subscribe
- Join me on Facebook: http://Facebook.com/ValerieBowmanAuthor
- Follow me on Twitter at @ValerieGBowman, https://twitter.com/ValerieGBowman
- Reviews help other readers find books. I appreciate all reviews whether positive or negative. Thank you so much for considering it!